CLOSE TO HEAVEN

A COLORADO HIGH COUNTRY CHRISTMAS

USA Today BESTSELLING AUTHOR

PAMELA CLARE

CLOSE TO HEAVEN

A Colorado High Country Christmas

Published by Pamela Clare, 2017

Cover Design by © Carrie Divine/Seductive Designs
Image: ozimicians/Depositphotos
mppriv/Depositphotos

Copyright © 2017 by Pamela Clare

This is a work of fiction. Names, characters, places, and incidents are products of the author's imagination or are used fictitiously, and any resemblance to actual persons, living or dead, business establishments, events, or locales is entirely coincidental.

All rights reserved.

No part of this book may be reproduced, scanned, or distributed in any printed or electronic format without permission. Please do not participate in or encourage piracy of copyrighted materials by violating the author's rights. No one should be expected to work for free. If you support the arts and enjoy literature, do not participate in illegal file-sharing.

ISBN-10: 0-9987491-4-1

ISBN-13: 978-0-9987491-4-3

Merry Christmas and Happy Holidays to all of my readers around the world. May you be blessed with abundance and health, and may peace and wisdom prevail on this Earth.

Pamela Clare

Christmas 2017

Acknowledgments

Many thanks to the usual suspects for their unfailing support of me as a writer and a person: Michelle White, Jackie Turner, Shell Ryan, and Benjamin Alexander. I would not get through this without you. Additional thanks to Pat Egan Fordyce for always being willing to read my stuff at the last damned minute.

Special thanks to Left Hand Brewing Company for the tour and for answering my many questions. I am now a huge fan of your Milk Stout.

Chapter One

Twenty-seven days till Christmas

Joe stood behind the bar of his brewpub, Knockers, watching the news on one of the muted overhead TVs, waiting for the weather report. He reached up absentmindedly to stroke his beard only to find it gone, five o'clock shadow in its place. He'd lost a bet with his head cook Rico about last week's Broncos game, and he'd had to shave it off.

Bastard.

He forgot about the bet and his missing beard the moment the forecast appeared on the screen. "We're in for it."

The National Weather Service was predicting another three to five *feet* of snow in the mountains. That was on top of the thirty-eight inches that had fallen in the past twenty-four hours. The governor was asking all but essential emergency personnel to stay home and off the highways while the Colorado Department of Transportation—CDOT—did its best to clear the roads.

That was life in Colorado's Rocky Mountains.

Joe had already sent Marcia, his bartender, and much of the other staff home, keeping on hand only those who lived nearby. He had wanted everyone else to get safely home before CDOT closed the highways. "It's time to close up."

"Hell, Joe, it's not even nine yet." Hank Gundry, Joe's only customer, took a sip of his whiskey, his love of liquor apparently stronger than his fear of driving in the snow. "Can't a man enjoy the drink he paid for in peace?"

Leave it to Hank to put pleasure before safety. The man had blown up his own house trying to extract hash oil from marijuana a couple of years back.

"As much as I like your company, Hank, buddy, I can't risk the safety of my staff. You can stay till you finish that drink, but then it's time to go."

Hank gave a slow shake of his head. "You're a hard man, Joe."

Joe chuckled, reached for a cloth, began to wipe down the bar. "Aren't I just?"

Rain walked out of the kitchen carrying a plastic dishwasher tray of clean shot glasses, her long blond hair hanging down her back in a French braid, her red Henley shirt and jeans hugging curves that Joe tried hard every day not to notice. She was his general manager, a valued member of his staff. He'd be no better than the drunk hunters and skiers who came in for dinner and leered at her if he allowed himself to see her in a sexual way. In fact, he'd be worse, because she trusted him.

But, *damn*. It wasn't easy.

She had a body that turned heads and an angelic face with big green eyes, high cheekbones, and a full mouth that smiled easily. A tiny silver ring graced her right nostril, tattoos of skulls, roses, and ivy adorning her forearms. She'd had her dreadlocks taken out a few months back, her blond hair thick and shiny. But what made everyone in Scarlet love her was her goodness. Joe had never met a woman more generous or caring than Rain. In a world that was growing darker and more selfish by the day, she followed her heart.

But something was bothering her lately. She denied it, but Joe knew her better than that. They'd been working side-by-side for twenty years now. He had hired her not long after he'd opened the place. She'd been only seventeen with a new baby and no family or man around to help her raise the child. He'd given her a job, watched over her. Which brought Joe to the other thing he always tried hard to remember.

Rain was *ten years* younger than he was. She deserved a man who could love her, maybe raise a couple kids with her, give her a happy life. Joe was congenitally unsuited to that task, the last in a long line of assholes. He had no damned business thinking about her the way he was trying not to think about her.

She went to work putting away the glasses. "What's the Weather Service saying?"

Joe finished wiping down the bar and tossed the cloth into the laundry bag. "They're calling for another three to five feet of snow. It's time to close the place up and make sure everyone gets home."

"I'll let the kitchen staff and servers know." Rain gave him that brilliant smile of hers, but it didn't quite reach her eyes. "You're such a good boss."

God knew, he tried. "Thanks."

Rain disappeared into the kitchen again.

"You're not so good to your customers though," Hank muttered.

"Come on, Hank. You going to give me a hard time? My customers are better off staying home tonight than getting stuck in a snowdrift—and that includes you. You want to make Hawke come out with his crew to fish you out of a ditch?"

"I guess not." Hank pushed an empty shot glass across the counter. "Give me one for the road."

Joe took Hank's empty glass. "I thought you didn't like jail. You want to risk getting a DUI and ending up there again?"

"Hell, no." Hank got to his feet, slipped a worn parka over his wiry frame. "See you when the snow lets up."

"Be safe out there."

Joe locked the front door behind Hank, then walked over to the control panel near the stage to shut off the music. He glanced over and saw it—another notch in the wooden post to the left of the stage. "What the hell?"

He examined it then crossed to the other side of the stage and ran his fingers over the notches in the wooden post there. Nothing new here.

These things had started showing up years ago. At first, he'd thought they came from the gear that bands who played Knockers lugged up around. But they were too uniform, too deliberate to be accidental dings. Besides, they hadn't had a live band in a week. How had the new one gotten here?

Well, he didn't have time to unravel this mystery now.

He took the receipts and cash drawer and disappeared into his office, leaving it to his staff to finish the cleanup. He was almost done preparing the bank deposit when Rain stuck her head through the open doorway.

"Cheyenne and I finished with the front end. We're heading out." She wrapped a purple hand-knitted scarf around her neck. "Rico and Vicki are almost done in the kitchen."

Joe got to his feet. He needed to check on the brewery and see how Libby was doing. "You sure I can't give you and Chey a ride?"

"Chey just left, and I'm good." She pulled a woolen hat over her head. "I snowshoed in this morning. I'll be home before you can finish scraping your windows."

"Smart." Joe ought to have thought of that. "Be safe."

"You, too. Goodnight."

"Goodnight." Joe walked back to the brewery and found Libby, his brewmaster, cleaning up. The brew crew ran in two shifts, arriving earlier than the rest of the staff and staying later. But not tonight.

He raised his voice so Libby could hear him over the machinery. "We're closing early."

"Rain told me." Libby was petite with freckles that made her look like a kid, but she moved the big hoses with ease and was a beer genius. "I just got a batch of milk stout moved into the fermentation tanks, so I can shut down as soon as I'm done cleaning up."

That was a relief. If the wart had been at an earlier stage in the process, shutting down would have meant dumping the entire batch, a loss of thousands of dollars.

"Do you need a ride?"

She shook her head. "I'm good."

"Stay safe."

"Will do, boss."

Joe left the brewery and walked back to his office, where Rico found him.

Rico pulled the hairnet off his beard. "We're done, boss. Vicki just left. I'm heading home. You need anything?"

An oak of a man with thick biceps, Rico was as kind as he was rough-looking. He had worked for Knockers for most of the twenty-one years it had been open, using the culinary skills he'd learned as a kid while doing a nickel in prison for auto theft.

"No, I got it. Thanks. You just get yourself home. Rain snowshoed in. I hope she makes it home okay. I offered to give her a ride, but…"

Rico shook his head. "When are you going to tell Rain how you feel about her? I've been watching the two of you dance around this for years."

Joe glared at him. "Where did that come from?"

"Oh, come on. Out of all the staff making their way home tonight, you're worried about her. It's obvious that you have a thing for her."

"*Why* did I hire you?"

Rico grinned, stroked his beard. "For my looks."

Joe scratched the stubble on his jaw. "Go ahead. Rub it in."

"Go, Broncos!" Rico chuckled all the way out the back door.

Rain Minear made her way home through quiet streets, Christmas lights glowing from beneath the snow, the sounds of the world muffled. Scarlet's single snowplow hadn't touched the side streets, only the main highway, so she had to break trail the entire way. This storm was carrying a lot of moisture from the Gulf of Mexico, which meant the snow was heavy. At least the exercise kept her warm.

She reached her street, rounded the corner. "Nice."

A four-foot snowdrift covered her front porch, blocking her front door, snow hanging in cornices over the eaves. She tromped up to the front porch, pulled her shovel free of the snow, and began to dig out her door.

Snow was still falling hard, fat flakes sticking to her eyelashes, melting against her exposed cheeks, saturating her hat and hair. By the time she'd cleared a path to her door, an inch-deep layer of snow covered the front steps where she'd started.

She knew what she'd be doing tomorrow morning.

She reached up with the shovel, knocked the overhanging snow free of the eaves in the areas she could reach, knowing she would have to deal with that tomorrow, too. She didn't want the snow tearing off her gutters. But for now, damn it, she wanted a hot shower, a glass of wine, and a good night's sleep.

She kicked off her snowshoes, propped them up against the house, then stepped inside, warmth spilling over her. She yanked off her boots and stripped off her winter gear, hanging her parka, gloves, hat, and scarf over a kitchen chair to dry. Then she walked to the bathroom, shed her clothes, and stepped into the shower.

The hot water felt wonderful as it sluiced over her skin, rinsing away the day's tension and the odors of fryer fat, beer, and food. It had been a slow day, and slow days were long days. A shift passed much more quickly when the tables were full. Also, busy days gave her less time to think. Lately, that's all she'd been doing—thinking about her life, or lack of a life.

She was a thirty-seven-year-old mother of an adult daughter, an empty-nester with no education, no savings, and no love life. She worked two unskilled jobs—managing Knockers and cleaning rooms at the Forest Creek Inn—and she still lived in the weird little mountain town where she'd grown up.

Scarlet Springs—one square mile surrounded by reality.

You are going nowhere.

It would help if she had some idea how to make things better for herself, what direction to go. Move to Boulder to be closer to Lark? Rent was crazy expensive there, and she'd be competing with students for restaurant jobs. Get a GED and some kind of degree? She didn't have the money to put herself through school right now. Voice lessons so she could take up singing again? She had no real connections in the music world and no clue how to make a name for herself. Besides, singing in a band had been the dream of her teenage self, and it had almost ruined her life.

As for her love life, well, Joe would never break the rules and date a member of his staff. If he hadn't tried to sleep with her when she was in her twenties and hot, he wasn't going to do it now. She needed to get over him and move on.

Easier said than done.

Some people were intimidated by him and thought him reclusive and eccentric, and Rain supposed he was. He kept to himself and never talked about his own life, never let anyone inside. Still, he was one of the kindest men she knew, decent to his core. Doing the right thing mattered to Joe, not because of what people would think, but because it was the right thing to do. While too many of the men Rain had known had thought only of themselves, he was generous to a fault.

On top of that, he was completely bonable. He was as good-looking as a man could be—tall, well-built, with a gorgeous face. Big brown eyes. Long eyelashes. A gentle nose. She'd found him incredibly handsome with the beard, but without it, he was lethal. She could see the hollows beneath his cheekbones and the square cut of his jaw now—not to mention that full, kissable mouth. The fact that he also had long hair—thick dark hair with just a touch of gray at his temples—was the cherry on top for Rain, who'd always been drawn to rock-star types.

And how has that worked out for you?

Ah, hell. Rain needed to get out of this place. She needed to leave Scarlet, start over somewhere, build a real life for herself doing something that mattered.

Everything had made sense when Lark had lived at home. Rain had built her life around providing food, shelter, clothing, and love for her daughter. Every paycheck had been a victory, a step forward for their little family of two. Now that Lark had moved to Boulder, nothing seemed to make sense at all. Rain hadn't even put up Christmas decorations this year. It didn't feel like Christmas without Lark in the house.

Snap out of it. You succeeded. You should be happy.

Yes, she had succeeded. She had raised her little girl, watched her grow into a beautiful, intelligent, independent woman. Lark hadn't made any of the mistakes Rain had made. She'd be graduating from college in May, and these years of struggle would be behind them. Rain should be celebrating, not feeling sorry for herself. But then she hadn't expected success to feel so damned … *lonely.*

She finished her shower, dried off, and slipped into her softest flannel pajama bottoms and a tank top, too tired to haul in wood for a fire. She settled on the sofa with a glass of red wine and the TV remote. After a few sips and five minutes of channel surfing, she turned off the TV and reached for her smartphone.

It was almost eleven, but Lark was a night owl. Rain sent her daughter a quick text message, not wanting to intrude but missing her too much not to reach out.

Hope you are safe and warm. How was your day?

She waited ten minutes for a reply, but it didn't come.

To hell with this day.

She finished her wine, brushed her teeth, and crawled into bed, cell phone on her nightstand just in case Lark called. She was almost asleep when her phone buzzed.

She reached for it, saw that Lark had sent a photo of herself standing outside in front of what looked like a giant snowman. Her cheeks were pink from the cold, a bright smile on her face, snow in her hair.

A text message followed.

We made a snow giant. Hope you're warm up there. Love you! XOXOXOX <3

Rain smiled, texted a quick reply.

Looks like fun! Love you too! XOXOX

She looked at the photo again, the momentary connection to her daughter easing some of the ache inside her.

From the front of the house came a loud creaking sound.

Rain sat bolt upright. "Is someone there?"

Who in their right mind would be breaking into houses in this weather?

"I'm calling the cops!" She dialed 911.

Breaking glass. A strange groan. A loud crash. A rush of cold air.

On a surge of adrenaline, she jumped to her feet and ran to her bedroom door to look out. Her mouth fell open, her heart slamming in her chest. "Holy shit!"

For a moment, all she could do was stare, her phone still in her hand.

The roof. It had collapsed.

It was *still* collapsing.

The groan of bent and breaking lumber. Another flurry of snow.

Phone still in hand, she dropped to the floor and crawled beneath her bed, unable to keep from screaming as the roof that had sheltered her bedroom crashed down.

Joe lowered the plow on the front of his Land Rover. He wanted to get a jump on clearing the parking lot. Three feet of snow would be a hell of a lot easier to move tonight than seven or eight feet would be tomorrow morning. He drove lengthwise across the parking lot, piling the snow up at the far end. It would cost him a handful of parking spaces, but there was nothing he could do about that.

Sirens.

He backed up, caught a glimpse of a fire engine making its way slowly through town toward the roundabout at the center of town.

Well, hell.

This was a bad night to have an emergency. How were Hawke and his crew going to make it through the unplowed streets? If they got stuck...

Shit.

Joe made his way out of the parking lot and headed toward them, plowing the street as he went. Whoever was at the wheel of the big engine stopped when they saw him and flashed the headlights—a signal that they needed his help.

He drew even with the driver's side window, found Eric Hawke, the town's fire chief, at the wheel.

"Where am I headed?" Joe asked.

Hawke pointed. "Rain's house. Her roof collapsed. She's trapped under her bed."

Joe's heart gave a hard knock. "Fuck!"

Not needing to hear more, he backed up and turned around, clearing a path for Hawke and his men as he drove, his thoughts on Rain. Was she hurt? Hawke hadn't said so, but they hadn't exactly had a long conversation about it.

It seemed to take an eternity to cross town. The big engine was wider than Joe's Land Rover, which meant that Hawke was driving with one tire on the plowed surface and the other on deep snow. More than once, the heavy vehicle slid, its lights jerking in Joe's rearview mirror as Hawke got it under control again.

Joe willed himself to focus on the road and not what was happening behind him. No one had more experience driving that big apparatus than Hawke no matter what the weather. This wasn't his first rodeo.

Joe turned the corner onto Fourth Street.

Rain!

Ice slid into his blood when he saw her house—or what was left of it. The entire structure had collapsed except for her garage, which leaned sideways as if it might fall at any moment. How the hell were they supposed to get to her?

That's Hawke's job.

Joe's job was to move this snow so that Hawke and his crew could reach her. He plowed not only the street in front of her house, but also her driveway, then parked across the street and climbed out into the wind and cold. Hawke's team were already moving around the structure, the truck's scene lights illuminating the wreckage of Rain's home.

"Shut off her propane! I don't want this place to blow!" Hawke shouted above the wind to Brandon Silver, one of his shift captains, who disappeared around the back. "Ryan, find the emergency electricity shut-off. There's no way we're getting into her garage to shut it off with the circuit breaker."

Joe wanted to help. "What can I do?"

Hawke looked Joe right in the eyes. "I know you care about her, but I need you to stay back while we do what we can to stabilize the place and get her out. You've already been a big help."

"Right." It wasn't in Joe's nature to be a bystander.

He moved back to his vehicle, crossed his arms over his chest, and willed himself to stay the hell out of the way. The minutes dragged as Hawke and his crew worked in the bitter cold and snow to brace the garage and the roof against further collapse and then began to cut through the back wall to get to Rain.

Whatever the town paid Hawke, it wasn't enough. Joe had long considered him a hero, but he'd never watched him in action. The man knew what he was doing, his cool-headed leadership setting the tone for his crew. Joe supposed it was in his DNA. Still, the man deserved a raise, and Joe would do what he could to make sure he got one.

Neighbors peered out windows or stood on porches to see what was happening.

Mrs. Beech, the retired English teacher, opened her window. "Is she dead?"

"No, Mrs. Beech. She's okay." Joe hoped to God that was true.

"What if my roof collapses? This house has been in my family for four generations."

Joe looked up, saw cornices hanging over her eaves. Her house, like Rain's, was among the older homes in town. If Rain's had collapsed, there was every chance that other roofs in this neighborhood would collapse, too. "You got a ladder and shovel?"

"In the garage. But I can't climb up there."

"I'll do it." He waited for Mrs. Beech to open her garage door, then grabbed the ladder and climbed up onto her roof.

Rain was trapped in a nightmare—a freezing, icy nightmare. She lay on her belly beneath her bed, shivering, her cell phone in hand. The weight of the roof and the snow made the old iron bedframe creak.

If it broke, if it collapsed, too, she might be crushed.

She'd heard the sirens, and the dispatcher had told her that Eric and his crew were there. Now she thought she could hear men's voices from outside. She called out to them, wanting them to know where she was. "Eric?"

The dispatcher's voice came over her phone. "Rain, are you okay?"

"I'm c-cold, and I'm afraid my b-bed is going to break. If it d-does… Wh-what's taking s-so long?"

"They're doing everything they can. They had to shut off the power and the gas."

Rain hadn't thought of that. If there'd been a gas leak…

Don't think about it.

"I'll let the FD know how you're doing. Stay on the line, Rain."

Rain fought back a growing sense of panic, the cold seeping into her bones along with the bleak reality of her situation. Her house, the house she'd bought just last year, was in ruins. She'd heard breaking glass and knew most of her dishes must be smashed. What the collapse of the house hadn't destroyed, water from snowmelt would. Her books. Her houseplants. Her grandmother's crystal vase. The photo albums that held Lark's baby pictures. All the little drawings Lark had made for her through the years, the birthday and Mother's Day cards she'd given her.

Oh, God.

She could replace the dishes, books, and plants, but the vase and her keepsakes from Lark's childhood were priceless. If they'd been damaged...

Rain swallowed the lump in her throat. Crying wouldn't fix anything.

She wished she'd grabbed a blanket before crawling under the bed. She'd never been cold like this, so cold that her teeth chattered uncontrollably. Was she becoming hypothermic?

From outside, she heard men's voices again and the sound of splintering wood.

Thank God.

It wouldn't be long now.

In the dark and cold, Rain shivered and waited.

Joe had just climbed down and stowed both ladder and shovel in Mrs. Beech's garage once more when he heard the sound of cheers coming from behind Rain's house. A moment later, Hawke rounded the corner, wading through deep snow with Rain in his arms, an emergency blanket wrapped around her.

Sweet Jesus.

Joe met them on the front sidewalk, his gaze on Rain. "Are you okay?"

She nodded, teeth chattering, her face pale.

"She's not hurt, but she's hypothermic. Can you get her to the ER? We don't have everything she needs on the truck. With that plow, you'll get her to the hospital before an ambulance can arrive."

"Sure thing." Joe took Rain's weight into his arms, relieved to be able to *do* something. "Thanks, Hawke."

"Thank you for clearing the road for us. Take care, Rain." Hawke turned, shouted something to his men about working through the night to clear rooftops.

Yeah, the man ought to get a raise.

Joe turned toward his vehicle. "You're going to be okay, honey." *Shit.* Had he just called her *honey*? "My SUV's all warmed up. In five minutes, you'll be in the ER."

"Th-thanks."

Not wanting to set her in the snow in her bare feet, he managed to open the passenger door with one hand, then settled her in her seat and fastened her seatbelt. Then he climbed into the driver's seat, started the engine, and cranked the heat. "I don't suppose this will make much difference."

She needed warmed oxygen and heated IV fluids, not just the heater.

"It f-feels g-good."

"God, Rain, I'm so damned glad you weren't hurt." *Or killed.* He thought the words but couldn't speak them. "When I saw your house…"

Damn.

"It's t-trashed—the h-house. Lark's b-baby pictures… All her d-drawings… E-everything I w-worked for."

Joe could hear the shock and grief in her voice. He could see it on her pale face—that stunned surprise that so often came with tragedy. He reached over, gave her icy fingers a squeeze. "I'm so sorry, Rain. We'll take care of all of that as soon as we can, but first, we need to take care of *you.*"

Hypothermia could kill.

He kept the plow down as he made his way through the center of town to the hospital, clearing a path for anyone who might need it, then parked outside the emergency entrance and carried Rain inside.

Chapter Two

Of anyone had told Rain that she'd be homeless by night's end and that Joe would be carrying her across the threshold, she'd have called them crazy. But here she was, her home and everything she owned in ruins, Joe carrying her through the open doorway.

Too bad it was just the ER.

Still, it was nice to be in his arms, his body hard and strong and warm. He'd been afraid for her. She'd seen it on his face. He'd even called her *honey*.

Lolly Cortez, one of the registered nurses, met them just inside. "Hawke called and told us what happened. I've got a bed set up for her. Put her down in here."

Joe followed Lolly into an exam room and set Rain down on the bed.

Rain moaned. "It's w-warm."

"There's a heating pad beneath you." Lolly reached inside a steel cabinet and pulled out two heated blankets. She tucked them around Rain, cocooning her in warmth. "Does that feel better?"

Rain nodded, still shivering.

Lolly reached for an oxygen mask. "The oxygen is warm and humid. It will help us get your core temp up again. So will the IV. How are you with needles?"

"I-I'm g-good."

"How about you, Joe?"

"Don't worry about me." He moved to the other side of the bed to make way for Lolly, who wheeled over an IV cart and went to work on Rain's left arm.

On impulse, Rain reached for him with her right hand.

Warm fingers closed around hers, his touch reassuring.

"Ouch!" The IV hurt more than Rain had expected.

"Sorry, sweetie." Lolly finished setting up the IV. "We'll let these fluids run and warm you up from the inside out."

"Th-thanks."

"Hawke asked dispatch to call out the Team," Lolly told them. "He's hoping they can help him and his crew clear off some of the older, flatter roofs around town before this happens to anyone else."

The Team—what locals called the Rocky Mountain Search & Rescue Team—was usually called out to rescue injured climbers or lost hikers. Shoveling snow off people's roofs would be a new one.

"They need to call out everyone who has a plow," Joe said. "No one is going to get anywhere with three feet of snow on the roads."

"Whatever you clear, you'll have to plow again tomorrow. I hear it's supposed to be seven or eight feet by the time the storm passes."

"Wow," Rain managed to say, her eyes closing. "Eight feet."

As her shivering subsided, she began to drift, fighting a losing battle to stay awake, their conversation floating over her.

"It's completely normal," she heard Lolly tell Joe. "Hypothermia makes people sleepy. Her body has been fighting to maintain its core temp, and that takes energy."

"Are you going to keep her overnight?"

"Probably not. Once we get her temp stabilized and are sure she's out of the woods, we'll discharge her."

"Is the hospital going to be okay?" Joe asked.

"This place?" Lolly chuckled. "It's a concrete and steel box. The hospital has withstood storms like this before. We've got a crew clearing the helipad and roof, just in case. A big storm like this usually brings a few heart attacks, some hypothermia, and people with back pain. It's going to be a busy day here tomorrow, then, in nine months, we'll have a baby boom."

Rain fell into a dreamless sleep after that—until Joe squeezed her fingers.

"Rain?"

She opened her eyes to find him looking down at her, concern in his brown eyes, his face impossibly handsome. "Sorry to wake you. I'm going to clear the streets for Hawke and his guys."

She held onto his hand a little bit longer. "Thank you for bringing me here."

She didn't want him to go. She didn't want this to end. For a short time, he'd dropped the barriers he always kept around him. He'd carried her, held her hand, stayed by her. He'd been afraid for her. Now he was leaving. The next time she saw him, he would be her boss again, all zipped up and proper, and she would be his employee.

"I'll be back in a couple of hours," he said. "You can stay at my place until we figure out what's next. How does that sound?"

The thought lifted Rain's spirits. Maybe this wasn't over. "I'd like that. Thanks. Be careful out there."

She was asleep before he left the room.

Joe called the fire department's non-emergency number to let Hawke know what he planned to do.

Jenny Miller, one of Hawke's crew, answered. "Scarlet Fire and Rescue."

"Joe Moffat here. Can you let Hawke know that I'm going to plow the streets around the hospital? After that, I'll make my way around town. If he needs me, he can reach me at this number."

"Sure, Joe. I'll let him know. He'll be grateful. How's Rain?"

"She's hypothermic, but the ER staff is taking good care of her." He'd hated to leave her alone, but there was nothing he could do for her, especially when she was asleep. But if he cleared the streets, he might make a difference for someone else. "Do you have a list of people with snowplows?"

"I've never seen a list like that, but I can make a few calls."

"Thanks. I appreciate it."

"Thanks for your help. Stay warm out there, and stop in for some hot coffee if you get a chance."

"I just might take you up on that."

Joe cleared the few blocks around the hospital and then made several passes through the roundabout, where the road had become treacherously icy. After that, he fanned out, moving down Scarlet's main street and then onto its residential streets, lights in red, green, blue, yellow, and white twinkling from beneath the deep snow, all but the tallest Santas and mangers buried.

Yeah, Baby Jesus was freezing his butt off tonight.

Joe spotted Austin Taylor on First Street where he was busy plowing the driveway of the Forest Creek Inn, the old bed-and-breakfast owned by his in-laws. Taylor was a park ranger and a lead climber with the Team. Like Hawke, he was a hero.

Joe pulled over, waited for Taylor to reach the mouth of the inn's long driveway, hoping he would agree to join the little volunteer plow crew.

Taylor stopped when he saw Joe, climbed out of his truck, and walked to Joe's driver side window. "How's Rain?"

"How'd you hear about that?"

"Hawke had dispatch tone out the Team to help clear rooftops, and dispatch told us what had happened."

Oh. Right.

"Rain has had one hell of a rough night, but she's in good hands. I'm taking her to my place when they discharge her. She can stay with me until she's got a new home."

Taylor nodded, a strange grin on his face. "Good."

What the hell did that mean?

Joe didn't get to ask because at that moment Bob Jewell, owner of the inn, stepped outside and walked down the plowed stretch of driveway toward them, wearing only a velour bathrobe and a pair of snow boots. He waved to Joe, then turned to his son-in-law. "You're not leaving, are you? The front walkway still needs to be shoveled, and the driveway—"

"I'm just talking with Joe. Please tell me you've got something on beneath that robe. You look like a damned flasher."

Bob chuckled and opened the robe, giving them a glimpse of his hairy chest and belly—and a pair of white men's underpants.

Joe shook his head. "I could have gone my whole life without seeing that."

"You and me both," Taylor said.

Bob chuckled. "You're just jealous. It takes a lot of single malt to build a one-pack like mine."

Taylor pointed toward the inn with a gloved hand. "Get inside before you catch pneumonia. If you get sick, Kendra will kick your butt."

Bob got a worried look on his face. "True enough."

Satisfied that his son-in-law wasn't abandoning him to the snow, he made his way back toward the house.

Joe got to the point. "I was hoping you and I could team up to clear the main streets around town. It will be a lot easier to deal with now than it will be tomorrow."

Taylor nodded. "I'm game. I need to finish here and then clear my parents' driveway."

"Sounds good to me." A person had a right to look out for their own.

"I'll have to get Megs to approve it, too."

Megs Hill, the director of the Team, could be a hard-ass at times, but Joe had a world of respect for her.

"Fair enough."

From behind him came the sound of an opening door.

"Is it true that Rain's roof collapsed?" Rose Ellery shouted from the shelter of her front porch, wearing a parka over her nightgown, her long silver hair hanging loose. The owner of Rose's New Age Emporium, she was the town expert on tarot and astrology—and the hub of Scarlet's gossip.

"Yes, Rose, it's true," Joe answered. "But she's okay."

"Thank the Goddess! What about my place? Do you think it will cave in?"

Rose lived in one of the town's old Victorian buildings—one of only a handful to survive the 1878 fire that burned most of Scarlet to the ground. Its steeply pitched gabled roof made it unlikely to collapse.

"I think you'll be okay, Rose," Taylor said.

"Could I ask you to shovel my driveway?" There was a coquettish tone to Rose's voice now. "You men are so strong, and this wet snow is heavy."

Taylor shared an amused glance with Joe. "I'll be happy to plow it for you, Rose."

"Thanks! If Rain needs a place to stay, I've got an extra bedroom. It's cold out here! Goodnight." With that, Rose disappeared inside again.

"Your parents live on the east side of town, don't they?" Joe asked Taylor.

Taylor nodded.

"Why don't you stick to the east side, while I take the west side—if it's okay with Megs, that is."

"Sounds good to me."

"You know anyone else with a snowplow?"

"The Team has one that's attached to its UTV. Herrera is at the Cave clearing the parking lot right now."

The Cave was the Team's nickname for their headquarters.

"Do you think Megs would be okay with having him join our little plow brigade?"

Taylor grinned. "I'll ask her—and I'll tell her it was your idea."

"I'm okay with that."

"See you around." Taylor turned and walked back to his truck.

Joe headed off again, finishing First Street and then turning onto Moffat Street, which had the misfortune of being named after his great-great-grandfather, Silas. It was going to be a long night.

It was three in the morning when Joe got a text from Rain that Dr. O'Brien was discharging her. He headed back toward the hospital, arriving twenty minutes later to find Lolly going over Rain's discharge instructions. Rain gave him a little smile when she saw him, but she couldn't fool him. He could tell she was shaken and overwhelmed by what had happened tonight, her face still pale. Who could blame her?

Not wanting to intrude on her privacy, he made his way over to the coffee, poured himself a cup, and waited until she stepped out of the exam room, wearing a borrowed parka over her pajamas and boots that were a bit too big for her.

"She's good to go." Lolly hurried off toward the ringing phone at the nurse's station. "Just keep her warm."

"Will do. Thanks." Joe stayed close beside Rain as they walked out to the Land Rover. "Where did they get the coat and boots?"

"Lolly said they raided lost and found."

"Clever." He opened the door for Rain, helped her inside, then hurried to the driver's side and climbed in beside her. He started the vehicle and cranked the heat, wanting to make sure that Rain didn't get chilled. "The guest room has a gas fireplace, so you'll be plenty warm."

"Thanks, Joe."

"Hey, we take care of each other here."

"Yeah."

"Does Lark know?"

Rain shook her head. "I didn't want to ruin her night. I'll call tomorrow. I'm so damned glad she wasn't home. I was able to crawl under my bed, but it's an antique. Her bed is low to the ground. If anything had happened to her…"

"Yeah." Joe couldn't even go there.

He drove through the plowed streets toward the highway, telling her what had happened during her time in the ER. "I ran into a handful of Team members—Sasha, Moretti, Nicole, Belcourt, Megs, and Mitch. They seemed to be having a great time climbing around on rooftops with shovels. Moretti had his skis on."

Rain didn't even smile. "I suppose this is a nice change from injured climbers, lost kids, and dead bodies."

Joe hadn't thought about it like that. "Yeah, I suppose it is."

"Does anyone know where Bear is? I'm worried about him."

Leave it to Rain to think of others in the midst of a personal crisis. Bear had lived in the mountains west of Scarlet for as long as Joe could remember. He was a big man with unmatched survival skills and an in-depth knowledge of the Bible, but he had a child's mind. No one knew why he was the way he was. The townsfolk did their best to watch over him, giving him hot meals in exchange for blessings.

Joe told his phone to call the firehouse again. "Hey, has anyone had eyes on Bear since the storm started?"

"You're the third person to call and ask me that," said Miller, her voice distorted by Joe's speakers. "He's here. Hawke spotted him walking down the road this morning and invited him to stay in an empty bunk tonight. He's sound asleep and snoring like, well, a bear."

Yeah, Hawke more than deserved that raise.

"Good to hear. Thanks. Talk to you later." Joe ended the call, gave Rain the news, relief easing some of the tension on her face.

"Thank goodness."

"Yeah. Good old Bear." Joe turned onto the highway.

Rain looked out the windshield, Joe's headlights lighting up the blowing snow, his plow scraping along the road. She didn't know what felt more unreal to her at the moment—the fact that her house was now a pile of broken lumber and shattered glass or the fact that she was on her way to Joe's house in her pajamas.

"God, I hope you have wine."

He glanced over at her. "I've got stronger stuff, too."

"Thank God for that."

"Thank God you're okay."

"Yeah." She didn't really feel okay, but she knew he was right.

She could have lost a lot more tonight than her house and everything in it.

"I've got a couple guestrooms. You can take your pick."

"Thanks." Rain had never been to Joe's place. She knew he lived somewhere north of Scarlet close to his family's old silver mine, but that was all she knew. He never invited staff over, instead holding staff get-togethers and meetings at Knockers. He spent most of his time at the pub, so it wasn't as if he were a recluse.

Then again, he'd lived alone for as long as she'd known him.

"You warm enough?"

"Yeah." She sank deeper into the borrowed parka.

"Liar." He turned up the heater. "This drive usually takes about ten minutes, but I think it's going to take me ten minutes just to get to the turnoff."

"I'm in no hurry." She was exhausted and desperately wanted to sleep, but she wouldn't be able to sleep if they ended up in a snowdrift.

Soon, Rain found herself fighting to stay awake, exhaustion dragging at her as they crept down the highway. Joe said something about Bob Jewell flashing him and Austin, but the words washed over her. After what felt like an eternity, a change in the vehicle's motion roused her. Joe had just made a left turn onto the unplowed dirt road that led to Moose Lake. Ahead of them, the road headed uphill toward the ghost town of Caribou and the old mine.

"Can you imagine leading a mule train up this road in winter or driving a team of oxen and a supply wagon?" he asked.

She fought to wake up. "Didn't they use the narrow-gauge railroad for supplies?"

"The railroad didn't arrive until 1883. Caribou was built in 1868."

Rain stared at him. "You know that off the top of your head?"

"I guess you could say I'm a student of local history."

"What history? Mine opens. Town booms. Mine closes. Town goes bust. End of a very short story."

He chuckled. "There's a lot more to it than that."

Something dark stepped onto the road ahead of them. Joe brought the SUV to a clean stop. A moose. It froze in its tracks, stared at them for a moment, snow on its back, then moseyed to the other side as if it didn't have a care in the world.

"Don't hurry on our account," Joe muttered.

Five minutes later, the forest on either side of the road opened up to reveal the open meadow where the town of Caribou had once stood. Most of the houses had been salvaged for timber by the time Rain was a little girl. Only the walls of the post office, which had been built of stone, proved that this was the site of a once thriving town.

"It's amazing to think that three thousand people used to live here."

"Three *thousand?* That's twice the population of Scarlet."

"And you say you can't do math." Chuckling, Joe turned right onto a road that led them through a stretch of dense forest. He motioned to the left. "The mine is a few hundred yards that way."

She glanced through the forest but saw only pine trees, their branches weighted with snow. On any other day, she would have thought it beautiful, but tonight she was too tired and too cold to care.

Joe made another right. "Here we are."

Rain stared open-mouthed. "You live *here?*"

He grinned. "I live at the pub—that's what people tell me anyway."

Rain missed the joke, her gaze fixed on his house. It was one of those mountain contemporary homes built to blend in with its surroundings. It stood two stories high, about the height of the surrounding forest. Its supporting walls were made of Colorado flagstone that was the same red color as the native soil, the rest of it floor-to-ceiling windows. "Wow."

He drove around to the back, pushed a button on his dashboard, and slid into a three-car garage. There were no other vehicles, just a snowmobile, a sled, a workbench with tools, and a ski rack full of gear. "Are you hungry? I can make something quick to go with that wine."

"No, thanks." The food and the wine would have to wait. "All I want is a warm bed and a roof that won't fall in on me."

"Good enough. Let's get you inside."

She climbed out of his SUV and followed him into a utility room that doubled as a mudroom. It had polished maple floors, a washer and dryer, a rug for snowy or muddy boots and shoes, a bench to sit on while putting on shoes, and a closet for coats, hats, and gloves. The room was as big as her kitchen.

Not that she had a kitchen any longer.

Joe took the parka she'd borrowed, stopping mid-motion to frown at something on her face. "You're bruised."

She rubbed her cheek, surprised to find it sore. "I must have hit my face when I dove under my bed."

"The bedrooms are upstairs. We can go up the back way. It's faster." He opened a door to a stairway and flicked on the light.

Rain followed him up two flights of stairs to a dark hallway.

He flicked on the hallway lights, opened a door, and turned on the lights in what must have been a bedroom. "Let's put you here."

Rain stepped through the doorway into the pages of a magazine. Recessed lighting cast a warm glow over the room with its polished maple floors. An upholstered platform bed stood against one wall, its headboard covered in soft gray fabric, a plump duvet folded at its foot. Across from the bed, a gas fireplace and large flat-screen TV were recessed side by side into an accent wall of burnished stainless steel. To the left of the bed were floor-to-ceiling windows that looked out onto the storm, a plush chaise set before them. The door to the bathroom stood a few feet to the right of the fireplace.

"You can adjust the heat here. I'm going to turn it up." Joe touched a dial on the wall. "There's radiant heat in the bathroom. The fireplace turns on with that light switch. Do you think you'll be comfortable?"

Rain was too tired to laugh. "This will do. Thanks."

"Let me know if you need anything. I'm at the other end of the hall." Joe turned to go. "Goodnight."

"'Night." Rain shut off the lights and crawled into bed.

Chapter Three

Twenty-six days till Christmas

Joe let himself sleep a good few hours, then dragged his ass out of bed, put on a T-shirt and went downstairs to the kitchen to make coffee, his gaze moving toward the door to Rain's room. He needed to get something in his stomach and call Hawke's crew for a SITREP. Snow was still falling, and there were probably lots of folks who needed help digging out this morning. On top of that, someone needed to get into the wreckage of Rain's place and pack up some clothes and personal things for her.

He got coffee brewing, then reached across the counter for the TV remote, listening to the weather report while he whipped up some biscuits, eggs, and bacon. Another thirty-two inches of snow had fallen in the mountains overnight, with high winds and as much as six to twelve inches expected today. DIA had cancelled all flights. The buses and light rail weren't running in Denver. All government offices and schools across the state were closed for the day. Even the ski resorts had closed. Mother Nature had shut Colorado down.

It didn't happen often, but when it did, locals treated it like a holiday. It was a chance to play outdoors all day—or stay in bed and screw.

You would like that, wouldn't you?

Hell, yeah, he would. Who wouldn't? But he hadn't had a woman in his life for a while now, and that wasn't going to change before the roads were cleared.

He'd given up on hookups and dating apps and websites. The last woman he'd dated hadn't understood why a man with a master's degree in mining engineering and a private fortune would waste his time running a brewpub. She hadn't been willing to leave her Denver condo to live in Scarlet, and he'd gotten sick of her condescension. Scarlet was his home. It was also a tough place to meet women, especially when almost eight percent of the town's single females worked for him, making them off limits.

Yes, he'd done the math.

Joe finished mixing the biscuits, plopped the dough onto a cookie sheet, and slid it in to bake in the top oven, while bacon sizzled in the lower one. He would eat and head out, leaving a plate for Rain on low in the oven.

"Wow!"

Joe looked up, saw her standing in the hallway at the top of the stairs, eyes wide, her gaze moving over the large open area that was his kitchen, dining room, and living room. "Hey. Did you get some sleep?"

She nodded, her gaze now on the vaulted ceiling. "This is amazing."

"Thanks." He glanced into the oven to check the bacon, then started cracking eggs. "You hungry?"

"Famished." She made her way down the staircase and over to the windows, her hair tangled, the bruise on her cheek darker now. "I usually love snow. But right now ... I just want to get my stuff out of the house and see what I can save."

Yeah. That wasn't happening. "Coffee?"

"God, yes." She turned and walked toward him.

Joe's mouth went dry.

Her pajama bottoms rode low enough to expose her navel, his gaze moving from the gentle curve of her belly to the tuck of her waist to the flare of her hips.

Damn.

He poured coffee into a mug and handed it to her. "There's cream in the fridge."

She glanced around. "Where's the fridge?"

He stepped over to the wood-paneled refrigerator door, gave it a light push to open it, and took out the cream. "Here you go."

"A camouflaged fridge. Nice." She poured some cream and put it away, then came and sat in one of the bar stools, sipping her coffee and watching while he finished scrambling the eggs. "I can't believe how beautiful your place is."

"I inherited all of this—the mine, the land—when my father died. I figured I might as well do something with it."

"Building a cabin with an outhouse is 'doing something with it.' *This* ... This is incredible. You designed it yourself, didn't you?"

How did she know that? "I worked with the architect, sketched out some ideas. She did the rest. We used a lot of repurposed materials. Want a tour?"

He had a few minutes before he needed to pull the biscuits and bacon out of the oven. He could take the time.

"Sure."

He gestured to the space around him. "Well, this is the kitchen. There's the dining room, and over there's the living room. Follow me."

He opened the door beside the pantry. "That wine you wanted? It's down here."

They walked together down the stairs and into his wine cellar.

"Gosh, Joe. Next time Marcia runs out of booze at the bar, I know where to send her. You've got a liquor store down here."

"Reds are here. Whites are there. Hard liquor is—"

"Macallan 1940?" She lifted the bottle carefully into her hands. "I don't even want to know how much this cost. Okay, yes, I do. How much was it?"

"My father bought that the year before he passed. I think it cost him thirty grand."

"Thirty thousand *dollars?*" Rain looked horrified and held out the bottle to Joe, as if she no longer trusted herself to hold it. "How could anyone drink that? You might as well pee liquid gold."

He chuckled, took it from her, and settled it back in its cubby. "I'm saving it for a very special occasion."

"Like what?"

"I don't know. We'll have to wait and see."

Next, he showed her the gym with its weights, exercise bike, and treadmill. "Feel free to work out. There's a stereo system and a TV."

"Good heavens, Joe. If this were my house, I would never leave. How can you spend so much time at Knockers when *this* is your home?"

"Hey, I like Knockers." He led her upstairs and showed her the library. "This is my favorite room in the house."

It wasn't large, but its shelves were packed with his books, including his despicable great-great-grandfather's leather-bound journals. There were two leather wingback chairs and a big leather sofa chosen for comfort. There was a wood stove in here, too. He preferred its heat to that of a gas fireplace.

Her gaze traveled over the old photographs on the way. "You must really love history to collect so many old pictures."

"Those aren't just any old photos. They're photos from Scarlet and Caribou, part of a collection my great-great-grandfather Silas commissioned. He wanted to dazzle his investors with images from the wild west or some damned thing."

"Really?" She stepped closer, peered at one of the photos.

Joe pointed to the man standing to the left of the kibble—the big iron bucket used to lower and hoist miners from the mine. "Do you recognize this guy?"

Rain studied the image. "He looks familiar, but…"

"That's Cadan Hawke, Eric's great-great-great-grandfather. He was the mine foreman." Until Silas decided he was too much of a rabble-rouser.

Rain's face lit up with a smile that made it hard for Joe to think. "Seriously? Wow. He looks so much like Eric, doesn't he?"

From downstairs in the kitchen came the sound of beeping.

"Sounds like the biscuits and bacon are ready."

After Joe left for town, Rain contacted her insurance company, more than a little afraid they were going to tell her she was out of luck. The woman who took her call was sympathetic and understanding and assured Rain that damage to her house and her belongings was covered by her policy. That was the good news.

The bad news was that her policy didn't cover a rental car, so she'd be without wheels until her SUV was liberated. Also, she had a deductible of a thousand dollars, so she wouldn't be able to replace everything. And the cherry on top? She would have to keep paying her mortgage—even if her home no longer existed.

The representative had assured her that they would send a claims adjuster as soon as they could. The woman hadn't been able to tell her when she'd be able to get to her belongings or how to hire a company to remove the wreckage of her home or how she would be able to afford rent together with the mortgage.

The entire situation sucked.

Knowing she'd done all she could do for today, Rain walked upstairs to take a shower. What would she wear when she got out? She didn't want to wear her PJs for the next two months. Joe had said he'd talk to the fire department about getting access to her clothes and personal stuff, but Rain knew Eric. He wouldn't risk anyone's life so she could have clean panties.

She turned toward her bedroom—and stopped. Maybe she could borrow a T-shirt and some jeans from Joe. He had told her to make herself at home and given her the run of his house. Surely, he wouldn't mind if she borrowed some clothes.

She changed directions, walked to the other end of the hallway, and slipped inside his room. She stood there for a moment, allowing herself to take in the sight of it—the king-sized platform bed with its black leather headboard, the pile of books on his nightstand, the overstuffed black leather chair in the corner. Oh, yes, this was the Joe she knew and lusted after—masculine, unaffected, graceful. The room even smelled like him.

She inhaled his scent again, her gaze fixed on the bed. She had fantasized about sleeping with him a thousand times, but she'd never made it into that bed.

You never will. Get used to it.

She gave herself a little tour, walking to the window and then stepping into his bathroom. "Wow."

It was even bigger than hers with a fireplace, a glass shower stall the size of the women's bathroom at Knockers, and an enormous marble bathtub. She walked over to the tub, ran her hand along the cool stone, her mind filling with images of Joe making love to her here, that mouth on her skin, those arms holding her close, his big hands working to please her.

Dream on.

She left the bathroom, walked over to his closet, and opened it to find herself smiling. It was the most organized closet she'd ever seen. Jeans hung here, casual shirts there, dress shirts near his neatly hung ties. Shoes ranging from running shoes to cowboy boots to formal dress shoes sat on shelves. Was that a tux? Yep, it was.

God, she'd pay money to see him in that.

Get what you need and leave. You're not here to snoop.

Couldn't she snoop just a little? She'd never been this close to the private Joe Moffat, and it fascinated her. She opened drawers in the built-in dresser, telling herself that she was looking for T-shirts. Instead, she found boxer briefs. She reached inside the drawer, ran her hands over them.

Oh, for God's sake! Stop! You're not this desperate.

Maybe she was.

Feeling a little ashamed, she took out a pair of briefs, figuring she had to wear something, then picked a shirt and a faded pair of jeans and headed to her own room. She dropped the clothes on her bed and hooked her phone to the sound system she'd discovered this morning. Then she flicked on the gas fireplace, which was double-sided, the fire visible both from the bedroom and from inside the bathroom. Just because she'd been forced to abandon her home didn't mean she couldn't enjoy staying here.

She stripped, tossed her pajamas on the bed, and walked into the bathroom. The tile floor was warm against her feet. Yeah, she could get used to radiant heat.

She found small bottles of shampoo and conditioner in one of the drawers, along with bars of soap, travel-sized tubes of toothpaste and several unopened toothbrushes, and a bag of disposable razors. "You think of everything, Joe."

She took shampoo, conditioner, and soap to the shower, which was big enough for four adults to stand together without touching, its floor and walls made of gray stone tiles, its half-dozen chrome fixtures promising her a massage as well as a shower. She studied the knobs for a moment, then turned the largest of them.

Ice-cold water sprayed at her from all directions.

She shrieked, scooted back against the wall, and fumbled with the knob in a rush to turn off the water. "Let's try that again."

This time, she stayed out of the way of the nozzles, testing the water with her hand until it was warm before stepping into the spray.

"*Ooob!*" She couldn't help but moan, warm water raining down on her from above and hitting her spine from behind, the warmth and the gentle rhythm of it as relaxing as a massage.

This was luxury.

She'd grown up without money and had needed to work for every penny she'd earned, but that didn't mean she couldn't appreciate nice things.

She took her time washing her hair and skin and shaving her legs and underarms, turning so that the massage heads worked over her entire body. Best. Shower. *Ever.*

She stepped out and dried off with a fluffy gray towel, tying it around her body before grabbing a second smaller towel to dry her hair. Humming to the music, she danced her way out of the bathroom and began to dress.

She stepped into the boxer briefs. They were a bit tight around her hips, but not uncomfortably so. His jeans fit, too, though she had to roll them up at the ankles. The shirt was too big for her, so she rolled up the sleeves and let it hang like a tunic.

She didn't have a bra, which meant that the tips of her nipples stood out beneath the soft white fabric. Ah, well. There was nothing she could do about that. Joe never looked at her anyway. He wouldn't notice.

She'd just combed her hair when her cell phone rang. She hurried to the shelf, unplugged it. "Hey, baby, how are the snow sculpt—"

"Why didn't you call me?" Lark sounded truly angry. "The roof collapsed on our house, and you didn't even call me? You could have been killed!"

"It was the middle of the night, and there was nothing you could have done. I didn't want to worry you."

"I'm your daughter. I'm your only family. It's my job to worry about you."

Rain told Lark what had happened and how she'd been able to take cover under her bed. "I can't get in to get anything out or see what's been damaged. Joe said he would talk to the fire department about that for me."

Lark's tone of voice changed from angry to intrigued. "Oooh! So Joe rescued you? He likes you, Mom. I know he does. The whole town knows he does."

"Eric and his guys rescued me. Joe is just being kind. He'd do this for anyone."

"I'm not so sure about that. Where are you staying?"

"Joe's place." She was about to tell Lark how amazing Joe's house was, but before she could get a word out, Lark cut her off.

"Excellent! See? He likes you."

Rain felt a niggling of irritation. She had waited for twenty years for him to notice her, wasted the best years of her life pining for him. "If he likes me, why doesn't he say something?"

What about last night?

He'd called her *honey*. He'd seemed genuinely worried about her. He'd stayed with her, held her hand in the ER.

"How am I supposed to know, Mom? Men are weird."

Lark's call was the first of many, as news of Rain's situation made its way through town. Apparently, the newspaper had done a front-page article on the collapse of her roof, and people wanted to help. Kendra called and told Rain that she could stay in Lexi's old room at the inn. Rose called, too, asked a lot of questions about Joe, then told Rain she was welcome to stay in her spare bedroom. Lexi, and Vicki, called, too, and Cheyenne—all of them offering her whatever she needed, whether it was a place to stay or clothes to wear or a shoulder to cry on.

Their kindness touched Rain. She thanked them all but told them she was staying with Joe for now. As for the clothes... No one could drive to her, and she couldn't go anywhere. That would have to wait.

Rain wasn't used to having an entire day off. With no job to go to and no house to clean, Rain didn't know what to do with herself. She wandered downstairs to the kitchen, wondering what there was to eat for lunch. She searched Joe's pantry and refrigerator—and then inspiration hit her. She found the ingredients she needed and got busy making a big pot of chili. She turned on music, dancing while she thawed and browned the bacon and beef, chopped onions, garlic, celery, and tomatoes, and measured out spices. It was a recipe she'd made a hundred times in her crockpot and perfect for a snowy day.

Her phone buzzed—again.

Joe.

She answered. "Hey, how's it going?"

"Most of the streets in town are slick but passable, but a lot of people need help with their sidewalks and driveways. How are you doing?"

"I called the insurance company, and I'm covered, so that's a relief."

"I bet. I'm glad to hear it."

"I love that shower in your guest room. I could live there."

"In the shower?"

"Absolutely."

He chuckled. "I left a message with Hawke about getting into your place to get some clothes and personal stuff. He hasn't called back yet. He's probably still asleep. I'll let you know what he says."

"Thanks, Joe. Be careful. Nothing in there is worth your life."

"I'll check in a bit later. I'm off to clear the parking lot at the pub again and check on the roof. Talk to you later."

Rain went back to the chili, adding a bottle of Glacier Stout she found in the fridge. Soon, it was simmering in a big cast iron pot on the stove, the scent making her mouth water. She ate a quick bowl for lunch, added a little more chili powder, and then left it on low on the stove so that the flavors could cook together. She would make cornbread and a salad to go with it later.

She drifted through the house, retracing the steps of the tour Joe had given her, still amazed by the luxury and beauty of his place. What a humble man he was. He never let on that he was wealthy. His family had earned a fortune off their silver mine. Everyone knew that. But Joe didn't behave like a spoiled rich kid, the heir to a fortune. He rarely mentioned his family or his ancestry. He was just a normal guy—okay, a very *hot* guy with a successful business who was ethical to a fault, as demonstrated by his disappointing refusal to hit on her.

She found herself in his library, looking at the old photos on the wall. Eric's great-great-great-grandfather with dust and grime on his face, a steel drill propped over one shoulder, the stub of a candle stuck to the brim of his helmet. A building of wooden planks with the words *Caribou Silverlode* painted on the side. Five miners holding sticks of dynamite. A woman making a meal on a barrel stove, a baby lying on a blanket in the dirt nearby. A man standing on a scaffold about to be hanged, a hood covering his head, the noose already around his neck. She found herself wondering who he'd been and what crime he'd committed.

She walked over to the bookshelves, perused the titles. Shakespeare. Byron. Dickens. Austen. Faulkner. Hemingway. Shelley. Fitzgerald. Tolkien. Lewis. Wharton. He had all of the classics, but they weren't there for show. The bindings were worn, and some still had bookmarks.

Deciding she might as well read, but not interested in anything heavy, Rain moved to another set of shelves, her fingers tracing the leather-bound tomes. These were labeled only with Joe's last name and gold embossed numerals. Curious, she drew out the first volume and opened it.

It was a journal, but not Joe's journal. The date at the top of the page was June 15, 1868, the handwriting meticulous. This wasn't the original. It was a bound copy of an original. Joe must have had it copied and bound it so that he could read it without risking the original. In the margins were notes written in pencil in Joe's familiar cursive.

Rain set the diary on a nearby chair, built a fire in the woodstove, then settled herself on the plush leather sofa with a fresh cup of coffee and began to read.

Chapter Four

June 15, 1868

I arrived yesterday afternoon in Scarlet Springs in the Colorado Territory. I have come to this rough frontier town to invest my inheritance in the gold and silver buried in these Rocky Mountains. As Father said, "The noblest use for wealth is the procurement of greater wealth."

Those who are not affluent decry the pursuit of capital, calling it avarice, but they would snatch up gold with both hands if it were offered to them. There is nothing that advances a man's prospects more surely than lucre. To a wealthy man, all doors are open, and no one, from priest to politician, turns him away. I intend to elevate my fortunes so that the name of Moffat is spoken with reverence in the halls of power and so that my descendants might live like kings.

I traveled with the Central Overland California and Pikes Peak Express from Leavenworth, Kansas, as the railway has not yet reached Denver City. I was told by a fellow traveler, a newspaperman named Greeley, that dueling railways are under construction—one from Cheyenne and one from Kansas—and that I could do far worse than to invest in one or both. Indeed, this area must have the railway to prosper. The journey of six days by stagecoach passed through lands best described as desolate and over roads that are unworthy of the name. Though the drivers worried ceaselessly about Indian attacks, I saw not a single Indian the entire way—a disappointment, I must admit.

Denver City itself is as squalid a frontier town as one could ever hope to see. Wagon trains and oxen share the muddy streets with horses, carriages, and those who have no means of transportation but their feet. Even so, a man of means can find comfortable lodgings and a good meal. If he is not too particular, he can satisfy his baser needs among the tents and Indian huts set up along Cherry Creek. One such tent had a crude wooden sign out front that read, "Men taken in and done for." As ineloquent as it is, the advertisement seemed to work, as some twenty men stood in line, each waiting his turn at whatever pock-scarred, toothless strumpet plies her trade there.

Yet, one might well consider Denver City a metropolis compared to Scarlet Springs, this little mining town high in the mountains. The town can only be reached by wagon over a steep and winding road. This will make getting supplies difficult and costlier, especially in the winter. While this rugged country presents challenges, it is rich beyond measure in opportunity for men of vision and determination. These untamed mountains will surrender up whatever treasures a man's will can wrest from them— lumber, quarried stone, meat, pelts, silver, and gold.

As for Scarlet Springs itself, the town boasts but a single inn, which stands near the center of town. Mr. O'Hara, the owner, is an educated man at least, despite being a flame-haired Irishman who talks too much. Brothels far outnumber other businesses. There are two dry goods stores, three saloons, a mercantile, a blacksmith, a wheelwright, a stable where a man can rent a horse or a mule, and a newspaper. In addition to these respectable enterprises, there are at least a dozen brothels, which cater to the miners.

Edward Gundry, the drunken Cornishman who brought my luggage via cart from the station to the inn, told me the town is named for its whores, scarlet being the color associated with soiled doves. Mr. O'Hara, upon hearing this, immediately denied it. Indeed, he grew scarlet-faced in defense of his town, claiming the name honors the bright red soil that is common in this area.

As tedious as these little people can be, I also find them amusing.

Gundry for his part quietly offered to procure me the services of one of these women of ill repute should I find myself in need. "For a silver coin, I'll talk to the madam and bring back the right maid for you. We'll bring her in through the back like, aye? No one need know." I thanked him for his offer, but declined.

Two months hence, I shall marry Louisa Beaulieau. I shouldn't like to risk a scandal that might outrage her father and end our betrothal. He owns steelworks in Pennsylvania, and I shall no doubt need his connections and his capital, along with a great deal of steel, if I am to succeed in Colorado. Truth be told, I find his money far more attractive than his daughter, but I shall have both, as he has no male heirs. Once the wedding is consummated—I am confident I can rise to the task no matter how plain Louisa's countenance might be—then I shall be free to dally where I will.

Tomorrow, I shall ride up to the area called Caribou to visit the mine I am here to purchase. My assayer and engineers assure me that one of the richest silver lodes in the West is trapped within its rock, waiting to be blasted free. The man who discovered it, a placer miner, lacks the capital to develop it. I will make him a wealthy man, at least according to his standards, and then we shall see.

Rain read until it was nearly dark outside and Joe had texted her that he was on the way home. She couldn't say she liked Silas Moffat. Still, his impressions of this area from long ago fascinated her. Her own ancestors had arrived in Scarlet Springs not long before he'd come, and she wondered if she'd read anything about them in his pages.

She tucked a bookmark in where she'd stopped reading and set off for the kitchen to bake cornbread.

Joe smelled it the moment he stepped out of his Land Rover, and his mouth watered. "Damn."

He grabbed the two large bags of belongings he'd managed to rescue from Rain's place and walked inside, stopping to take off his coat and boots before following that delicious aroma straight to the kitchen.

Rain looked up, smiled, her hair hanging loosely around her shoulders. "Hey. I made chili and cornbread. I hope you're hungry."

Holy hell.

Joe stared, his gaze raking over her. She wore one of his shirts and a pair of his jeans, but they looked a hell of a lot better on her than they did on him. His jeans hugged her hips and ass. The overly large shirt made her look small and feminine despite its masculine cut, her nipples dark and pebbled against the cloth.

He was hungry all right, but not for food. "Chili. Cornbread. Good."

You sound like an idiot.

He *was* an idiot, his mind unable to rein in his body's response to her. He cleared his throat, moved whatever was in his hand so that it covered the growing bulge at his groin, some part of his mind stuck on one thought: Her ass was in his jeans.

"I hope you don't mind that I borrowed some of your clothes." She smoothed her hands down the front of her shirt drawing his gaze back to those nipples.

He gave a shake of his head. "No. No. Not at all."

"I just grabbed a pair of your underwear, some jeans, and this shirt. I'll wash them when I'm done."

She was wearing a pair of his boxer briefs?

Goddamn.

Her gaze dropped to his crotch—or rather to whatever he was holding in front of it. Oh, yeah. The bags that held her clothes and a few other things. Right.

"I managed to get into your place—just the bedroom. Hawke brought in some beams to stabilize it, while I crawled in and grabbed a few things for you."

Her eyes went wide. "You went inside my house?"

He nodded.

"Oh, Joe!" She moved toward him.

He hesitated to offer her the bags, not wanting to give away his hard-on.

Shit.

She took the bags from him, set them down on the table, opened them.

He stepped behind the counter, willed his dick to chill out. "I couldn't get out of your room to the rest of your house, but I did make it to your closet. I hope I grabbed the right stuff."

"This is perfect." There were jeans, a couple of sweaters, T-shirts, a few blouses, her bathrobe, and the clothes she wore to work, as well as lacy underthings—and the framed photo of Lark she kept on her bedside table.

She gave a little gasp, pulled out the photo, held it to her breast. "Thanks, Joe. This means a lot to me. You weren't in danger, were you?"

"Do you honestly think Hawke would let me go in if I were?"

"Mmm... no."

The timer on the oven beeped.

She left the bags near the table, hurried to grab an oven mitt, and pulled a golden loaf of cornbread from the oven. "Dinner is ready."

"That smells incredible. I'll just wash up." He took the stairs up to his bathroom, washed his hands, and gave himself a stern look in the mirror.

Rain worked for him. She was a valued employee, and she was a decade younger than he was. He did not fuck around with his female staff. He did not try to romance them. She was off-limits, even if she was wearing the hell out of his Levis.

Got that, buddy?

Yeah. His mind got it. He wasn't sure about the rest of him.

He made his way downstairs again to find the table set, and dinner served, chili in bowls, cornbread on plates. "I'll go grab us a bottle of wine."

Down in the wine cellar, he closed his eyes, drew a deep breath. "What the hell has gotten into you, man?"

"What did you say?" she called.

"I said how about a 2012 Château Grand Traverse Pinot Noir Vin Gris." He reached for the bottle and headed back upstairs to open it.

"That sounds fabulous." Rain was lighting candles, which she'd arranged in the center of the table.

Hell. Was she trying to create a romantic atmosphere? Joe wasn't sure he could survive that.

Keep your shit together, man.

"Did you go out of your mind with boredom today?" He found his wine bottle opener, removed the cork, and poured them each a glass, then carried both glasses and the bottle to the table and sat.

"I spent the day in your library reading." She put her napkin in her lap. "I found Silas Moffat's journals, and I'm reading all about the early days in Scarlet."

Joe froze for a moment, spoon in mid-air, a hint of adrenaline making his heart beat faster. "Oh?"

It was on the tip of his tongue to warn her that she wouldn't like what she read, but he knew Rain. If he tried to stop her from reading the journal, he would only pique her curiosity.

"I just reached the point where he bought the mine and hired a photographer to document everything. I guess most of those photos on your walls are his."

"Yeah." Joe took a bite, barely noticing the mingled flavors of the chili flaring across this tongue. "Silas wasn't a good man."

That was an understatement.

The bastard had been ruthless, and Joe was ashamed to be his descendant—and the beneficiary of his cruelty. If Joe had anything to say about it, the name Moffat would die with him. Joe didn't plan to marry or have a family. When he died, his money would go into a foundation for the people of Scarlet Springs, and that would be the end of Silas' legacy. Some part of Joe wished he'd hidden the journals so that Rain wouldn't have found them. With any luck, she would lose interest before she got to the worst of it, the part of Silas' story that haunted Joe.

"O'Hara—that's the last name of Lexi and Britta's mother, isn't it?" Rain had gone to school with the two Jewell sisters and knew them well. Their mother had died in a car crash in the canyon when they were little.

"Yeah." Joe buttered his cornbread. "The O'Haras came west, built the Forest Creek Inn during the silver rush, and stayed. Bob Jewell took possession of it when his wife died. Unless Lexi or Britta takes over the operation, I'm not sure what will happen to the place. Someone will probably buy it, and it will leave the family."

That would be a shame after five generations.

"Is the Mr. Gundry that Silas mentioned related to our Hank?"

Joe nodded. "Hank is his great-great-grandnephew—or something like that."

Rain looked over at Joe, a knowing smile on her lips, wine glass in hand. "This is how you know so much about Scarlet Springs history, isn't it? You've got an eye-witness account of it in your library and all those photos."

"Yeah." Joe left it at that.

After supper, they did the dishes together, then moved to the living room, taking their glasses and the bottle of wine with them. Rain couldn't help but love the intimate feel of the moment. She was getting a glimpse of the private side of Joe, the side of him that no one except perhaps Rico got to see. She could get used to this.

Joe flicked the switch to start a gas fire in the fireplace, then sat with her on the gray leather sofa in the living room to watch the news.

Channel 12 led with a weather update, predicting high winds, blowing snow, and another nine to twelve inches of snow in the high country. The governor had yet to lift the state of emergency, and mountain highways were still closed due to a combination of icy conditions, blowing snow, and avalanche danger.

"Are you going to open tomorrow?" Rain couldn't remember a time when Knockers had been closed two days in a row.

Joe's brows drew together as he thought about it. "If the wind kicks up, we're going to have twenty-foot drifts blocking the roads. They're saying more snow. I guess we'll have to wait and see."

Outside, the sun had long since set, snow swirling against the windows as the wind picked up.

Rain thought of her house and the mess waiting for her there. "Maybe it's a sign."

"A sign? What's a sign?" He released his hair from its ponytail, letting it fall loose and free over his shoulders.

Rain's brain went blank, her fingers aching to run through that hair. Did he have any idea how good-looking he was?

She took another sip of wine, fought to pull herself together. "My house. Maybe it's time for me to start over somewhere else."

Joe frowned. "Why do you say that?"

"I'm thirty-seven. My only child is an adult and living on her own. I'm perpetually single." *Hint, hint, you big dummy.* "I've been here all my life."

Except for the year she'd spent on the road with Guy, but that had been a disaster.

"Here isn't so bad." Joe gave a little laugh. "I've seen what's out there, and, believe me, what we have in Scarlet is as good as life gets."

It was Rain's turn to laugh. "That's a depressing thought."

He studied her through narrowed eyes. "I thought you loved this town."

"I do." She did. Really. But… "I've been here all my life, and now my life doesn't seem to have much of a point."

A look of understanding passed over his face. "This is about Lark."

His words, like an arrow, shot straight to her heart.

Tears welled up in her eyes. She turned her face away from him, blinked. "No. Okay, maybe. Yeah. I miss her."

Joe reached over, took her free hand in his, gave it a squeeze, heat shivering up Rain's arm at the touch. "Lark is a smart, fun, caring, beautiful young woman, and *you* raised her. You raised her on your own even though you were just a kid yourself when she was born. You should be proud."

Joe knew the whole story, of course—how Rain had dropped out of high school to tour with Guy and his Grateful Dead cover band; how she'd gotten pregnant on the road and had given birth alone in the back of an old VW van while Guy was off drinking, doing LSD, and screwing some other woman; how he'd refused to drive her to the hospital because he was afraid he'd be arrested; how Rain had hitchhiked her way home with Lark in her arms; how her parents had rejected her, even moving to Florida to get away from the daughter that had shamed them.

It was Joe who'd given Rain a job and helped her find a place to live. He'd even held a baby shower for her at Knockers so that Lark could have clothes and a crib and all those things babies needed. When Guy had shown up at Knockers a few years later, wanting money and demanding to see Rain, Joe had punched him, thrown him out the door and onto his ass in the parking lot.

Rain had been hopelessly in love with him since that day.

"I *am* proud, but...." How could she explain this? "It feels like the center of my life just packed up and left. I don't know what I'm supposed to do with myself now. I didn't even put up a Christmas tree this year, though I guess that turned out to be lucky. If I *had* put up a tree, all of the ornaments Lark and I made together would have been broken. They're all in boxes in the garage."

"Way to find the silver lining there." Joe's gaze dropped to the floor, and she knew he was thinking about something.

Was he upset at her for reading Silas' journals? He hadn't said so over supper, but she knew him well enough to know that something about it bothered him.

He lifted his gaze to hers. "I have an idea. After work tomorrow, let's put up a tree here. I've got boxes and boxes of decorations somewhere around here. Some are antiques. Hell, some of them probably even belonged to Silas and his wife."

"Really? How cool is that?"

"We can decorate the place, make some hot chocolate, play some of that awful holiday music that everyone loves."

Rain stared at Joe. "Are you serious?"

He nodded. "Sure."

"I could make Christmas cookies, too, and fudge—well, if you've got the ingredients. I think you probably do."

Joe laughed. "All right, then. Let's get to it. Bundle up. You can borrow whatever outdoor gear you don't have from me. We can take out my snowmobile, cut down a tree, and have it waiting for us when we get back after closing tomorrow."

For the first time in what felt like a long time, Rain was excited about something.

Chapter Five

Joe attached the sled to the back of his snowmobile, then tied the chainsaw onto the sled, together with his snowshoes and a bundle of rope. He used the sled to haul back firewood that he cut on his property through the winter. He'd never used it to carry a Christmas tree.

Rain stepped into the garage and closed the door behind her, one of his hats on her head, his ski gloves on her hands, an old woolen scarf wrapped around her neck, his ski pants on her legs. "The socks make the boots fit better. Thanks."

"You're welcome." He studied her for a moment. "Are you sure you should be going out? You just got over hypothermia. I could do this and be back in a flash."

"I want to come."

"Okay, but promise me you'll say something if you start to feel chilled."

"Yes, mom." She looked up at him from beneath her lashes, a teasing gleam in those green eyes.

Damn, she was sexy when she was a smart-ass.

He opened the garage door, straddled the snowmobile. "Climb on."

Rain settled on the seat behind him, her arms going around his waist, her inner thighs pressing against the outside of his. Even through the layers of parkas and clothes, he could feel the heat of her body. Or maybe that was the heat in his blood.

"Hold on." He rode the snowmobile out of his garage and into deep snow, the sled with the chainsaw following behind.

The night was cold, but it was also beautiful. A thick blanket of white lay over the landscape, pine branches laden with snow until their boughs bent. The snowmobile's headlights illuminated the path ahead of them, snowflakes swirling in the wind.

"This is fun!" Rain called to him.

"Have you ever been on a snowmobile before?"

"No!" she called back.

Well, it was about time.

Joe went a little faster, found himself smiling when she squealed. He hadn't had a Christmas tree since he was a kid. He was rarely home, and there was no one to share it with. It seemed like a lot of work for nothing. Then again, Christmas had never meant much to him. It had always seemed like an empty holiday, a time when people got themselves into debt buying shit they didn't need. But that's clearly not how Rain felt about it. Her face had lit up the moment he'd suggested this, her eyes filling with excitement.

Hell, he'd have been willing to do almost anything to see that smile.

"Where are we going?" she shouted up to him.

"Just over here." He knew every inch of this forest and would have had no trouble finding his way even without the snowmobile's headlights. He knew right where he was taking her—a thick stand of young evergreens on the other side of the old shaft house that he'd planned to thin.

"What's that?"

The shaft house loomed out of the trees, a dark shape against the forest, the words *Caribou Silverlode* still visible on the side.

He waited until he'd stopped the snowmobile to answer. "That's the shaft house. It covers the entrance to the mine shaft. That's where you find the machinery that lowers the kibble—that big iron bucket you saw in the photo—into the mine. That's how miners got in and out with their tools and gear. Can you reach my snowshoes?"

Rain turned and climbed back onto the sled to untie the knot that held them in place. "Here you go."

"Thanks." He strapped into them, then stepped onto seven feet of new snow, sinking up to his ankles. "You probably ought to stay where you are. If you step out onto this stuff, you'll find yourself post-holing and be hypothermic again in no time."

He walked a short distance away to the stand of trees he'd had in mind, snow crunching under his snowshoes. He shook the snow off the branches of the tallest one. "What do you think?"

"It's perfect."

He started up the chainsaw, cut through the slender trunk, then took hold of the tree and dragged it back to the sled. "I'll just tie this down, and we'll get you back to the fire where it's warm."

He lifted the tree onto the sled, picked up the rope, but couldn't manage to tie it down with his gloves on. He pulled them off, accidentally dropping one in the snow.

Rain reached for it. The snowmobile tilted just a little, but it was enough to dump her into the snow. She laughed, floundered, sinking deeper until she was up to her hips in powder. "I didn't mean for this to happen. Sorry."

"Don't apologize." He walked over to her and took her hands to pull her up—only to lose his balance and fall into the snow almost on top of her.

Damned snowshoes.

She laughed, looking up at him through wide eyes, breathless, snow on her eyelashes. He laughed, too, unable to take his gaze from hers.

God, he wanted to kiss her.

His gaze dropped to her lips, his mouth only inches from hers now, close enough that he could feel the heat of her. It would be *so* easy.

Knock it the hell off.

He rolled off her, wallowing in the snow before he managed to get his snowshoes beneath him again. "We need to get you out of this."

By the time he was on his feet, she'd taken hold of the snowmobile and was trying to pull herself up. He walked to the other side and held it, acting as a counterweight so that it wouldn't flip over. The damned thing weighed almost six-hundred pounds, but it wasn't as stable as it seemed, especially not in deep snow. He reached for her with one hand, helping her into the seat.

"Thanks." She was still smiling.

"You okay?"

She nodded, laughed, gave him a breathless, "Oh, yeah. That was fun."

"How did I know you were going to say that?" He finished securing the tree to the sled, and drove their cargo back to the house, his mind reeling from what he'd almost done, what he still wanted to do.

"Head in and get warm while I stick the tree in a bucket of water."

She nodded, her cheeks red from the chill, then disappeared inside.

Joe let out a breath. He needed to get his act together. He had come so close to kissing her out there. She was going to be here for a while. He couldn't let his desire for her get the better of him.

He grabbed his snowshoes, went to hang them on their hook.

Would it be so wrong?

The thought surprised him, made his step falter.

Would it be wrong for him to tell her how he felt about her and to let her decide where this went? She wasn't that vulnerable sixteen-year-old kid any longer. She was an adult and more than capable of taking care of herself.

No.

There was right, and there was wrong. No matter what he felt for Rain, Joe was *still* her employer.

Resolved, he hung up his snowshoes then walked back to untie the tree.

Twenty-five days till Christmas

Rain knew the moment she opened the blinds in the morning that Joe wouldn't open the pub for business today. Snow had blown against her window in a drift that was more than ten feet tall, obscuring much of her view of the outdoors. Outside her bathroom window, visibility wasn't much better, snow blowing horizontally in the wind, white snow against a white background. She couldn't tell whether the state was in the midst of a blizzard or if the wind was moving snow that had already fallen.

She knew it wasn't good for business to be closed two days in a row. Even so, she couldn't help the sense of anticipation she felt at the prospect of spending the entire day with Joe and decorating the tree they'd brought back.

Joe had almost kissed her last night. For a moment, she'd seen desire in his eyes. She'd known he'd wanted to kiss her. Then he'd pulled away. Why? If he was attracted to her, why not give in to that attraction and see where it led them?

She showered, dressed, and went downstairs to find a note on the kitchen counter.

Hope you slept well. I'm heading into town to help clear streets. We'll decorate tonight.

Well, so much for spending the day together.

She made herself some toast and coffee, then decided to put her time to use making Christmas cookies and fudge. Using a recipe from her favorite online cooking site, she got to work on the cookie dough, measuring out flour, sugar, and butter, cracking eggs, mixing it together.

Why had Joe pulled back? Why hadn't he kissed her?

If she knew him—and she liked to think she did—he was probably worried about their working relationship. It would be just like Joe to get caught up on something like that. Or maybe she'd misread the entire thing and he'd never meant to kiss her at all.

No, that couldn't be it. She'd worked waiting tables all her life. She knew desire in a man's eyes when she saw it.

She set the cookie dough in the refrigerator to chill for a couple of hours. When she'd cleaned up the dishes, she made a batch of her Grandma's old-fashioned Christmas fudge, melting butter in a cast iron pot, adding sugar, cocoa, and stirring it as she brought it to a boil.

Her mind drifted to last night, sifting through the details. The feel of his hard body as he'd fallen on top of her. The sharp need in his brown eyes. The way his gaze had dropped to her lips. The desire on his face as his mouth had hovered just above hers.

Shit!

Had she let the fudge boil too long?

She tested it, dropping a bit into cold water, and was relieved to find it was still in the soft ball stage. She whisked vanilla into the fudge, poured it into a greased pan to cool, then loaded the dirty dishes into the dishwasher and started the machine.

Now what?

She walked to the window, looked out onto the landscape of churning white. Then she remembered Silas and his journals. She poured herself another cup of coffee, carried it to the library, built a fire in the little woodstove, then curled up beneath a soft, white throw blanket with the journal to read.

July 28, 1868

I depart Scarlet Springs tomorrow and journey back to Philadelphia for my wedding. How I wish the ceremony and the wedding night could be accomplished in my absence. After countless delays, we finally received the shipment of steel rails needed to begin work in earnest, and yet now I must abandon this enterprise to play bridegroom to a simpering, witless girl. With any luck, I'll get her with child on our wedding night and be able to leave her behind when I return.

John Craddock, whom I hired in Denver, is the superintendent of my mining enterprise, but he has no head for it. I had hoped that this exciting new venture would produce in him a man of will and vigor. Instead, he continues to earn my disfavor. Where I have learned much about silver mining these past weeks, he seems incapable of expanding his knowledge. He obeys me well, but he cannot reason for himself or anticipate my demands or the needs of the organization. If I do not tell him to do a thing, he does not think to do it. Yet, I must leave my mine in his hands these next two months no matter my misgivings.

Today, I hired a foreman. I sought a man who knows the mining trade well enough to run the underground operations in my absence and who knows how to get a day's hard work out of these damned Cornish. By all accounts, the man I hired is just such a man. He is himself Cornish, with the colorful name Cadan Hawke. He is a big man, all muscle like an ox, and came with letters of praise written by the last mine owner for whom he worked. I cannot say, however, that I am well pleased with him. He is bold in both manner and speech, as if he believes himself to be my equal.

His speech itself is as amusing as it is unintelligible. When I asked him how long he'd worked in mines, he said, "Me father was a tinner, you, and his father afore him. I was born with a gad in me hand. I been holin' like since I was a bearn o' nine."

I told him that I would expect him to make sure everyone on my payroll, from the hoist operator to the muckers—the boys who put ore into the carts—does a full day's work without shirking. He said, "I'll nae abide any sleuchin' at the wheal. The men will be good trugs and true."

Mr. Craddock informed me that this meant Hawke would not tolerate laziness but would only hire hard workers. I will admit that Craddock has a knack for their ridiculous dialect. I suppose that does commend him.

After that, Hawke looked me in the eyes as bold as you please and asked whether I was a "jest man, a fair man." He said he'd work his knuckles to the bone for such a man, but not for one who "knicks" his workers.

Is that not insolent?

I laughed and told him I was as just and fair as any man and that I was the one who ought to be afraid of dishonesty and thieving.

Next, he asked about the pay—not his pay, but the pay of the men. I asked him what he thought was fair, hoping the question would reveal whether he had my interests at heart or merely those of the workers. I had Mr. Craddock look into this matter and had learned that the going rate of pay for miners in the Colorado Territory was three dollars a day plus three candles. I waited for Hawke's answer, determined to send him away if he thought me a fool and asked for more.

"Three dollars a day, sir, and three tommy sticks," he said.

Why I should have to pay for the miners' candles is beyond me, but I saw no alternative but to agree. I informed Hawke that he had the job and that I expected him to have the mine completely operational by the time I return in September. He grinned and told me I'd be "right plaised" when I got back and that I wouldn't regret hiring him.

I do hope he's right on both counts.

For now, I must turn my attention toward my journey home and my coming nuptials. I received a letter from Louisa this morning in which she prattled at length about her love for me and her joy at the thought of becoming my wife. Do women have nothing better to ponder? I spent no more than a dozen hours in her company, and yet she writes eloquently of the deep love she has for me.

I have yet to purchase a gift for her. I find the whole business tedious, and yet a man must have an heir. Still, this wedding has begun to feel like the noose around my neck. Since there is no way word of any dalliance could reach my future father-in-law before I do, I have procured the services of one of Belle Ellery's girls for my last night in town. Belle owns the most fashionable brothel in Scarlet and is quite lovely for all that she is aged almost forty. For a handsome fee, she has promised me a virgin.

I warned her that I would have no problem discerning between a true virgin and an actress. I cannot hope to breed a healthy heir on my wife if I give her a disease. Belle asked if I wanted a white girl or whether a Mexican or Indian would suffice. I told her

I didn't care so long as no man has been between her legs before I. All women are the same on the inside.

Rain closed the journal, set it on the sofa beside her, and got up to stoke the fire, laughing to think that Rose's ancestor had run a brothel. She had no trouble imagining that. Rose, like Belle, had a penchant for seducing younger men. Though Rose never traded sex for money, she did sell illusions—tarot readings, astrological readings, and the like. What was prostitution if not the illusion of intimacy?

The description of Cadan Hawke's speech had also amused her. Most of the people here were descended from Cornish miners, and not all of their customs—or their unique words or ideas—had been lost. The pub, Knockers, was named after the tommyknockers, spirits that the Cornish had believed lived in the mines. Lexi Taylor even claimed to have seen one when she'd been trapped and injured in a collapsed mineshaft. She said the tommyknocker called himself Cousin Jack and kept her awake and alive until Austin and the rest of the Team arrived to rescue her. Rain had always figured that Lexi had hallucinated the tommyknocker, but who was she to say that what Lexi had seen wasn't real?

As for Silas, Joe was right. He wasn't a good person. Rain felt sorry for Louisa. The poor bride-to-be had no idea that her future husband was a pig who cared more for money than for her. Rain found herself wishing she could send a letter or a telegram to warn Louisa. But of course, all of this had happened long ago. Besides, if Louisa hadn't married Silas, there would be no Joe.

Rain had just put another piece of wood in the woodstove when she heard Joe enter the mudroom, stomping his feet to shake off the snow. She closed the woodstove, went downstairs, and walked down the hallway to meet him. The look on his face made her pulse skip. "What is it? What's wrong?"

Chapter Six

"I'm an idiot. That's what's wrong." Joe slipped out of his sodden parka, hung it on a hook to dry.

Rain walked toward him, concern on her face. "What happened?"

The sight of her blunted the sharpest edge of his anger. "I've spent the entire morning half a freaking mile from the house stuck in a damned ditch."

"What?"

Oh, she looked good, faded jeans accentuating her hips, the ties of her blue peasant top undone to reveal just a hint of cleavage, her hair hanging thick and beautiful down her back.

He pulled off his wet gloves, tossed them onto the bench, and flexed his freezing fingers. "I couldn't see the edge of the road and slid off at the first switchback."

"Oh, no! I'm sorry."

"I called the tow company, but they're backed up and won't be able to make it up until about seventy-two hours after the roads open again." He sat on the bench, yanked off one boot and then the other, his anger at himself flaring. "I've stopped being an asset and become a liability.

"You're too hard on yourself."

Joe didn't think so. He was supposed to be a leader in this community. Instead, he'd gone and done something stupid. "I tried digging my way out. That's what I've been doing all morning. I got soaked and had to give up. I wasn't making much progress anyway with this wind."

"Why didn't you text me or call? I could have come to help."

He got to his feet. "I didn't want you out in this."

She took one of his hands, her fingers warm. "Your hands are like ice. You need to get out of those wet clothes. I'll make some fresh coffee."

Coffee.

Damned if that didn't sound like the best thing ever. "Thanks."

Wanting to avoid dripping or tracking snow across the floor and up the stairs, he waited till she'd gone, then stripped down to his boxer briefs, tossing the clothes into the washer. He grabbed a clean towel from the dryer, wrapped it around his waist and headed up the back stairway, aching for a hot shower. The warm water was almost painful at first, stinging his cold hands and feet, warmth slowly seeping through his skin. But the water couldn't wash away his frustration.

He and Rain were stuck in this house until the tow company had the staff and the time to drive up, help dig him out, and tow or winch his Land Rover out of the ditch. Yes, he had the snowmobile, but he couldn't risk taking Rain out on that, not when the road to town would involve some serious steeps and a lot of sidehilling. He'd risk his safety, but he wouldn't risk hers.

So you're going to be snowed in for a few days with a sweet, beautiful woman who means a lot to you. Why is that a problem?

It was a problem precisely *because* he was attracted to her. No, that was a lie. He wasn't just attracted to her. He *wanted* her. He'd wanted her for a long time, and spending time with her had only made him want her more.

It's called self-control.

Yeah. Okay. Sure. It's not like Joe was a dumbass twenty-year-old who was controlled by his dick. He could spend time with a desirable woman without getting sexual. Hadn't he been doing that where Rain was concerned for years now?

This situation is different.

No, it wasn't different. He didn't have to let it be different. He could treat it like any other day at the pub.

Do you believe what you're saying to yourself?

Whose side was his brain on, anyway?

And ... he was talking to himself.

Great.

He finished his shower, dried off, and then, just for the hell of it, shaved. He'd had to buy razors when he'd lost the bet to Rico and might as well use them up. When he'd finished that, he towel-dried his hair, and dressed, slipping into some jeans and a long-sleeved T-shirt and leaving his hair down.

He found Rain sitting on a bar stool at the breakfast counter, sipping a cup of coffee and looking at messages on her cell phone.

She looked up, her lips curving in a smile. "Feeling better?"

"Yeah. Thanks."

She hopped down from the stool and poured him a cup of coffee. "This will warm you up the rest of the way."

He took the mug from her, sipped, the rich flavor of dark roast filling his head. "What have you been up to?"

"I made dough for Christmas cookies. It's in the fridge waiting to be rolled and cut. I also made chocolate fudge, and I read more of Silas' journal—the entry where he hired Cadan Hawke."

Damn.

Joe wished she'd lose interest. "You've been busy."

"Did you know that Rose has an ancestor who owned a brothel?"

"That's a true fact. Belle Ellery was a working girl herself until she set aside enough money to buy her own place." Joe didn't even want to know how much fucking and sucking that had entailed.

"I wonder what she looked like."

"I think there's a photo of her somewhere. I can try to find it later." He decided to change the subject. "Are you hungry?"

"Starving. Why don't you sit down and relax while I warm up some of my chili and cornbread from last night?"

Didn't that just sound like heaven?

Don't get lost in some fantasy of domestic life. This is temporary, just a product of circumstance.

Rain buzzed about the kitchen, reheating chili on the stove, popping cornbread into the microwave, clearly at home in his kitchen, the two of them talking mostly about the weather.

"I wonder how they dealt with storms like this one," she said.

"Who?"

"Our ancestors."

"I suppose a big snowfall shut the town down for a while. It would have been impossible to get supply wagons up the canyon. In long winters, most people went hungry trying to make supplies last. Lots of folks died, women and children, too. Back then, if you weren't prepared, you didn't last long."

"They didn't have the Weather Channel to warn them."

"We've got it easy."

"It doesn't always seem that way."

"Amen to that."

She put their lunch on the granite counter and sat down on the bar stool beside him. "Have you ever thought of putting all of these historic photos and Silas' journals in a museum or donating them to a library somewhere? I bet people would love to read—"

"No!" He barked the word, interrupting Rain, who froze mid-sentence. Surprised by his own response, he tried to salvage the situation. "Sorry. I didn't mean to bite your head off. It's been one hell of a morning."

"It's okay."

"I could probably share the photos, but not the journals. They're Silas' private journals. He never intended them to be made public."

That wasn't the real reason Joe didn't want to share them. He didn't give a goddamn how Silas felt about anything. The truth was far uglier.

There were things in those journals that might hurt people living in Scarlet today, people he cared about—including Rain.

While Joe set up the tree and retrieved box after box of Christmas decorations from storage, Rain rolled out the cookie dough, cut circles in the dough with a glass—Joe had no cookie cutters—

then sprinkled the dough with sugar and put the cookies in the oven. She watched Joe as he came and went. Some part of her wanted to pretend that they were a happy couple preparing for Christmas together, but she was too much of a realist to play that game. Besides, Joe was anything but happy. He seemed tense, even grouchy. He was probably still upset about his SUV being stuck in a ditch.

He was always the first person in town to help others in times of trouble, but he had a hard time asking for it. Worse, he hated being out of the action. Now, he was stuck here with her for a couple of days, sidelined by a storm.

Rain cleaned up the mess she'd made, wiping flour off the countertop and getting the dishes into the dishwasher.

Joe walked in, another big box in his arms. He set it down on the floor near the living room fireplace. "I think this is the last one. I had planned to donate all of this. I just never got around to it."

Rain dried her hands. "Maybe because it means something to you?"

He shrugged. "Nah. I've just been busy."

Rain rested her hands on her hips. "We don't have to do this, Joe. If this isn't fun for you, it won't be fun for me either. We can just chill and watch TV or do our own thing if that sounds better to you."

He drew in a breath, closed his eyes, the tension inside him palpable. "You're right. Sorry. I'm being an ass."

"I didn't say that."

He opened his eyes, his lips curving in a lopsided grin. "Maybe you should have."

"I'm sorry about your SUV."

"It's nothing. Compared to what you're going through…"

She wanted him to know she understood. "It's hard for you to ask for help, I know, especially when you want to be out there helping other people."

"Yeah. Pretty much."

"Okay, now, get over it. Everyone needs help once in a while—even the mighty Joe Moffat."

He raised a dark eyebrow. "Is that how I come across?"

"Only when you're beating yourself up for being human."

Some of the frustration left his face. "Good to know."

He walked over to his sound system, pulled out his iPod. "Christmas music. Let's see what I have on here. Andy Williams. My grandmother loved him."

Rain didn't want to be negative. "He's fine."

Joe frowned. "Okay, so not Andy Williams. How about the Chipmunks?"

"The Chipmunks?" Rain laughed. "You listened to the Chipmunks?"

"No to the Chipmunks?"

She had a better idea. "Do you trust me?"

"Sure."

Rain drew out her cell phone, found her Christmas playlist, then plugged her phone into the sound system and hit play. José Feliciano's *Feliz Navidad* spilled into the room. "I love this song."

She couldn't help herself. She sang along and then started to dance, the happy melody and the Puerto Rican rhythm calling to her.

Joe crossed his arms over his chest and watched her, a grin on his face, his gaze warm. "You have a beautiful voice," he said when the song ended.

The compliment hit a sore spot inside her.

"Not beautiful enough to make a career out of it." She walked into the kitchen, checked the oven timer.

One minute.

"Come on now. You don't know that." He was still watching her, and she knew he was trying to decide whether to let it go. He changed the subject, pointing to the speakers. "What's playing now?"

"Celtic harp. Kim Robertson." Rain searched for an oven mitt, grateful that he hadn't pushed her. "She's incredible. I saw her play in Denver a few years ago."

The timer beeped, and Rain took the cookie sheets out of the oven, the sweet scent of fresh sugar cookies mingling with the bright pine scent of the tree. She left the cookies to cool, joining Joe in the living room, where he was going from box to box as if trying to decide where to start.

He glanced over at her. "Let's open these up, and see what we have."

"You don't know what's in them?" She found this funny.

"They belonged to my mother. They were handed down to me after she passed, but I haven't opened them."

Was that it? Was that why he'd seemed so tense?

"If this is going to dredge up unhappy memories for you or make you sad, we can decorate with popcorn or ribbons or old socks for all I care."

"Old socks?" He chuckled. "It's fine, really. I wasn't close to my parents. At Christmas, staff decorated the trees—several of them—for my mother's Christmas parties. They also did all of my mom's Christmas shopping. I was away at boarding school until right before the holiday. By the time I got home, everything was decorated, and the gifts were under the tree. It's not something we did as a family."

An ache in her chest, she watched as he chose a box and lifted it onto the coffee table. It made her sad to think that he had no real attachment to any of these decorations, no happy memories of putting up the tree with his parents and hanging his favorite ornaments year after year. The stuff in these boxes was just stuff to him. No wonder he'd planned to donate it.

"Let's see what we've got." He lifted the top off the box he'd chosen.

"Oh!" Delight washing through Rain. "They're precious."

On top sat a box of old European-style blown glass ornaments in pastel colors with glittering white, gold, and silver details—angels, Kris Kringles, shimmering birds with feathers for tails, elves, a little church, a trumpet, a cello, a violin. Each ornament was tucked carefully into tissue paper.

Joe took out one of the angels, turned it over in his hand as if it were a Rubik's Cube. "How do you hang them on the tree? There are no hooks."

"What do you mean?" Rain gaped at him. "Have you never decorated a Christmas tree before?"

"I told you. We had staff for that."

"Well, it's about time." She found a small box of ornament hooks and opened it. "You take one of these and pass it through that little loop there. See?"

"Okay. Yeah. I get it." He took it from her, started toward the tree.

"Oh, no, you can't put it up yet. First, you have to put up the lights."

He stopped mid-stride. "Lights? Right. I wonder where those are."

Putting Christmas lights on a tree could test the patience of a saint. They found two big boxes of the damned things—dozens of strands of white lights—and went to work replacing old bulbs and putting the strands on the tree one by one. Rain took charge, imparting her vastly superior experience in Christmas tree decorating to him.

"You don't want to drape the lights over the ends of the branches. You need to weave them through the tree, get them deep inside."

She showed him how this was done, starting at the bottom of the tree and passing the lighted strand around its girth to him, their fingers brushing as they handed the strand back and forth. Awareness sang through him at her touch. Their gazes met through the tree's green branches, the warmth in her eyes a provocation.

Twinkling lights. Soft music. The scent of pine.

Damn.

Joe was in trouble. He knew he ought to distance himself from her somehow, maybe go back outside and try digging out his Land Rover again, but he couldn't get himself to step away. Their fingers lingered now, the touch deliberate.

They put strand after strand on the tree until it glittered and Joe was about to lose his mind. Then they moved to the ornaments—a new kind of torture. Every time they opened a box, a look of wonder came over Rain's face, her smile and happiness putting a hitch in his chest. His pulse was tripping, and he wasn't even touching her.

Jesus.

He got to his feet, walked to the window, needing some distance.

"These must be antique." She held up a trio of angels. "Look. The faces are made of painted wax, not plastic."

"Yeah." He turned to look out onto a windswept world of white, working to get his emotions under control, while she continued to rummage through the box.

"Oh!"

He heard her exclamation, recognized the excitement in her voice, but didn't turn to see what she'd discovered, too caught up in his own feelings.

"Do you have any tape or thumbtacks?"

He answered without facing her. "They're in the drawer next to the fridge."

When are you going to tell Rain how you feel about her?

Rico's words came back to him. Damn Rico anyway. What the hell did he expect Joe to do? Was he supposed to pull Rain aside and admit to her that he'd had sexual fantasies about her for far too long? Should he tell her that her smile, her laughter, the very sight of her put a warm feeling in his chest or confess that he spent more time at Knockers than he needed to so he could be close to her?

Listen to yourself. You're pathetic, man.

When this storm passed, he would make an effort to meet someone again. He'd sign up on one of those online dating sites and—

"Oh, Joe." There was a sing-song tone to her voice that cut through his thoughts.

He turned to find her standing in front of the sofa, a teasing smile on her lips, a look of expectation on her face.

She looked up at the ceiling, drawing his gaze with hers.

Hell.

Mistletoe.

It was plastic, but she didn't seem to care.

"Rain." He shook his head, but his feet began to move. "I'm your boss."

Her gaze held his, an almost pleading look in her eyes. "Oh, who cares? It's Christmas. I'm not going to sue you, if that's what you think."

"It's not that." Joe had come from a long line of assholes, and he was trying desperately not to become one himself.

Just give her a quick peck on the cheek.

Okay. Yeah. Sure. He could do that.

He closed the distance between them, hesitated for a moment, then ducked down to press his lips to her cheek. But his body betrayed him, and his mouth found its way to hers. It was just a brushing of lips, but the shock of it brought him back for another pass and another. Her lips were warm, soft, pliant, the sweet scent of her skin intoxicating. But he *was* going to stop. Any moment now, he would draw away from her and end this *incredible ... exhilarating... foolishness.*

It was her little sigh of pleasure that undid him.

He drew her against him, claiming her mouth in a hungry kiss. She came alive in his arms, arching against him, matching his fervor, her tongue meeting his stroke for stroke, her fingers curling in his hair. God, she tasted like heaven and felt perfect in his arms, her breasts pressing against his chest, her body soft in all the right places.

Joe's heart thrummed, blood surging to his groin. Some part of him realized that he hadn't stopped, that he was still kissing her, but he didn't care, not when kissing her felt so... damned ... *right*. He nipped her lower lip, drew it into his mouth, felt her tongue graze his upper lip, her fingers fisting in his hair.

Whether she stumbled backward onto the sofa or whether he urged her, he couldn't say, but one moment they were standing, and the next he was lying on top of her, pressing kisses along her throat, her pulse frantic beneath his lips.

She whimpered, her hips moving beneath his, grinding herself against his erection. She reached for the top button on his jeans. "*Joe*. I want you."

"*Yes.*" What the hell had he just said? "*No.* No, Rain, we can't."

"Why not?" Rain stared up at him, disappointment and desire naked in her eyes. "We're adults. I want you. You want me."

As if the hard-on in his jeans left any doubt about that.

"I'm your employer, Rain." Joe pulled away from her and got to his feet, everything inside him protesting the abrupt loss of contact. Not sure what to do or say, he started packing together the empty boxes.

"Seriously? *That* is your excuse? I told you. I'm not going to sue."

"Do you really think I've got some kind of risk assessment going on in my head right now?" He glanced over at her. "I'm trying to be fair to *you*."

Her expression fell, and she broke eye contact.

Shit.

He'd hurt her. He didn't want that. "Rain, I—"

"It's okay, Joe." She stood, smoothing her hands over her blouse. "Let's get these boxes put away and have some cookies."

Joe said what he'd been trying to say. "I care about you."

"I know. You care about all of the staff." She packed tissue paper into two empty boxes then closed them, shutting herself off from him, too.

This is what happened when he ignored his own better sense. He shouldn't have kissed her in the first place. What the hell had he been thinking?

Chapter Seven

Rain tried not to notice the ache behind her breastbone while they cleaned up, but it didn't go away. It was there when they stowed the last of the boxes in his storage room. It was there when she made hot chocolate and fixed them each a small plate of sugar cookies. It was there when they closed the blinds, turned off the lights, and sat down to enjoy the sight of the lighted tree in relative darkness. White lights twinkled, sparking off colored glass ornaments, making them glitter.

"My first Christmas tree in this house."

"It's beautiful." Rain had always loved the sight of a Christmas tree in the dark. It usually felt so peaceful, the lovely ornaments, the scent of pine, and the lights bringing her a sense of contentment—but not today. "Can I ask you a favor?"

He glanced over at her, a hint of wariness in his eyes. "Sure."

"If you decide to donate all your ornaments, please donate them to me. I'd hate to see beautiful antiques like those end up in a thrift store."

He chuckled. "It's a deal."

She took a bite of her cookie, watched him do the same.

"These are great. Is that your recipe?"

She shook her head. "I got it from a cooking website years ago. They're Lark's favorites. I usually cut them into Christmas shapes and frost them."

"Have you heard from Lark today?"

Rain shook her head. "She's having fun with her friends."

The thought of her daughter brought back all of Rain's loneliness in a rush, dark thoughts spiraling inside her. Her daughter had moved out. Her house was destroyed. If that wasn't enough, she had finally proved to herself, in case there'd been any doubt, that Joe was not interested in her in a sexual way.

Well, it was good to have that question answered at long last.

They finished their hot chocolate and cookies, the conversation staying far from anything personal. Then Joe got to his feet, said he had work to do, and disappeared into his office, leaving Rain in the living room.

I'm trying to be fair to you.

That had been his way of telling her he wasn't truly interested in her, that having sex with him was a dead-end street, no matter how the passion in his kiss—and the wood in his jeans—had made it seem. What else could it mean?

Hadn't she told Lark a thousand times that a hard-on wasn't a measure of a man's true feelings for a woman? But it had seemed genuine—the way he'd kissed her, the way he'd dragged her against him and then pushed her onto the sofa, the delicious ridge of his erection. For a moment, she'd thought her dreams were about to come true.

And then…

Don't cry. Don't cry. Don't cry.

She'd brought this on herself.

Stupid mistletoe.

She carried their plates and cocoa mugs into the kitchen and put them in the dishwasher. She wondered for a moment what she might make for supper and then decided that she just didn't care.

When life sucks, eat cookies.

That rule had sustained Rain through a lot of hard times. Right now, she wanted to hide in her room, do something mindless, and eat *all* the cookies.

She walked to the library to get Silas' journal. It wasn't on the sofa where she'd left it. Joe had put it back on the shelf, her bookmark removed. He really didn't want her to read this, did he? Well, too bad. She had started the story, and she couldn't stop now.

She carried the book to the kitchen, grabbed the entire plate of sugar cookies and headed up the stairs, where she turned on the gas fireplace, climbed onto the bed with the plate of cookies, and began to read.

May 15, 1872

My wife informed me last night that once this child is out of her body, she will take it and my son and return to her parents' house in Philadelphia. Do all women speak thus to their husbands? The night before, she berated me for taking my leisure at Belle's place. What else is a man to do when his wife is bloated like a cow? Louisa is bold only because her father has invested heavily in the mine, making me obliged to retain his favor. But I am her husband, and she must obey me, not her father. I informed her that I would not give my permission for her to travel unless this child, too, is male. Only when I have two sons—my heir and a spare—shall she be free to leave. She seemed to be in a hurry to settle the matter and began having pains this morning. Perhaps even now, my second son is making his arrival.

Today's business involved the mine inspector, who arrived mid-morning. We spoke in my office, where Hawke, that bastard, defied me to complain to the inspector about timbering. For the past two years, it has been our custom to inspect and replace timbers in the mine after every third explosion. Each time we do so, work comes to a halt as fresh lumber is brought in to replace those cracked by the blasts. Now, Hawke says we must inspect timbering after every other blast or risk a cave-in. He would see me increase by almost one third the idleness of my workmen. If, however, I were to suggest that we cut the miners' pay by one third to compensate me for their lack of productivity, he and the others would think themselves ill-used.

When I asked him to defend this, he said, "Men get back to the lode quicker, you, when they're nae afeard the hratticin' will crash down upon their 'eads."

I informed him that any man too **afeard** *to do his job ought to lose his position. A mine is no place for cowards. I asked the mining inspector his thoughts on the matter. He said we ought to discuss it over a meal, as he had not eaten since leaving Boulder City early that morning. I took him to the inn, saw to it that he received a warm meal and some whiskey, at which point he confessed that he was of the same mind as I. After that he was content to leave for Boulder City once more, having never set foot in the mine.*

To think a government official can be bought for the cost of a meal and a few shots of whiskey.

Once I was rid of him, I sent Mr. Craddock to find the pretty girl Hawke had hired last week. As Belle cannot continually provide girls who are truly virgins, I have found it necessary to procure my own. Though I had Mr. Craddock serve the little bitch tea and a bit of chocolate, she did not trust me. I asked her how old she was. She said fourteen. I asked if she was a virgin. She blushed to the roots of her hair. I asked for her name, and she said, "Jenny Minear." I then offered her the usual—one silver dollar in exchange for her virginity. When she refused, I dismissed her, making it clear that she was not to report for work in the morning.

She stared at me through big green eyes and begged me not to take her job. She told me her father would throw her out if they found out she'd been with a man. I said I certainly would not tell them. She seemed to have some idea of what was to come, lying back on my desk and lifting her dusty skirts. The silly girl had tears in her eyes and complained that it hurt. I told her that was normal the first time. Her crying ceased the moment I held out the coin.

"Is that all there is to it?" she asked.

If I'd had the capacity, I'd have tumbled her again right then to show her true male prowess. Instead, I made her an offer. If she promised to keep only to me, there would be more coins in her future. She curtsied, thanked me, and left, her trepidation gone, a smile on her face.

As I cannot go home unless I wish to listen to Louisa moan and wail, I have it in mind to find a game of cards at the new saloon that opened last week. Scarlet Springs is a thriving town now due to the success of my mine. Every man here owes his livelihood to me, and well they know it.

A post-script for the day: Mr. Craddock found me at the saloon and told me that Louisa gave birth to twins, both stillborn. Louisa died moments after the birth of blood loss, leaving me alone with the boy. I shall have to decide what to do with Joseph, whether to send him back east to his grandparents, who will surely coddle him, or keep him here with me and find a nurse to look after him.

Rain slammed the journal shut, blinked back her tears, rage a knot in her chest. The bastard's wife had died giving birth, and he hadn't spared a thought for her. He'd married her for her father's fortune, used her for sex and children, and hadn't seemed to care at all for her when she'd died.

The poor woman!

Rain had thought herself in love with Guy, too—until he'd left her alone to have their baby, refusing to drive her to the hospital for fear they'd arrest him for statutory rape. Giving birth to Lark had been one of the worst experiences in her life, the pain tearing her apart, giving her nightmares for weeks afterward. It had also made her see Guy for who and what he was.

Louisa had clearly come to see Silas for what he was, too. She'd wanted to go back east to be with her family, but she'd never gotten the chance.

Rain didn't just dislike Silas. She *loathed* him.

And what about Jenny Minear? She must be one of Rain's ancestors. No one else around here had that last name. Rain knew nothing about her heritage. Until this moment, she hadn't cared, but now she wanted to learn everything she could.

Would Joe know? Could she ask him? It would be a little awkward.

So, your ancestor coerced a woman who had the same last name as I do into having sex with him. Do you know what connection I have with her?

Not that she blamed Joe, of course. He was nothing like Silas. Joe would never bully one of his female employees into having sex or…

Was *this* why Joe wouldn't touch her?

The thought struck her—and stuck.

I'm trying to be fair to you.

Is *that* what he'd meant?

No, it couldn't be. He had to know that they were in no danger of repeating history. He was no Silas, and she was no fourteen-year-old virgin. He certainly hadn't forced her to kiss him. The kiss had been *her* idea.

Then again, it would be just like him to go overboard trying to balance out a wrong that had been done. This was the same guy who secretly donated to fundraisers at Knockers, seeding the donation jars with thousands from his own pocket to help others in the community because he felt he somehow owed the people of Scarlet Springs a debt. He'd never told her this, but she knew it was true from the little things he said.

She'd caught him stuffing a fat roll of hundreds into a donation jar for victims of that awful bus crash. When she'd started to say how generous she'd thought this was, he'd cut her off, dismissing her praise.

"My family took a lot from this town, so I give back when I can," he'd said.

Then another possibility came to her. What if Silas had gotten Jenny pregnant? What if Rain and Joe were *both* descended from Silas? They'd be half third cousins or something—not related closely enough for it to get them arrested.

Oh, Joe, you sweet, wonderful idiot.

If he thought he was going to keep her at arm's length because of Silas, he was in for a surprise.

Joe looked at the figures on his computer screen. It had taken him a lot longer than it usually did to catch up with the accounting, perhaps because he couldn't get his mind off a certain beautiful green-eyed woman. He willed himself to focus, looked at the bottom line. Knockers was almost certainly going to break even this month, and that was good enough for him. He didn't run the place to make a profit.

Still, they'd had a profitable fall, and that would more than make up for being closed these few days. Even if they remained closed for the rest of the week—and he doubted that would be necessary—he'd be able to meet payroll on Friday and hand out Christmas bonuses without dipping into his capital gains.

Not wanting the staff to worry, he sent out a group email, assuring them all that everyone would receive their regular salary and that they'd be open again as soon as the roads were safe and the state of emergency lifted. Then he scrolled through his emails, not really seeing the words on his screen.

You can't hide in your office all night.

Was that what Joe was doing? Was he hiding?

Coward.

He needed to face Rain sooner rather than later and apologize for letting things get out of hand. Yes, the kiss had been her idea, but he'd ignored his better judgment and turned what could have been a friendly Christmas kiss on the cheek turn into a full-blown make-out session. Then again, maybe apologizing wasn't a good idea either. He would probably end up hurting her feelings more than he already had. Besides, he wasn't sorry—not really. That kiss had been the best kiss of his life.

He'd seen the desire in her eyes. He'd watched it melt into disappointment and hurt when he'd pulled away from her. But, damn it, what was he supposed to do? If he slept with her, he'd be little better than Silas or any of his male ancestors. Joe's father had faced more than one sexual harassment lawsuit for groping female employees.

But Rain wanted it. She wanted you. She said so.

He supposed that *did* make it different, though it didn't change the fact that she was his employee. If he had sex with her, he'd be breaking his own rules. Even as he told himself this, his eyes drifted shut, a fantasy of her filling his head, her breasts bared to his touch, her face flushed from arousal, her body closing around him like a fist. The hard-on that strained against his fly wasn't imaginary, however, his jeans uncomfortably tight.

You're not making this any easier on yourself.

Ah, hell.

He waited until his erection had subsided, then got to his feet and opened his office door, the scent of something delicious hitting him in the face. He found Rain in the kitchen, dancing to and singing along with the Timberline Mudbugs while she made a pot of spaghetti. Her voice slid over the notes like silk as she filled out their melody with her own sweet harmony.

Joe stood for a moment and watched her, knowing she hadn't yet seen him. God, she was beautiful, her blond hair swinging as she moved, her motions sensual, her sense of rhythm innate and flawless. If not for that bastard Guy, who'd used her dreams to manipulate her into his bed, she might have had a chance. But she'd gotten pregnant and had set aside everything she'd wanted in life to raise her little girl.

Joe had always admired her for that, but, *damn*, that had been a big price to pay for trusting someone. She refused even to talk about it now, the loss of that dream still painful for her.

She glanced up, smiled when she saw him. "Hungry? I made pasta with marinara sauce. It's late, so I figured we should have something light. Want to make the salad?"

"I can do that." He walked up behind her, sniffed the sauce, the scents of onion, tomato, oregano, and garlic making his mouth water. "That smells incredible."

"It's one of Rico's recipes."

"Good old Rico." He walked to the sink, washed his hands, then went to work on cleaning and chopping the salad fixings she'd set out on the counter. If she wouldn't bring it up, he would. Then he noticed the empty plate sitting in the sink. "Hey, what happened to the cookies?"

"I ate them."

"All?" *Shit.* If Rain had binged on cookies, it meant she was upset. Joe thought he knew why. "About what happened earlier…"

"Do you know who Jenny Minear was? Is she my great-great-great-grandmother or something?"

The question caught Joe unprepared, but it shouldn't have. He'd known she'd find the journal and keep reading. She was caught up in the story, just as he'd been the first time he'd read the journals. "Jenny was your great-great-great-grandmother's older sister."

"You and I aren't third or fourth cousins?"

"No." He sliced tomatoes, tossed them into the wooden salad bowl. "We might have been. Silas got Jenny pregnant. She had a couple of girls, but they died. After he left her pregnant, she went to Belle seeking help and died from a botched abortion."

"What?" Rain stared at him, eyes wide, rage turning her cheeks pink. "What a stinking rat bastard! That poor girl."

"Yeah." Silas had coerced Jenny, used her poverty and the power he held over her as her boss to bend her to his will.

Rain's gaze grew soft. "You're nothing like him, you know."

Once again, her words caught him off-guard, this time sparking his temper. "Of course, I know that."

"It's not your job to pay for his crimes."

"He got away with all of it—*all* of it, Rain. He made a lot of money, too, and I inherited that wealth."

"You inherited his money, not his guilt."

"It's blood money, Rain."

"Oh, bullshit!" Rain stepped in front of him, wooden spoon in hand. "Just stop! It's *your* money now. In your hands, that money has made life better for a lot of people in Scarlet. You gave me a job when no one in town would hire me, when it wasn't even legal for me to serve alcohol. You helped me find a place to live, paid my first month's rent, gave me a bed and a crib, held a baby shower for me."

Joe hadn't forgotten. She'd walked in to apply for a job waiting tables, newborn Lark in her arms, her belly still swollen from pregnancy. She'd promised to work hard, looking up at him, her green eyes filled with desperation and hope. It had broken his heart to see someone so young in such dire straits.

"I did what anyone would do."

"Not true, and you know it. I had applied everywhere. No one wanted to hire a teen mom with a two-week-old baby—until you."

Then it dawned on him.

He'd tried to talk about the kiss, and Rain had deftly changed the subject. He couldn't let her get away with that. "So, about what happened earlier—"

"Don't you dare apologize. We're both adults. You know I wanted that kiss, and I think you wanted it, too. I think you enjoyed it and wanted more, just like I did."

What the hell could he say to that? She had him figured out.

"Okay, you're right. I wanted it. I enjoyed it, and, yeah, I wanted more. But that doesn't mean it was the right thing to do. It won't happen again."

Her lips curved in a little smile, her gaze lingering on his as she turned back to the stove and stirred the sauce.

Holy hell.

Chapter Eight

Twenty-four days till Christmas

Rain awoke the next morning feeling a renewed sense of hope and determination. She reached for her cell phone, checked her email, and found a quick message from Lark asking how she was doing. There was also a handful of messages from people in town asking her how she was doing and two emails from Joe. The first assured her and the rest of the staff that they would get paid no matter how long Knockers was closed, while the second told them that Boulder Canyon wasn't yet open and the pub wouldn't reopen for at least one more day. That was Joe in a nutshell, putting the worries and needs of his staff before his own.

She typed out a reply to Lark, then climbed out of bed and, still in her pajamas, followed the sound of classic rock downstairs to the home gym and peeked inside. Her pulse skipped, a shaft of heat piercing her belly.

Oh. My. God.

Joe stood, shirtless, doing bicep curls, his dark hair drawn back in a ponytail. Not once in twenty-one years had she seen him without a shirt. She wasn't disappointed. The man was *ripped*, all lean muscle without being bulky. Dark curls peppered well-defined pecs, his abdomen an honest-to-God six pack, his biceps bunching as he worked.

And tats. Bands of Celtic knotwork encircled his biceps. Who had known he had tats on his biceps? Not Rain.

She wasn't sure she'd need coffee if she got to look at this every morning. Some part of her—she thought it was probably her ovaries—could have stood on this spot and watched him all day, but her brain had a better idea.

She tiptoed back upstairs and searched through the clothes Joe had brought from her place, pulling out a pink V-neck T-shirt and a pair of navy yoga pants. She dressed, brushed her teeth, put her hair up in a deliberately messy bun, and checked her reflection. She'd opted for her white lacy pushup bra and was happy with the results. She adjusted her boobs for maximum effect and went downstairs again, walking into his gym as if she did this sort of thing every day. "Hey, mind if I join you?"

He looked up, his gaze sliding over her and stopping at her cleavage. "Yes. No! I mean no, yeah, sure."

Tongue-tied, Joe?

Good.

Rain had never been a gym rat. She preferred hiking outdoors or climbing at the rock gym to running on a treadmill or lifting weights. She hadn't spent much time in the regular gym and wasn't sure where to start. She glanced around, her gaze passing over him once, twice.

He pointed, a hint of a smile on his lips. "The dumbbells are over there."

She walked over to the rack that held his set of dumbbells, grabbed two thirty-pound weights. Yeah, no. She put them back, trading them for two twenty-pound weights. Even that was a stretch. She turned toward him and did what she'd seen him do.

"Try to hold your upper body still."

"Am I moving?"

"You're using your back and shoulders to help lift the weight." He walked over to the rack, picked up two smaller weights, and brought them to her. "Try these."

She traded him, twenty-pound dumbbells for the seven-pounders, looking up at him from beneath her lashes. "Are you saying I'm weak?"

"Weak? No. A beginner? Yes." He carried the heavier weights back to the rack, then came to stand beside her.

She raised the weights.

"Try alternating sides, and don't let your upper body compensate for your motion." He pressed a hand to the middle of her back and one to her upper abdomen, his touch making her belly tense. "Make your motions nice and smooth."

He was so close now that she could smell the male scent of his skin, feel the heat radiating off his body. Her brain went blank, but somehow she managed to do as he'd asked, alternating left and right while he counted to twelve.

He stepped back, drew his hands away. "That's a good start. Give your muscles a few minutes to recover, and do another set."

His voice was deeper now, softer, something in his dark eyes telling her that she wasn't the only one feeling this spark between them. Then his gaze dropped to her lips, and she knew he was going to kiss her.

Instead, he turned away, walked to a bench where a barbell rested, large weights already attached on each side. "We can't open the pub today. Boulder Canyon is still closed. It doesn't make sense to open when half the staff can't make it in and most of our clientele is still hunkered down."

"I got the email." She set the dumbells on the floor and followed him. "It was good of you to reassure the staff about their paychecks. I'm sure the newer folks were starting to worry."

He lay back on the bench, situated himself beneath the barbell.

"Should I spot you?" Her dad had always had her brother spot him when he bench-pressed with free weights.

Joe raised his head, an amused grin on his face. "Do you think you could lift this off me if I needed help?"

"How much does it weigh?"

"Two-ten."

Two-hundred and ten pounds? "Oh, hell, no. You're on your own."

Chuckling, he lay back again, raised the barbell, and pumped out nine slow reps, exhaling as he lifted, his pecs bulging with the effort.

Rain's knees went weak.

Joe willed himself to focus on the burn in his pecs and triceps and not the beautiful woman who stood just a few feet away, staring at him as if she were starving and he were dinner. Why hadn't he thought to wear a shirt?

He was used to being alone in the house. That's why.

He finished this set, lowered the barbell back into its rest, then drew in a breath, resolved to behave no differently than he would if he were lifting weights with Rico. Hairy, bald, tattooed Rico. Rico who belched like a damned hog after a good meal. Rico who'd kept his beard while Joe had been forced…

Joe sat up, stared at her.

Damn!

Rain had turned away from him and was doing another set of bicep curls, her blue leggings clinging to her sweet ass like a second skin, leaving no doubt that she wasn't wearing a thing beneath them. The thought sent a surge of blood toward his groin.

Oh, no. No, no. He was *not* getting a hard-on. Without a shirt, he had no way to hide it. His running pants weren't tight, but she'd be sure to notice.

He stood, turned away from her, and croaked out words of encouragement. "You're doing great. Much better."

The rest of his workout was agony—a sweet kind of agony. He did his best to keep his eyes off her ass and her cleavage, but it was pointless. Even the littlest things, the smallest details, turned him on. The flush in her cheeks. The bead of sweat that trickled down her nape. The delicate sweep of her eyebrows. The notch at the base of her throat. The light in her green eyes. And it came to him in a rush that it wasn't her ass or her breasts that had him burning up. It was she herself.

It was Rain.

He shut that thought away and coached her through the rest of the workout, spotting for her when she bench-pressed the barbell without weights, showing her how to do dumbbell flys and pushups, lifting her to the bar so that she could attempt to do a pull-up. He had to be a masochist because he was *enjoying* this—the recklessness of being near her, the heat in his blood, the knowledge that he was walking the razor's edge.

You'll be fucking your fist in the shower, dude.

Yeah. So what? That was nothing new.

He was feeling pleased with himself for his self-control when she caught the toe of her shoe on the edge of the floor mat and tripped, falling face-first toward the weight rack. It was instinct to reach out and catch her... instinct to draw her against him... instinct to lower his mouth to hers.

God, yes.

The moment their lips met, the lust in his blood ignited, and he forgot. He forgot that he hadn't meant to kiss her. He forgot he was her boss. He forgot everything but Rain—her soft lips, the lush curves of her body, the sweet scent of her skin.

Oh, she could kiss, her mouth as ravenous as his, stealing control of the kiss from him, taking as much as she gave. She whimpered, slid her hands up his sweat-slick chest and locked them behind his neck.

He reclaimed control of the kiss, reaching with both hands to cup her luscious ass, crushing her against him, her body pliant in his arms.

Do you know what you're doing, man?

Somewhere in his mind, alarm bells were ringing, but they were drowned out by the roar of his pulse, years of suppressed desire for her slamming through his veins. She gave a little hop and wrapped her legs around his waist. He moaned into her mouth and turned, walking her to the wall, pressing her against it with his weight. He ground himself against her, his cock aching to be inside her. Needing more, he reached up, cupped one of her breasts through her T-shirt, the nub of her nipple hard against his palm.

You're really going to fuck Rain against the wall in your smelly gym?

He ignored the thought, kept kissing her, his thumb teasing that nipple.

She deserves better than this.

Okay, true. He could take her upstairs, make love to her on his bed. Lots of room. Soft sheets. Plus, he had condoms there.

You're her boss.

That thought pierced the fog of pheromone in his brain.

He dragged his mouth from hers.

She whimpered in protest. "Don't stop."

"We can't, Rain. I can't." He lowered her to her feet, stepped back, his body still burning for her. "I'm sorry."

She hugged her arms around herself. "I don't understand. Lots of couples meet at work. If it's consensual, what's the problem?"

"I'm your employer. That's the problem."

She glared at him. "You sound like a damned broken record. Do you think anyone would hold that against us?"

"I don't care what other people think." How could he make her understand? "When a man starts breaking his own rules, what does he have left? Besides, I'm ten years older than you are. You could have any man—"

"Do you see me trying to sleep with just any man?"

"No."

"Do you know *why* that is?"

Was this a trick question? "I guess you're waiting for the right one."

"Oh, Joe!" She shook her head. "You admit that you want me, but the fact that I work for you means you will never have sex with me. Did I get that right?"

He narrowed his gaze. "Yes."

Where was she going with this?

She nodded, hurt and frustration naked in her eyes. "Okay. Fine. I quit."

She waited for a moment, then she turned and walked out of the gym.

Rain made it to the kitchen before Joe caught up with her.

"You don't mean that, Rain."

"Oh, yes, I do." She didn't turn to look at him but reached for a pen and the pad of paper he kept on the kitchen counter. She scrawled a hasty resignation on the page, tore it off, and handed it to him. "Take my job, and shove it."

He glanced at her note, fury on his face. "You can't just quit."

"Oh, yes, I can." She fell back on the orientation speech she gave new servers. "Colorado is an at-will state, which means that an employment arrangement can be terminated by either party with no notice."

She hurried toward the stairs, wanting to get away from him before her fury dissolved into tears.

"That's not what I mean." He stepped into her path. "How are you going to support yourself?"

She poked his chest with her finger. "That's not *your* problem, Mr. Former Boss."

"Jesus, Rain." He put his hands on his hips, gave a slow shake of his head. "This is exactly why I shouldn't have kissed you. Sex ruins work relationships."

"We haven't had sex!" She pushed past him, continued toward the stairs.

"I don't want you to quit, Rain."

She stopped, turned to face him. "Why not?"

He stammered after an answer. "Why? Well, you…. you're one of my most valued employees. You're the heart and soul of Knockers."

His answer hurt.

"I *was* one of your most valued employees. Knockers will go on without me." She turned away from him and continued up the stairs. "As soon as the roads open up, I'll go stay with Bob and Kendra. They offered me Lexi's old room."

"Now you're leaving my house, too?" There was genuine hurt in his voice.

This time she didn't stop. She didn't want to see his face. "Yes."

Stunned silence followed her to her bedroom. She slammed the door, threw herself down on her bed. Her body still thrummed with arousal, her lips tingling from his kisses. But he cared more about the fact that she'd quit than the fact that she wanted him—and he wanted her.

No man could kiss a woman like he had kissed her unless he meant it. That's what she told herself anyway. But she'd never been a good judge of men.

What was she going to do now? She still had her part-time job cleaning rooms at the inn. It didn't pay nearly as much as Knockers, but it was something to tide her over. She'd planned on giving Kendra her notice at the end of January. She would have paid Lark's last tuition payment by then. She'd only taken the job to help Lark with school. Now she would have to keep that job.

She glanced toward the bedroom door. She'd hoped he would follow her upstairs and ask to talk so that they could cut past all the bull and get to the heart of this, which was that she loved him and he ...

Did he love her? Lark said he did.

Why don't you just ask him?

Then she heard the sound of an engine.

She hopped from the bed and glanced outside in time to see him ride out of the garage on his snowmobile. He'd left her by herself rather than face this.

Oh, Joe.

Heart aching, she filled the bathtub, turned on the gas fireplace, and settled in the tub with Silas' journal.

March 5, 1874

Our new sheriff, Kit Taylor, came to visit me today. He's a Cornishman like the rest of them but one who speaks clear English. He said he was concerned that my men are running rough-shod over the good people of Caribou and Scarlet Springs. I offered him a drink, which he refused, and assured him that whatever stories he'd heard had been exaggerated. He laid before me claims of a bruised and bleeding scarlet lady who told him my men used her, beat her, and then failed to pay her.

"Is our sheriff a pimp, charged with collecting a whore's fee?" I asked.

Oh, what a dour man! He did not laugh or even crack a smile. "A workin' girl has a right to get paid same as any man who works in your mine. I won't tolerate your hired men raisin' havoc in my town."

His town? Oh, the audacity. I was of a mind to throw him out on his ear, but he is the law. Instead, I informed him that there would be no town without me and made certain he knew that everyone in Scarlet owed their wealth and well-being to me, including the whores. I told him that my hired men are necessary only because this country is overrun with thieves and outlaws. In truth, they serve to keep the miners in line, for I cannot trust Hawke to do so.

"I've said my piece," Sheriff Taylor said. "You watch your men. We've enough sorrow and hardship to face with this epidemic. We don't need them stirrin' up trouble."

I told him that I was not insensitive to the current suffering as I had lost a child, too. True, she was a bastard and only a girl, but Jenny was quite distraught. Taylor offered his condolences and wished me a good day.

I watched through my window as he left and spied him talking with Hawke as if the two of them were friends. I like that not at all.

As it happened, Hawke was on his way to speak with me. It seems this epidemic of scarlet fever that killed Jenny's child has hit miners hard with scarcely a family in Caribou or Scarlet Springs that hasn't lost at least one child. "Tobias Stephens and his wife Elizabeth have lost ten of their fifteen children. Poor Elizabeth. I've ne'er seen a woman so distraught."

I told him that I had lost a child to the fever just last week. Sometimes one must appear to commiserate if one wishes to control.

He removed his hat, something he never does out of deference to me. "Jenny's daughter? I'd not heard. I'm sorry. It's a good thing you sent your son back east, aye? It's safer there than here in these mountains."

I asked if he had any children.

He said that he had eight—five boys and three girls.

The lower classes do breed like rabbits.

"God has spared them all," he said.

I asked him what he wished from me. He said that the miners hoped I could make some provision for those with sick children, as the cost of so many doctor's visits have left some families with an empty purse. They also hope that I will help those who've lost children by contributing granite for grave markers.

"Most families can scarce afford the cost of one headstone, let alone three or ten at once," he said.

I cannot see why I should spend my coin on gravestones for other men's children. If one is poor, one must suffice with a simple wooden cross or bury the dead in unmarked graves. I did not say this, however, as the sound of Jenny's weeping was still fresh in my mind. More than that, Mr. Craddock has brought me news of grumblings and discontent since I started making the miners pay for their own candles. I discerned here a chance to win back their favor.

I assured Hawke that I would find some means of enticing more doctors to the miners' camp and would pay the cost of their visits for families who could not afford it. Then I shouted to Mr. Craddock that he should have a stonecutter brought up from Boulder City, along with granite for headstones for all the children lost to this plague.

Hawke could scarce hide the surprise on his face at this. He bowed his head and thanked me repeatedly, then hurried off to tell the men.

I'm certain I shall not like the expense that this incurs, but bereaved men can be dangerous. Better to spend the coin and pacify the miners that way than to be forced to hire more men.

On my way home, I stopped at Belle's. I had asked her to procure a gift to give to Jenny to assuage her loss. As strange as it may seem, I care more for Jenny, who is little more than my private whore, than I ever did for my wife. Jenny is quite fair, but more than that she knows her place. She seeks ever to please me, where Louisa sought always to assert her own interests. Louisa came from a wealthy family and believed herself to be above me on the social ladder, while Jenny knows that everything from the roof over her head to the food in her belly depends on my good will. She is pregnant again, and this time she assures me it will be a son. It is of no consequence either way, as I could never marry her.

Rain's heart ached for the miners. She couldn't imagine giving birth to fifteen children and watching ten of them die. Her heart ached for Jenny, too. She couldn't imagine sleeping with Silas, either, and wondered what Jenny would have done had she been given any real choice. The bastard had coerced her into sex, ruined her reputation at a time when women paid a terrible price for such things, and then kept her in a cottage, giving her gifts and food and shelter in exchange for using her body. Thanks to Joe and his big spoilers, Rain knew how Jenny's story ended.

Rain climbed out of the tub, dried off, then crawled, still naked, beneath a blanket on a chaise near the fire, skimming through boring entries about Silas' earnings and his accounts to read more of the personal history. She stopped when she heard an approaching engine. Blanket wrapped around her, she ran to the window and saw Joe's Land Rover disappear into the garage, towing the snowmobile behind him.

Her heart sank.

He'd gotten his SUV out of the ditch. Life would be going back to normal.

It was time for her to leave.

Chapter Nine

Joe pulled slowly into the garage, watching the snowmobile in his side mirror. He parked, unhooked the chain he'd borrowed from Taylor, then rode the snowmobile inside and parked it. At least that was done.

News had spread that he'd gone off the road—of course, it had—and Taylor had texted him, asking if he needed help. Joe met Taylor and Moretti at the pile of snow that was his SUV, and the three of them had dug it out, chained it to Taylor's vehicle, and towed it out of the ditch. At one point, Joe had been certain the damned thing was going to roll, but at last, they'd gotten it up on the road.

The men had waved off his thanks.

"Hey, I miss my brew," Taylor had said.

Moretti had nodded. "Don't forget the pizza."

Joe had promised the men he'd open tomorrow if the weather held. "Your next meal is on me."

Both men had asked about Rain. Joe had told them she was fine and had left it at that. What had happened between them was no one's business.

Joe closed the garage door, stepped into the mudroom, and stripped off his gloves, coat, and snow boots. The physical exertion had helped him work off his frustration and that lingering sense of arousal. Now all he wanted was a hot meal and a shower.

Rain wasn't in the kitchen or the living room. Maybe she was taking a nap—or reading Silas' damned journal in the library. He hoped she'd come to her senses. He couldn't believe she truly wanted to quit.

Jesus!

How would she support herself? What would she do?

Joe couldn't stand the thought of her leaving Knockers, but he had an even harder time imagining Scarlet Springs without her. What did she stand to gain? Everyone loved her here. In any other town, she'd be among strangers, and he would never see her.

He made his way upstairs, his mind on a hot shower. His gaze fell on her closed bedroom door, and he couldn't resist. He wanted to make things right.

He walked to her room, knocked on the door. "Rain? Can we talk?"

"Sure."

He opened the door and froze, his heart slamming into his sternum.

She stood beside her bed, completely naked.

It was in his mind to look away or step out and close the door, but he stood rooted to the spot, heat surging to his groin, his gaze moving over her from her lush breasts with their full pink nipples to the curve of her hips to her gently rounded belly to the dark blond curls of the landing strip between her thighs.

Holy fuck.

She turned, walked to the closet, giving him a view of her delicious ass. There were small, dark bruises on her creamy skin. Had he done that?

She didn't so much as look his way. "Did you want something?"

"You ..." He cleared his throat. "You didn't say you were naked."

"You didn't ask."

It was then he realized what she was doing. She was taking clothes out of her closet and packing them back into the plastic bags.

"You're really doing this?"

"Yes." She walked back to the bed, T-shirts draped over her arm. She bent over, folded the shirts, and slid them into the bag, her breasts swaying as she worked, the bright colors of her tattoos a contrast to her pale skin. "Bob said he'd call Austin and ask him to come pick me up."

Wasn't she going to stop and put something on?

You could look away, leave the room.

No. No, he really couldn't.

She was the most beautiful woman he'd ever seen.

"Taylor and Moretti helped me dig out my Land Rover. I'll drive you."

"Are you sure? You've done enough to help me as it is. I don't want to be more of a pain than I already have been."

"Jesus, Rain. Did I say you've been a pain?"

"Can I ask you a favor?" She reached beneath one of the bags and pulled out Silas' journal. "I'm up to 1878 now. May I borrow this?"

"You won't like how it ends."

"I think I can handle it. I promise I won't let anything happen to it. I'll drop it by Knockers when I'm done."

"So you're going through with it. You're quitting." He couldn't believe it, a cold, hollow sensation spreading behind his breastbone.

"I'll pick up my last check on payday. I've got some vacation time."

He shook his head. "I don't understand why you're doing this."

At last, she met his gaze. "You're right about that."

What the hell was that supposed to mean?

Rain could tell Joe was furious. They said little as he drove her into town, his jaw tense, his lips a hard line. But when the SUV slipped and she gasped, he was quick to reassure her, his voice soothing despite the anger in his eyes.

"It's okay. We're good. Are you warm?"

"Yes. Thanks." She'd let him walk into the room while she was naked. She had exposed herself to him, and he'd acted like it was nothing. She'd thought he might crack and jump her bones or at least kiss her again, but he'd stood there talking to her as if nothing out of the ordinary was happening. God, she'd been an idiot. She'd loved him for so long, and she'd never been more than an employee in his eyes.

How could he kiss her like that if…

Stop. Don't do this.

Guy had kissed her, told her he loved her, made her feel like a queen—and he'd left her to give birth alone in a minivan.

She stared unseeing out the window until they got into town. "Wow!"

Immense piles of snow stood in the corner of every parking lot and people's front yards, most of the roads limited to a single, icy lane. Some of that snow had been transformed into sculptures—lots of snowmen, a naked couple entwined, a sea monster, a Darth Vader head, a Tyrannosaurus, a snow Christmas tree with real lights, a giant snow penis. Someone had stuck a painted sign in the middle of their yard that read, "Hey, Ullr, is this the best you can do?"

Ullr, the Norse god of snow, was a favorite of local ski bums.

"Looks like people have kept themselves busy," Joe said.

They were still busy, kids playing, adults skiing and shoveling their walks, folks standing in the middle of the street and talking with their neighbors. The wintery joy of the scene would ordinarily have made Rain's spirits soar. Instead, she felt like crying. The whole town seemed to be happy, while her heart was breaking.

Joe turned onto First Street. The Forest Creek Inn stood tall and proud halfway down the block, its paint bright yellow against the white snow. The largest Victorian building in town, it looked like something from a postcard, decked with wreaths, garlands, and lights to celebrate the season. It was strange to think that it had stood here since the days when Silas prowled the streets of Scarlet.

"You are always welcome at my place. If you need anything, just call. I mean it."

She couldn't look at him. "Thanks."

He turned into the long driveway and parked. "Your job is still there, too."

He wasn't going to make this easy, was he?

She unbuckled her seatbelt, swallowed the lump in her throat. "You've been good to me, Joe. You gave me a job when no one else would. You helped me get on my feet. You've been a great boss for every one of these twenty years. You helped me through this mess like a true friend. Thanks for all of it."

She pushed open the door, dropped to the ground, and opened the rear passenger door to get her bags, blinking back tears she did not want him to see.

He was there before she could make her retreat. "Nothing will be the same without you."

She willed herself to smile up at him. "You'll be fine."

Bob opened the door behind them. "Need a hand?"

Rain turned toward him, grateful for the interruption. "Thanks, but I've got it."

"Good. I don't feel like putting my boots on again." Bob chuckled.

Rain waved to Joe. "Drive safe, and thanks again."

She was inside before he started the engine, her heart in shreds, so many things between them left unspoken.

"Oh, honey, what's wrong?" Rose sat at the kitchen table with Kendra, a bottle of wine between them.

"Nothing. I'm fine."

"Her roof collapsed. What the hell do you think is wrong?" Bob answered for her.

"Take her bags to Lexi's room, Bob, and then find something to do with yourself. We women need to talk," Kendra said. "You sit here with us, sweetie. I'll get another glass, and you can tell us all about it."

Bob muttered something to himself and disappeared down the hallway.

Rain looked at the two women and felt like the fly being lured into the spider's web. She knew Rose was the hub of gossip in this town and that nothing she said would stay in this room, but she couldn't stop herself. She sat, took the glass of wine from Kendra, and burst into tears. "My life *sucks*."

Rose reached over, took her hand. "Tell us all about it."

Joe drove from the inn to Knockers, where he plowed the parking lot again, an ache in his chest where his heart ought to have been. Rain couldn't seriously mean to leave her job after *twenty years* because he refused to sleep with her. Had she expected that he would fuck her on the floor right then?

Now that he thought about it, that wasn't such a bad idea.

No, it was a terrible idea.

He had wounded her pride, left her feeling rejected. But she would snap out of it. She would come back as soon as she had time to think it through. When she did, her job would be waiting for her.

Joe finished with the parking lot and then got to work clearing a large snowdrift from the walk in front of the entrance one shovelful at a time. People waved to him from their cars, offered to help, asked when he'd be open.

"Tomorrow," Joe called back.

When he'd finally cleared the doorway of snow, he took out his keys, unlocked the door—and was hit in the face by Led Zeppelin's *Dyer Maker* playing on the sound system. He stepped inside, glanced toward the stage, and stared open-mouthed.

Son of a ...!

Some big guy was fucking a half-naked Libby from behind, his pants around his knees, ass bare, the two of them in the spotlight, their cries audible as *Dyer Maker* came to an end and they climaxed.

Why were all the women in his life naked today? And why was Libby fucking some dude onstage?

Libby looked over her shoulder toward her boy toy, saw Joe, and shrieked. The two of them hurried to dress, Libby reaching for her T-shirt, her breasts still bare, the guy yanking up his jeans.

Joe turned his back.

"I didn't know you were coming in today," Libby said.

"I can see that." Joe walked toward the door. "I'm going outside for a minute. When I come back in, I want you dressed and lover boy gone."

He stepped outside and stood there in the cold wondering what the hell else happened at his pub when he wasn't here.

The door opened behind him, and a man strode past him.

"Hey, Joe."

Jesus!

Brandon Silver?

Shaking his head, Joe turned and walked back inside. What was he supposed to say to Libby? It wasn't in the employee handbook not to have sex in the workplace, but that's only because Joe couldn't have imagined anyone doing it.

Libby was waiting for him, her face flushed, but not from embarrassment. "Sorry, Joe. If I had known... Sometimes you've just got to have it, you know?"

Oh, he knew. He just rarely gave in to the impulse.

"Can't you get it at home?"

"Well, yeah, but you know."

"I don't think I do."

"It's kind of a thing in this town to have sex on your stage."

Joe couldn't have heard that right. "It's ... what?"

"Sex in the Spotlight."

He glared at her. "Marcia's drink?"

Libby rolled her eyes as if he were an idiot. "People try to have sex on your stage in the spotlight. Marcia made the drink in honor of that. It's like the Mile High Club, except we call it the Sex in the Spotlight Club. Eric and Vicki have done it."

Joe gaped at her. "Eric and Victoria have had sex *on my stage?*"

"Lots of people have." She started listing names. "Austin and Lexi. Of course, they've had sex everywhere. Ellie and Moretti. Rico and that woman he used to date. Creede Herrera and, well, every female he's dating. Marcia and her hubby. I think Megs and Mitch started it, and then Rose—"

"Megs and Mitch have done it, too?" Joe's head was starting to ache.

Libby nodded. "You didn't know? That's what those notches in the wooden posts on either side of the stage are for. It's kind of like proof of membership. When a couple does it onstage in the spotlight, they carve a little notch in one of the posts."

"You have got to be kidding me." Joe finally had the answer to that mystery. Hell, there were *dozens* of them. "How do they get in?"

He couldn't have the entire town sneaking into his place after hours to bone.

"I guess they stay late and wait for the dining room to be empty and then try to do it before anyone steps out from the kitchen or the back offices to catch them."

"Jesus." Why hadn't he known this?

"I've been cooped up here for three days and Brandon—"

"Three days? Weren't you supposed to go home?"

Her face lit up. "On my way out that night, I got an awesome idea for a new special edition milk stout. I figured I might as well use the pilot tanks to brew it up and see if it tasted as good as I thought it would. Want to know what it is?"

"If you say 'pumpkin spice,' you're fired."

Libby laughed, clearly not taking him seriously. "It's an orange-chocolate peppermint milk stout. It's in the fermenting tank now, but I've had a little sip. It's going to be amazing. I named it Plow Me Blizzard 2017 Limited Edition Milk Stout."

"Plow Me?"

"Everyone in town has been trying to get plowed one way or another this weekend, right? Come on. I'll show you."

Wondering how his life had gotten so beyond his control, Joe followed Libby back to the brewery, his gaze falling on Rain's locker as they walked down the back hallway. She would come back. She had to come back.

Rain wiped her eyes with the tissue Kendra had handed her. "I stood there naked, and for all he seemed to care, we might have been at work. I've waited *twenty years* for him to notice me, and even that didn't do it. I think it's all a sign that I should move on, leave Scarlet, figure out what I'm supposed to do with my life. There's no point hoping for something that's never going to happen."

She hadn't told them anything too personal—just that she and Joe had kissed, but that he wouldn't do anything else because he was her boss and that her being naked and quitting hadn't changed anything, which must mean that he didn't really care about her.

Okay, so maybe that was more information than she'd intended to share.

Hell.

Rose gave Rain's hand a squeeze. "The two of you have never…?"

Rain shook her head. "Never."

Rose looked surprised. "Joe is a good guy. Give him time. He'll come around. That man has so much pent-up sexual energy. Everyone knows he's crazy about you."

Rain gave a little laugh. "Yeah—everyone except him."

"That's because God gave men balls instead of brains." Kendra poured more wine in Rain's glass. At 63, she was still an attractive woman, slender with sleek shoulder-length brown hair and impeccable makeup. "He'll figure it out."

"Even if Joe doesn't change his mind, why would you want to leave Scarlet?" Rose asked. "This is your home."

Kendra shrugged. "Hell, why shouldn't she leave? It's about time someone besides Britta escaped. You could go to California, maybe stay with her for a while."

Britta was Lexi's younger sister, one of Bob's two daughters by his first wife.

Rain took a sip of her shiraz. "I hadn't thought of that. Is San Diego nice?"

Kendra's face lit up. "No snow. Beaches. Palm trees. You could get a job tending bar or waiting tables near Coronado and maybe hook up with a Navy SEAL."

Rain loved beaches and the ocean, but she also loved snow and aspens and cool mountain air. The idea of meeting a Navy SEAL didn't excite her as much as it seemed to excite Kendra because ... well, *damn it*, she loved Joe. "I'd be so far away from Lark."

"You know what this is? You're lovesick, and you've got a case of empty nest syndrome at the same time." That came from Bob, who stood in the doorway, beer in his hand. "That's the thing about raising kids. You put your whole heart into them, and if they grow up and leave you behind, you've done your job right."

Rain's eyes filled with tears again. "It sucks."

"Lexi and Britta aren't mine, but I helped raise them." Kendra took another drink. "When they were little, I couldn't wait for them to grow up and leave, and then when they did ... It got awful quiet around here."

"You can always have another baby," Rose said. "Men give sperm away for free. It's the cheapest substance on earth."

Rain stared at her, shook her head. "Another baby? I don't think so. It's hard work raising a child by yourself. Plus, being pregnant and giving birth again? Nope."

She'd gone through that once, and that had been enough.

Rose smiled indulgently. "You've got powerful Empress energy—the Empress symbolizes fertility in the tarot—and such a strong second chakra."

Maybe it was the wine, but suddenly Rain had to ask. "Rose, what do you know about your ancestor, Belle Ellery?"

She didn't mention the journal. She wasn't sure anyone knew about it and didn't feel it was her place.

"The madam?" Rose sat up a little straighter, tucked a strand of silver hair behind her ear. "She ran the best brothel in Scarlet Springs. She was a woman before her time, skilled when it came to working with sexual energy."

Bob gave a noncommittal grunt. "She was a whore."

"Sex worker," Rose corrected him. "She all but ran this town."

"Are you going to sit around talking all night, or are you going to make dinner?"

Kendra glared at him. "How about you get off your hairy butt and make dinner?"

Bob chuckled. "I love you too much to force my cooking on you, darlin'."

"Yeah, right." Kendra shook her head, but Rain could see the hint of a smile on her lips. "We're running a bit low on things, and the shelves at Food Mart are all but empty. How does leftover pot roast sound to everyone?"

Rain stood. "I'll help."

She wanted to get this evening behind her so that she could go upstairs to be by herself and sleep—or maybe read.

Joe took a sip from the glass Libby had handed him, let the complex flavors play over his tongue. Chocolate malt. The bright tang of orange. The cold bite of peppermint. The warmth of yeast. He nodded. "I guess you can keep your job."

It was a malt-forward brew, rich and quite sweet, but then it wasn't finished fermenting. The yeast would eat a lot of that sugar, transforming it to alcohol.

Libby beamed. "I knew you'd like it."

He'd shoot Kari, his designer, an email so she could start work on art for the label. "Do we have to call it 'Plow Me'?"

"Everything with 'snow' in it is taken. Snowstorm. Snow day. Blizzard. Snowblind. Snowed in. I spent hours on Google and *Beer Advocate*."

That was the hardest part about brewing beer. There were so damned many breweries these days that all the good names were taken.

"I guess 'Plow Me' it is." He handed Libby the glass. "Can you do me a favor? No more 'Sex in the Spotlight'—the activity, not the drink. I don't ever want to catch you or anyone else *in flagrante* again."

Was he a prude?

Libby gave him a disappointed look that told him she thought he was. "Okay."

"You should head home, get some rest. We open again tomorrow. Good work ... on the brew, that is."

He left the brewery, made his way to his office, and sat at his desk, that ache in his chest like a weight. He sent a quick email to Kari, then emailed the staff to let them know the pub would open at eleven tomorrow and that everyone should report for their regular shifts. He debated for a moment whether to delete Rain's email from the message. The recipient list was suppressed so the other employees wouldn't notice if she was included or not. But he didn't want to seem pushy. At the same time, he couldn't believe she had truly quit. In the end, he deleted her email address out of respect for her decision, and hit send.

He puttered around for a while, deleting old emails, cleaning his desk. He was tucking a ledger away when a yellow sticky note caught his eye. It was the note Rain had left him almost a year ago when a bus crash in Boulder Canyon had killed one little boy and injured many more, all of them kids from Scarlet Springs. Joe had been torn up by it. The whole town had been devastated.

Joe picked up the note, read it again.

Breathe. We can only do what we can do. You will make a difference. XO.

He exhaled, rubbed his face with his hands.

Shit.

There was no one like Rain, no woman who touched him the way she did.

He shut the drawer, locked it, and left for home—after checking to make sure no one was hiding in the building. He drove home to a dark house, the emptiness of it pressing in on him in a way it never had before. He turned on the fireplace and the Christmas tree and poured himself a glass of scotch.

Then he sat in the darkness, an image of Rain, naked, fixed in his mind.

Chapter Ten

August 12, 1878

I was forced to leave Boulder and my new hotel last evening after Mr. Craddock sent word that my miners defied me and voted in secret to join that accursed union. The ungrateful bastards are demanding that their workday be limited to eight hours with no decrease in pay and are threatening to cease work if the mine owners refuse to acquiesce to their demands. This is blackmail and an affront to the natural order of society. It ought to be the mine owners who set conditions for work, not the riffraff.

I had hoped that by discharging known troublemakers, as I have repeatedly done, and decreasing my labor force with the use of mechanical drills, we might avoid the conflict that has plagued this mining elsewhere. I can see now that I was naïve. It is the very nature of these men to be belligerent, a trait passed on to their children, who scrap in the dust and mud like animals.

I have dispatched telegrams to the other mine owners in this state to hear what they would do. I further sent word to Governor Routt, asking him to prepare the National Guard in the event of violence. For my part, I see no choice but to hire more men who are loyal only to me to act as my private guard at the mine.

I will not let a rabble compel me into conducting business in any way that is not profitable for me. They grumbled when I required them to pay for their own candles. They complained when I brought in mechanical rock drills. I did not let their ill-mannered whining dissuade me. It shall not move me now.

Upon reaching Scarlet Springs, I sent for Hawke, who arrived, filthy to his skin, and stood, coughing, in my office.

"That drill kicks up an awful dust, so it does," he said.

I asked him whether he'd known of this secret vote, and he said that he had but that he, as underground foreman, had not been permitted to participate. Upon hearing this, I berated him, shouting in his face, demanding to know why he had not warned me or found some means to prevent the vote from taking place. I reminded him that he worked for me and not for the men.

He was not in the least bit cowed but told me that the miners have a right by law to assemble peaceably and to form unions if they believe it necessary.

When I asked him why I should not immediately replace him, he answered, "So you're after more difficulty with the men, then, aye?"

The arrogance! Still, I know he is right. The workers respect him in a way they do not respect me. I've seen him talk an angry crowd of miners into silence and get the men back to work after an accident when not one of them would listen to me.

It is not right that someone in my employ should hold a greater sway over my workers than I. Yet I have not the patience to mingle with their type, to listen to them prattle, to pretend that they are not lesser men than I, whose coin feeds, clothes, and houses each man among them and their whores and brats.

"Those men would be wise to thank me every day that I provide them with employment. Without me, there would be no town at Caribou, no schoolhouse. They would be working in some filthy coal mine or begging for work back in Cornwall."

Hawke glared at me, a hard glint in his eyes. "You ought to thank them that their back-breakin' labor brings up the ore that makes you wealthy. Are you thinkin' you could do it by your lonesome?"

I told him that for the sake of his wife and eight children, he'd best watch his tongue. No man in my employ speaks in such a haughty tone to me. He laughed and said it was past time that someone put me in my place.

I might have struck him right then had not Mr. Craddock burst in to tell us that a fire was sweeping down from the mountainside and headed straight for town. He said that we should gather those things most dear to us and flee before the fire caught us in the canyon. I ran outside and saw a conflagration moving toward us, carried by the wind.

Hawke dashed off after his own family, our conversation unfinished, while I grabbed my ledgers and this journal and sent Mr. Craddock after the contents of my safe. Gundry, who is now in my employ, made a wagon ready.

"Go, man, go!" I shouted when we were aboard.

"Oughtn't we to get your lady?" Gundry asked.

I had forgotten about Jenny. I've grown so weary of her company. Since losing her second daughter, a sickly little thing that lived only a few days, she seems to have lost *her spirit, insisting that she is unwell and taking to her bed each day with laudanum. I would have long since set her aside for another were it not for a lingering fondness I feel.*

Mr. Craddock dashed upstairs, dragged her from her bed, and carried her to the wagon. We made our way with most of the town down the canyon toward Boulder as if fleeing the scene of some terrible battle. As we left, I saw O'Hara dousing his inn with buckets of water.

Postscript: I was told that Scarlet has burned to the ground. Only a few buildings remain. One of those is O'Hara's inn—the clever bastard. The rest of us shall have to rebuild before the winter snows arrive.

Twenty-three days till Christmas

Rain woke to a bright blue sky, her arms and chest muscles sore from yesterday's workout, her life in pieces. She read a little from Silas' journal, then went to work cleaning the six guestrooms, which were split between the two upper floors of the inn—four on the second floor and two large suites on the third. The guests had been snowed in, too, and had checked out all at once when they'd heard the canyon was open.

As Rain went from room to room, she found herself wondering what the place had looked like back in Silas' day. He'd stayed here, eaten here, put up his guests here. Which room had been his?

Not that she liked the man. She was just curious.

She ran her fingertips over the woodwork on the oak handrail at the top of the stairs on the third floor, noticing the detail in a way she hadn't before.

"It's beautiful, isn't it?" Kendra came up from below. "As much as I say I hate this place, I love every square inch of it."

"It's lucky that the inn didn't burn down in 1878 along with everything else. Do you have photos from that time?"

Kendra stopped in the middle of the stairway and shouted at the top of her lungs, "Hey, Bob! What happened to the old photos of the inn? Rain wants to see them!"

Rain soon found herself sitting in the living room with Bob, looking at carefully preserved photos from Scarlet's earliest days. The inn. Main

Street with its saloons. Lexi and Britta's ancestors. Belle's brothel. "Is that Belle herself?"

"Yeah, that's her—the sexual energy worker." There was more than a hint of sarcasm in Bob's voice.

Rain studied the image. Belle had a little cupid's bow mouth and dark curly hair and was quite pretty, but didn't look like Rain's idea of a prostitute in the Old West. The high collar of her black gown was buttoned almost to her chin, her cleavage covered, her expression stern. "She looks like a school teacher."

"As far as the young men in this town were concerned, she was." Bob chuckled at his own joke. "The inn belonged to my first wife Emily's family, you know. I'm hoping to pass it to Lexi. So far, she's showing no sign that she wants to take over."

"That's sad." Rain couldn't stop the next question. "Do you have any photos of Silas Moffat, Joe's great-great-whatever-grandfather?"

"I think so." He turned a few pages, pointed. "There. That's him, standing next to the bank. Emily's old man said he was a real asshole."

"It's true." Rain studied the image, surprised to see not a big man like Joe, but a small, slight man. His features were hatchet-like, sharp and hard, his eyes cold, his bushy sideburns looking ridiculous. A woman stood beside him, sadness in her gaze, her young face heavy with sorrow despite the smile on her lips.

Jenny.

Rain didn't have to ask to know it was true. The woman in the image resembled her grandmother from her cheekbones to her nose to the shape of her mouth. "That's Jenny Minear. My great-great-great-grand aunt. I'm not sure about the number of greats."

"Really?" Bob stared at Rain. "I had no idea you were such a history buff. I've got other things around here, some antiques, some old newspapers."

Rain was about to say she'd like very much to see it all when her phone buzzed. A text message from Rico.

You okay? We're open.

She hadn't had time to reply when she got another message and another, the staff at Knockers checking up on her, wanting to know where she was, worried that something had happened to her because she hadn't shown up. There was nothing from Joe.

She swallowed the lump in her throat, typed a message back to Rico.

I quit yesterday. Thanks for everything. I loved working with you. XO.

Rico's reply was almost instantaneous.

WHAT. THE. FUCK!

"Ha!" Bob sat there, peering over Rain's shoulder. "Rose must be off her game. I'd figure everyone in town would know by now. Joe hasn't told the staff you quit. He must be hoping you'll come back. He must really value you as an employee if he'd rather have you work for him than have you in his bed."

Rain's head snapped up, and she glared at Bob, pain lancing through her chest at his words. She opened her mouth to say something—then realized Bob was right. That was precisely the problem. Joe valued her as an employee, but he didn't feel for her the way that she felt for him.

"I can't go back."

Not now. Not ever.

Knockers was busy from the moment Joe unlocked the front entrance. People who'd been cooped up in their own homes wanted to get out, hear the news, talk with friends they hadn't seen for the past few days. But it was surreal to go through the workday without Rain. She had always been the heart of this place. He tried to pretend that nothing was wrong, that nothing had happened.

But he wasn't fooling anyone.

Joe knew the moment the staff got word that Rain had quit. Marcia quit speaking to him. Cheyenne openly glared at him. Libby told him she was too busy to talk when he came in to discuss art options for the labels of the new brew.

"Just pick whatever," she said, her voice cold.

Shit.

Hank reappeared just after noon, asked Marcia for a whiskey. He shook his head when he saw Joe. "What's wrong with you, Joe? Rain is a special woman. I thought you were smarter than that."

So now he was being lectured by Hank?

But it was Bear who was the last straw. He came in just before the lunch rush, asking for Rain, clearly hoping for a hot meal.

"She quit, Bear," Cheyenne said with no tact. "She won't be coming in again."

The tears in the big man's eyes felt like an indictment.

Joe threw the towel he'd been holding onto the bar. "See to it that Bear gets a good meal on the house. I'll be in my office."

He stomped to the back, sat at his desk, checked his email. Lots of messages, but nothing from Rain.

It was just after the lunch rush when Rico appeared in Joe's doorway, hairnet on his beard, chef's knife in one hand, sharpening rod in the other. He scraped the blade slowly over the steel, his gaze meeting Joe's, his lips pressed into a thin, angry line. "Well, you really blew it, didn't you?"

Not Rico, too.

Steel scraped steel.

"Come in, shut the door, and say your piece."

Rico nudged the door shut with his shoe. "Rain quit because of *you*."

Joe had had it. "I didn't want her to quit. It would be bad for business. Whatever goes on between Rain and me is no one's business."

"Don't give me that." Rico slid the blade over the steel once more, the sound grating on Joe's nerves. "I've worked alongside the two of you almost since the beginning. That girl has been crazy in love with you for twenty years, and you're too damned stupid to see it."

"What?" Had everyone gone insane?

"You're in love with her, too." Rico's words hit Joe in the face.

He stammered out the first thing that came to him. "I'm her employer—or I was. She quit because of her own stubborn pride because I wouldn't sleep with her."

Joe couldn't believe he'd just told Rico this.

Rico passed the blade over the steel again. "That wasn't pride. She quit so that you'd have the freedom to choose."

Joe's pulse throbbed in his ears. "What? What are you saying?"

Rico rolled his eyes. "She chose *you* over her job, and what did you do? You let her walk away. Now she's talking about leaving Scarlet, maybe going to San Diego to live with Britta."

Jesus! Could that be true? "Leaving Scarlet?"

He couldn't let her do that. He couldn't imagine this town without her.

Then it hit him.

Wait just a damned minute…

"How do you know all of this? Did Rain call and vent or something?"

"You know Rain would never do that, but Rose … I guess she was at Bob and Kendra's when you dropped Rain off. Rain was crying, and, well, word has gotten around. Kendra told Lexi. Lexi told Victoria."

Rain had been crying? *Ouch.*

If Rose knew, that meant everyone in Scarlet had the details by now.

Fuck.

"You know what I think?" Rico ran the knife over the sharpening steel once more.

"Could you sit and put down that damned knife?"

Rico sat, laid the knife on Joe's desk. "I think some part of you is punishing yourself because you've wanted her since she came to work for you."

Joe couldn't deny that last part, guilt sliding through him, dark and jagged. There was more to it than Rico knew. Not only had Rain been seventeen, but she was also a Minear, while Joe was Silas' great-great-grandson. Joe would have cut off his own dick before he'd followed in Silas' footsteps.

Rico wasn't finished. "You knew it was wrong for a twenty-seven-year-old guy to hook up with a seventeen-year-old. She was vulnerable, alone with a new baby. Wanting her made you feel like you were as much of a scumbag as the guy who'd abandoned her. Wasn't he about your age?"

He had been *exactly* Joe's age.

Rico didn't wait for an answer. "You tried to bury those emotions, shut off your feelings. You set her aside in your mind as the girl you could never touch. But I've got news for you, Joe, buddy. Rain hasn't been a child for a long time. She's not the girl you hired. She's a sexy adult woman, and she loves you, man."

"She and I have always been close, but—"

"Close?" Rico laughed. "Do you know why she's still single? She's been waiting—for *you*."

Joe stared at Rico, dumbfounded. "She … she told you that?"

Rico went on. "Do you know why no man from Scarlet hits on her? They're all afraid you'll kill them."

Joe opened his mouth to object, but had nothing.

"Yeah. Don't try to deny that one." Rico stood, picked up the knife and the sharpening steel. "If you're not careful, man, you're going to lose more than a valued employee. You'll lose *her*. Got that? If you can't figure out what to do from here, you're dumber than you look."

He opened the door and walked away, leaving Joe to stare after him.

October 7, 1880

Today has been a most rewarding day. Late last night, Sheriff Taylor arrived with the shocking news that striking miners had attacked the guards I set to protect the replacement workers and that one man was shot and later died. Immediately, a witness among my guards stepped forward to tell Sheriff Taylor that the man who'd pulled the trigger was none other than Cadan Hawke.

Taylor found the bastard at home with his wife and children and asked where he'd been. Hawke told Taylor that he'd been summoned to my office just after supper but hadn't found anyone. He claimed that he didn't even own a pistol.

Taylor returned to question me, asking whether Mr. Craddock or I had called for Hawke. I told the good sheriff that we had not and informed him that we had been at the inn dining at the time. Taylor returned to Hawke's home, where one of Taylor's deputies then discovered a Colt Peacemaker hidden in the rafters of Hawke's chicken coop, proving him a liar. Taylor had no choice but to take him into custody.

His wife, I am told, wept inconsolably as they led Hawke away.

Mr. Craddock was amazed by this turn of events. "How fortuitous it is that the man responsible for these recent misfortunes is about to meet his end."

I then admitted to Mr. Craddock that I had orchestrated the entire affair—the attack, the shooting, summoning Hawke to my office, and hiding the pistol in Hawke's chicken coop. I hadn't intended for the guard to die, but I shall compensate his widow.

It is not an exaggeration to say that Mr. Craddock was awed by my actions, the smile on his face that of a man who has just had a great revelation.

"Great men make the world as they wish it to be," I told him. "When the miners see Hawke swinging in the wind, it will break their spirit—and end this strike."

Hawke is behind these agitators. I know it. They look to him as their leader, do as he bids them. He claims that he did not press for the strike, that the changing times and my refusal to meet the miners' demands is the cause. But he has always put their needs ahead of mine.

Well, now he shall pay the price. Taylor tells me it will be a month before the judge is next in town. There will be a jury trial, but I do not see how Hawke could be found innocent, not with the Colt and a witness—a well-paid witness, I might add. In the meantime, I wait for the National Guardsmen the governor promised me should there be an outbreak of violence at the mine. The troops will break the back of this strike and restore order. Without Hawke to rally them, the miners will fall into line.

I am not heartless. I have assured Sheriff Taylor that I will see Hawke's family well cared for as long as he remains behind bars.

"He is innocent until proved guilty," I said.

I saw in Taylor's eyes that he suspects me, and I know him to be a friend of Hawke's. Both men are Cornish, after all. But Taylor is an educated man of the law. He will do his job and, in so doing, rid me of this rabble-rouser.

I am troubled by one thing, however. As Mr. Craddock left, I spied Jenny standing at the top of the stairs in her nightgown. She looked frightened. When I asked her how long she'd been standing there, she stammered something about needing water.

I fear she overheard me. Given her penchant for laudanum, I doubt very much she will remember this in the morning. Nevertheless, I shall send her to my hotel in Boulder straightaway to keep her far from Sheriff Taylor.

A knock jerked Rain back from the nineteenth century. "Rain?"

Kendra.

"Yeah?" Rain marked her place, then closed the journal, her stomach in knots for Cadan and his family.

Kendra opened the door, stuck her head inside. "Joe is here. He looks like a man who's had some time to reflect. He wants to speak with you."

Rain sat up, smoothed her hands over her blouse and jeans. "What time is it?"

They'd eaten dinner hours ago.

"It's just after ten. You look fine. Come on. He's waiting."

"He can wait a bit longer." She zipped across the hall, brushed and braided her hair, brushed her teeth, and put on a little mascara.

Why did she bother? Joe was probably there just to try to talk her into coming back to work for him.

She met her gaze in the mirror, resolved not to give in, then walked out to the kitchen to find him standing just inside the door.

His gaze met hers, an unfamiliar softness there. "Can we talk?"

She crossed her arms over her chest. "I'm not coming back to Knockers, Joe. If that's why you're here, save yourself the trouble and go."

There. She'd said it. She'd been strong.

"That's not why I'm here. Please, can we talk somewhere private?"

"We can go to my room." She led him down the hallway.

"No hanky-panky!" Bob called after them from the living room, laughing.

She shut the door, tried to sound casual. "What's up?"

He looked at the floor, gave a little laugh. "I guess I need to hear it from you."

"Hear what?"

He lifted his head, his brown eyes looking into hers. "Why did you quit, Rain?"

"I told you—I'm not coming back."

He nodded. "I heard that. I'm not here to bring you back. I just need to know. Why did you quit?"

Rain's pulse spiked. "Y-you were there. You know why."

He shook his head. "I know what happened, but I don't understand it."

Rain stared at him. Seriously? "Oh, come on!"

He took a step toward her and another until he stood only inches away from her. He tucked a finger under her chin, lifted her gaze to his. "Why, Rain?"

Did she have to spell it out for him? Did she have to make herself naked for him again? Well, why not? She had nothing left to lose here.

"You said you wouldn't ... be with me, not as long as I was an employee. I quit so that you would be free to do what you want, but that apparently doesn't include me." She steeled herself and laid the truth at his feet, certain she was about to ruin their relationship for good. "I love you, Joe. For twenty years, I've waited—"

Joe's mouth came down on hers in an almost violent kiss.

Chapter Eleven

Joe forgot where he was, his need for Rain driving everything else from his mind, his world shrinking until it held only her, his senses overwhelmed by her. The surprise on her sweet face. The taste of her lips. The silk of her hair. The soft curves of her body. Her feminine scent.

He slid a hand into her hair, drew back her head, pressed his lips to her exposed throat, the thrumming of her pulse a match for the pounding in his chest. "*Rain.*"

They stumbled backward onto the bed—which gave a loud *squee-eee-eee-eeak* as their weight settled.

Shit.

Remembering where they were, Joe pulled back, ran his thumb across Rain's cheek. "Come with me—unless you want to risk Bob or Kendra hearing."

She gave a little laugh, her lips wet and swollen. "Yeah, *nooo.*"

He stood, drew her to her feet. "Grab your things. You're not coming back here."

Not to be pushy or anything, but, damn it, if they were going to cross this line there would be no going back.

Rico had been dead-on. Joe had felt an attraction to Rain from the moment he'd seen her, and he'd felt guilty as hell about it—guilty for having sexual feelings about a vulnerable girl who'd already been hurt, guilty for being the same age as the man who'd used her, guilty for being her boss and yet wanting her. Loving her would have broken all the rules, would have made him no better than Silas or the bastard who'd gotten her pregnant. He'd done exactly what Rico had said he'd done.

He'd made her off-limits.

It had been the right thing to do back then… But now? She was no longer a child, no longer defenseless, and no longer his employee.

More than that, she'd said she loved him. Sure, he'd heard that from women before, but what they had really loved was his bank accounts. But Joe knew Rain. He'd known her for twenty years. He trusted her. She didn't give a damn about money. If she said she loved him, then she must truly love *him*.

That changed everything.

She hadn't unpacked her clothes, so it took just a few seconds to gather her toiletries and pajamas. Feeling like a teenager trying to sneak out of the house, Joe carried the bags down the hallway to the kitchen, following Rain.

She ducked her head into the living room, where the television was on, blue light flickering on the walls. "Thanks for everything. I'll come by and clean Lexi's room tomorrow. Can you thank Kendra for me?"

"Sure thing, and, hey, you're welcome." Bob chuckled. "Have fun, kids. Don't do anything I wouldn't do."

They left by the back door, walked through the snow to Joe's SUV and stowed Rain's bags in the back seat.

Joe fought to clear his mind, starting the vehicle and backing down the driveway to find Kendra and Rose huddled together out front. "I wonder what those two have to talk about this late at night."

"Us?"

"We are so on to you two," Joe muttered.

The two women waved, big smiles on their faces.

Oh, yeah. Play innocent.

The drive home seemed to take forever. Joe held Rain's hand, talking about little things to pass the time—the weather, how busy Knockers had been today, Libby's new brew. "She named it 'Plow Me.'"

That made Rain laugh. "Oh, that's perfect."

Which reminded him…

"Sex in the spotlight?" He glanced over at Rain. "Did you know about that?"

"The drink—or people having sex onstage?"

Damn. "You knew?"

"You didn't? Joe, you own the place." She shook her head. "You work too hard."

He couldn't stop himself from asking. "Have you done it?"

"Had sex onstage at your pub?" She looked over at him. "No. The man I wanted to do it with wasn't interested."

Oh, he'd been interested. "What an idiot he must have been."

"You have no idea." She gave his hand a squeeze.

Finally, they reached the house. He drew into the garage, parked, and glanced over at Rain, who looked tense. "Hey, what is it?"

She looked at him through those big green eyes. "It's not every day you have sex with the man you love for the first time. I've waited so long."

Her words hit him in the solar plexus.

Had she really waited twenty years for this?

Haven't you?

Now he was nervous, too. He ought to do what he could to make this special for her, for both of them. Tonight would change everything, and there would be no going back for either of them. His room was probably a mess. He couldn't remember if he'd made his bed or whether he'd left his clothes from yesterday on the floor. There was also the fact that he'd been at work all day and smelled like the pub.

Shit.

He grabbed her bags, and they walked inside together, hung up their coats, tugged off their boots. "Why don't you go sit in the living room by the fire where it's warm and give me a few minutes upstairs?"

She cocked her head, as if trying to figure out what he doing. "Okay."

He took the stairs two at a time, hurried to his bedroom, and picked up the dirty clothes off his floor. After that, he turned on the fireplace, changed his sheets and left the bed turned down. Then he took a fast shower to wash off the reek of beer and grease.

Nothing said romance like the odor of fryer fat.

He slipped into a pair of black boxer briefs, lit the candles on his nightstand, and went back for her. He found her sitting on the sofa, hands clasped tightly in her lap, the vulnerability on her face reminding him of the seventeen-year-old girl she'd once been. "Hey, beautiful."

She stood and turned to face him, her gaze sliding over him, vulnerability chased away by a look of naked longing.

His heart gave a thud.

She pointed at his torso. "That right there—that's all I want for Christmas."

He closed the distance between them and scooped her into his arms, gratified by her little shriek of surprise. "Santa came early."

Rain's pulse tripped. Could this truly be happening? This wasn't like the times they'd kissed and Joe had stopped them. They were really going through with it this time. He was freaking carrying her up the stairs to his room *right now*.

She rested her head against his shoulder, not hypothermic this time, awed by the way he made her feel—feminine, protected, desired. The clean scent of his skin filled her head, his heart beating, steady and strong, beneath her palm.

He reached the top of the stairs, turned down the hallway, and stepped through his bedroom door, where he set her on her feet.

"Oh!" Rain walked toward the bed, warmth spreading behind her breastbone as she took it all in—the fireplace, the candles, the turned-down sheets.

Joe had built a little love nest for her.

He came up behind her, slid his fingers into her hair, and began to unbind her braid, his lips pressing butterfly kisses against the side of her throat.

She inhaled his clean scent, tilted her head, making room for him, some part of her still stunned to think that this was Joe and that he wanted her.

"I love your hair." He ran his fingers through the last bit of braid, then buried his face against her nape. "I've always loved your hair, dreads or not."

Shivers skittered down her spine.

He drew her back against the hard wall of his chest and reached around to unbutton her blouse, then tugged it over her shoulders and down her arms, the fabric pooling at her feet. He cupped her shoulders, kissed them. "You smell so good."

Anticipation made it hard for Rain to breathe as he reached down, grazed the swells of her breasts with his knuckles, and unfastened the front clasp of her bra.

He moaned when the lace fell away to reveal her breasts, then took the weight of them in his big hands, cupping her, lifting her. "Perfect."

She started to say something about the little stretch marks left from when she'd had Lark, but he circled her nipples with his thumbs, making her entire body jerk, sparks of arousal darting straight to her belly.

But he was just getting started.

He teased her nipples with his thumbs, circled the very tips with his palms, caught them between his fingers, his touch unleashing a surge of liquid heat between her thighs. "Does that feel good?"

"God, yes." She closed her eyes, pressed her breasts deeper into his hands, her hips moving of their own accord, seeking relief from the ache inside her.

That's how she discovered the thick ridge of his erection. It pressed against her lower back, heightening her lust.

He slid a hand slowly down her belly, making her muscles tense. "Your skin is like silk."

He unzipped her jeans, slid his hands inside her panties to explore her, his other hand still busy with her breast. He had no trouble finding her clit and no uncertainty about what to do when he found it, his clever fingers stroking, teasing, flicking. Impatient for him, she parted her legs and was rewarded when he slid a thick finger inside her.

They moaned in unison.

"You're so wet." He stroked her inside and out, the angle of his hand ensuring that he grazed her clit with each thrust, his other hand still tormenting her nipples.

She met his motions with thrusts of her own, digging into the muscles of his forearm with the nails of one hand, the fingers of the other fisting in his hair as she reached behind her to steady herself. "Oh, yes."

How could this be *so* good already? She was on the brink of an orgasm, and they hadn't even reached the bed.

She was close … so close… and then…

He stopped and scooped her up, then carried her to the bed and peeled the jeans and panties off her body, tossing them aside. He stood beside the bed, his gaze consuming her, candlelight playing over the ridges and valleys of his muscles. "You are the most beautiful woman I've ever seen."

"You didn't seem to feel that way yesterday."

"Are you kidding? It took everything I had to keep my hands off you."

A thrill shivered through her. "I wish you hadn't."

"Yeah, me too." He knelt on the bed beside her, ducking down to kiss first her mouth, then an aching nipple, his erection straining against his boxer briefs. "I want to taste you."

Was he asking?

"*Yes.*"

He didn't do what she thought he was going to do. Instead of burying his face between her legs, he came down on her throat, kissing, licking, nibbling. He worked his way slowly down her body, so slowly that she didn't realize what he was doing. His lips, tongue and teeth spread fire over her skin as he tasted her clavicle, her breastbone, the underside of her breasts. Then he latched on to a nipple and suckled.

She arched beneath him, feeding him more of herself, every tug of his lips making the ache inside her sharper.

He fed on one breast, then the other. "I love your body."

In the next instant, his mouth was on her again, tracing a path over her ribcage and across her belly then ducking down between her legs, his hot lips brushing against the sensitive skin of her inner thigh.

She opened her eyes, found him watching her, his brown eyes dark with arousal.

He smiled, pushed her thighs wide apart—and flicked her clit with this tongue.

She gasped, watching as he parted her and went to work on her with his mouth, licking and suckling her clit. The intense pleasure took her by surprise, her eyes drifting shut, her fingers sliding into his hair. She'd enjoyed oral sex—or tried to—but this was something different.

Joe was *so... damned... good...* teasing her clit ... drawing it into his mouth ... tugging and sucking on her sensitive inner lips...

She bucked against his mouth, desperate now. He threw a strong arm across her lower belly to hold her in place, then slid his fingers inside her, stroking her, every thrust magic, his mouth and lips and tongue *killing* her. She couldn't help but moan, her response beyond her control, the pleasure almost unbearable.

Orgasm hit her hard, making her cry out, the ecstasy lifting her up and up and up... and leaving her to float somewhere close to heaven.

Joe stretched out beside Rain, awed by her, shaken to his core by the depth of his feeling for her. She lay motionless, and he chuckled to see her so far gone, her eyes closed, her brow still furrowed, her body limp. There was a reason the French referred to orgasm as *la petite mort*—the little death.

Her scent all over him, her taste still on his tongue, he went to work bringing her back to life, planting soft kisses on her hair, her temple, her forehead, caressing the curve of her hip, her belly, the underside of her breasts, tickling her ribcage, her inner thighs.

She smiled, a sleepy, sexy kind of smile, stretched, and opened her eyes. "That was *amazing*."

"Yeah?" He kind of figured she'd enjoyed it, given her scream—and the fact that she'd almost pulled his hair out by the roots.

She rolled onto her side, slid a hand up his chest. "Do you know how many times I've fantasized about this?"

"Mmm...twice?" God, it felt right to be close to her.

"At least a thousand times." She leaned in, kissed one of his nipples, the contact sending blood back to his groin. "I've wanted you since the day you punched Guy and threw him out of the pub."

She'd been eighteen then.

Jesus.

Joe hated even thinking about that bastard. "He's lucky that's all I did."

Rain pushed Joe onto his back, straddled him, splayed her hands across his chest, the sight of her breasts making him fully hard again. "Did you fantasize about me?"

What could he tell her but the truth? She'd been honest with him.

"Yes. I felt guilty as hell about it."

"Poor Joe. You are way too hard on yourself." She bent down, kissed him, her breasts pressing against his chest.

He yielded to her, let her do whatever she wanted with him, turned on as hell to see her reaction to his body—her darkened pupils, the lustful little smile on her face, the furrow on her brow when her gaze moved over his abs.

She did what he'd done to her, licking and teasing his nipples, kissing her way down his chest and over his abdomen, licking and nipping him until his skin seemed to burn. She nudged his legs apart, sat between his thighs, her hands still exploring him. Then she stepped onto the floor, lifted his boxer briefs over his erection, and pulled them off, tossing them God knew where.

Her gaze dropped to his cock, a quick gust of breath leaving her lungs. "I knew you'd be hung."

Wait. She'd spent time thinking about his dick?

He opened his mouth to ask what had made her think that when she took hold of him. The breath caught in his throat, making words impossible.

She stroked him slowly from head to root and back again, her fingers cool against his aching cock. "Show me how you like it."

He reached down, guided her, increasing the pressure. She caught on fast, so he released her hand, left her to it. "Just ... like ... *that*."

His eyes drifted shut—then flew open when she took him into the heat of her mouth. He gasped at the shock of it, his cock jerking.

She looked up at him, her gaze never leaving his as she devoured him, her mouth and fist moving in tandem over the aching length of his cock, her tongue swirling over its straining head. He willed his muscles to relax, wanting to enjoy this, wanting to make it last, but it felt too damned good.

"*Stop.* Rain. Jesus. Stop." This wasn't how he wanted tonight to end.

He wanted to be inside her.

He twisted, reached for his nightstand, pulled a condom out of the drawer.

She took it from him, tore the wrapper open with her teeth, and tossed it, then rolled the condom onto his erection. Her gaze met his again, her lips curving in a sexy-as-hell smile as she crawled up his body, straddled him, then guided him inside her, taking him slowly, inch by inch.

Holy ... hell!

She was slick and wet and tight, the feel of her blowing his mind, even through latex. She rested her palms against his chest and began to move, her hips undulating in a way that was blatantly erotic, her clit rubbing against the root of his cock. Her eyes drifted shut, her lips parting on a breathy exhale. "That feels ... so ... good."

Rain, sweet Rain.

He'd wanted her for so long... wanted this. He let her set the rhythm, her motions enough to keep him hard and aroused, but not enough to make him come. There was time for that later.

Would she be able to come again? God, he hoped so.

He reached up to take the weight of her breasts into his hands, palming her nipples, pinching them, teasing them. He knew now how sensitive she was, how much she liked that. She moaned, arched, her motions faster now, the tension inside her building again. He reached down with one hand to tease her clit. She rocked against the pressure, her head falling forward, her hair a curtain around her face, her nails biting into his chest. He kept one hand busy between her legs, reached up with the other to move her hair aside. He needed to see her face, to watch her come.

Her eyes went wide, and she sucked in a breath, then cried out, a look of carnal delight washing over her face.

That was it.

In a single motion, Joe flipped her onto her back, growled out her name. "*Rain.*"

It was a plea, need for her slamming in his chest like a heartbeat. His gaze met hers, green eyes looking up at him. "You are so ... fucking ... beautiful."

He drove himself into her, years of wanting her, years of fighting his desire for her breaking through his control. He loved her... loved Rain ... wanted her... needed her so fucking much. He shattered, the bliss of climax blasting through him, shaking him apart, leaving him breathless.

He sank against her, his head on her breast, her heart beating against his cheek. And for a time, he couldn't move. It was only later, when he'd come back to himself, that he realized something wasn't right. "The condom. It broke."

Chapter Twelve

Rain lay back against Joe's chest in his big marble bathtub, a little tipsy, her body replete, her heart singing. She hadn't felt this sexually satisfied or safe with a man since … ever. This had been better than any fantasy, better than anything her imagination could have invented. She'd never known what it felt like to love a man with her whole heart—and have him love her back. Not that he'd said those words, exactly …

For a time, they sat there in silence, the water warm against their skin, empty champagne glasses and flickering candles on the window sill, steam on the window.

"I'm sorry," he said.

"Sorry for what?" Oh. Right. "Condoms break. I'll stop by the pharmacy tomorrow to pick up Plan B and make an appointment with my GYN to get something long term."

"I'm paying for it."

"You don't have to do that."

"Women deal with more than their fair share when it comes to sex. You're the ones who have periods and deal with birth control and get pregnant and have babies and breastfeed. Men ought to do something. I want to do my part. Besides, you've got enough going on right now with your house."

When he put it that way…

"Okay. It's a deal. You can pay. But tonight was the most amazing sexual experience of my life, and I don't want to waste the afterglow worrying." She pushed all thoughts of an unwanted pregnancy aside. "You're incredible. You know that, right?"

"I'm glad you think so."

"Tonight was … " A lump formed in her throat. *"Perfect."*

"For me, too." He kissed her hair, the fingers of one hand lazily stroking her ribcage just beneath her breast.

"How did you get to be so good in bed? Or maybe I don't want to know."

"I had a female friend in college who overheard me say something really sexist and stupid about sorority sisters craving dick. She got in my face and broke the news that dicks alone don't do it for most women and that a lot of women can be sexually content without having a penis inside them at all. Whoa! For an 18-year-old guy, that was a shocker. She said for most women, good sex was all about the clit. When I challenged that, she told me to try jerking off without touching my dick and see how fast I came."

Rain laughed. "I like this woman."

He chuckled, too. "It had never dawned on me until that moment that women's experience of sex could be so different from men's. I knew about the clit, of course, but I hadn't understood how important it was for women's ability to enjoy sex. I'd always thought good sex involved a lot of ramming. It was fantastic for me, so it must be good for her, too, right? After that, I set out to learn everything I could."

Rain tried to imagine Joe saying something awful like that and couldn't. "You must have been a different person back then."

"I was my father's son and Silas' great-great-grandson. I was an asshole, the spoiled son of a mining mogul and his Playboy Playmate wife."

"Your mom was a Playboy bunny?" Rain hadn't known that.

"Miss June 1968. My dad showed me her centerfold when I was about ten."

"Ten?" Rain turned in Joe's arms. "He showed you nude photos of your mom?"

That was screwed up.

Joe nodded. "He was proud of them. He told me he'd known she was the woman for him when he'd heard her say she would never let herself get fat."

Rain's jaw dropped. "How shallow can a man be?"

"They were a perfect match. He married her for her body. She married him for his money. By the time I went off to boarding school, they hated each other."

Rain turned so that she was sitting in his lap, her legs around his hips. She ran a hand up the wet skin of his chest. "I don't think you were spoiled. I think you were neglected, mistreated. What kind of father shares nude photos of his wife with their son?"

"That's my family—a long line of selfish assholes. That's one reason I've never wanted kids. For four generations now, Moffats have married women they don't love, fathered one son, and passed on the asshole gene to the next generation."

"Then why aren't you an asshole?"

He raised an eyebrow. "Who says I'm not?"

She held his gaze, defied him to contradict her. "I do."

"My grandmother deserves most of the credit. She did her best to break the mold. My grandfather got her pregnant and had to marry her. Back then, even a rich man couldn't knock a woman up and walk away— not when her father was a US Senator. She was a genuinely good person. She didn't deserve my grandfather. She tried to raise my father right, and I think it broke her heart to see how much like his father he turned out to be. She tried again with me, did her best to instill some empathy and compassion. That's why she gave me Silas' journals."

"She gave you the journals?"

He nodded. "My grandfather had wanted them burned to protect the family's reputation. She hid them away, told him they were ash. After my father died—he was killed in a plane crash when I was twenty-four— she entrusted them to me. What I read made me sick, opened my eyes. My father's death and Silas' journals were like a slap in the face. I finished my master's degree, realized I didn't give a damn about mining or Wall Street. I bought a plane ticket and came to Scarlet Springs."

Rain sometimes forgot that Joe hadn't grown up in Scarlet like she had, in part because his ties to the town went back further than hers. "It must have been a shock after growing up in ... wherever you grew up."

How could she know him so well and yet know so little about him?

"Weston, Massachusetts." He moved a strand of wet hair off her cheek. "I was amazed by Colorado—the mountains, the people. It was a new world. I learned to ski and climb. I met people who lived life on their terms, who said what they meant and meant what they said, who valued freedom more than money. I decided to stay. I wanted to find a way to give back to the town, to make up for what Silas had done. I had no idea how to do that until I asked Bob Jewell where a person could get a good beer. He said, 'You want good beer? Go to Boulder.'"

Rain and Joe both laughed at that.

"So that's why you started a brewpub."

"At first, I was just thinking about the business side of it, filling a market niche and brewing good beer. Then this teenage girl walked in." Joe's gaze softened, and he ran his knuckles down Rain's cheek. "She had a new baby. Some asshole ten years older than she was had gotten her pregnant and left her to give birth alone in a minivan. She begged me for a job, promised me she'd work hard. She had the biggest, greenest eyes I'd ever seen. I caught her last name—Minear—and I couldn't turn her away."

Rain gaped at him. "Jenny. That's why you did so much for me."

Joe nodded.

She'd thought he'd done it all out of pity, but it had been guilt. He'd been trying to atone for Silas' sins. *Oh, Joe.* "You're not Silas. You didn't need to do that."

"Yes, I did." His lips curved in a soft smile. "Besides, you gave me so much more than I gave you."

"I ... I did?"

"I watched you throw yourself into the job, watched how you smiled and gave it your best even after a sleepless night with Lark. I saw how you interacted with people, how they gravitated toward you. Empathy, kindness, doing the right thing—I always had to think about it, to weigh things out before I knew what to do. It came naturally to you."

Rain shook her head. "You're one of the kindest men I know. You always try to do the right thing. I love that about you."

"Thanks for saying that, but it hasn't always been that way. When I came to Scarlet, I still had a lot to learn, and you were my teacher—one of them, anyway."

"What do you mean?"

"You hadn't been working at the pub for long when Bear walked in, hungry and cold. If it had been left to me, I'd have told him to get out, but you treated him like family and bought him supper even though you barely had the money to feed yourself. I watched you and felt ashamed. Why hadn't I thought to do that? That's when it came to me. Knockers wasn't just about making sure Scarlet Springs had good beer. It was about building community, giving the people of Scarlet a place to come together, helping them get a sense of this town as more than just a former mining town gone bust. You gave me a sense of purpose, Rain, and you were just seventeen."

Rain found herself blinking back tears.

Sex had never left Joe feeling like this before—his heart full, his mind empty, his body satisfied down to his very bones.

"Why did you change your mind?" Rain rested her cheek against his shoulder, her breasts pressing against his chest, her legs still wrapped around his hips. "One minute you made it clear we weren't going to sleep together, and the next..."

How could Joe explain it so that she could understand?

He traced the curve of her spine with his fingers. "I've wanted you since the first day I met you, and I *hated* myself for that. You were seventeen, so vulnerable and alone, and I was twenty-seven, the same age as that asshole who'd hurt you. You depended on me, trusted me. I didn't want to betray that trust. I didn't want to be him or Silas, so I shut that part of myself off—or I tried to."

"You're nothing like either of them."

Oh, but he could have been. "I'm not a saint."

"Do you think the things you've done matter less because you had to think them through?" She cupped his cheek. "You've *chosen* to do what's right. You gave up a lucrative career to try to set right wrongs that weren't yours. That tells me everything I need to know about you."

He looked into her eyes, the redemption she offered like a drug. "So much of what I've done here in Scarlet has been to make myself worthy of your respect. I'd be a different person without you."

"Worthy of my respect? I've always respected you. God knows where Lark and I would have ended up without you." She kissed him, then frowned. "I get why you couldn't get together with me back then. But I quit yesterday. I wasn't your employee, and you still wouldn't touch me."

"What did you think I'd do—ball you right there on the gym floor?"

"That would have been nice."

"How could I? I knew you needed the job. I couldn't accept your resignation, sleep with you, and then hire you back the next day."

"So what changed?"

Joe wasn't sure he was ready for this conversation, but he couldn't hold anything back from her, not after tonight. He told her how the staff had been angry with him when they'd learned she had quit and why and how Rico had gotten in his face about it. "He told me you were serious about leaving Scarlet, which scared the hell out of me. Then he said ... that you loved me."

Rain lifted her head, her green eyes wide. "He did?"

Joe owed Rico. "I had to find out the truth. The moment you said those words yourself..."

"That made sex okay all of a sudden?"

"Yeah." Couldn't she see? "All the women who've told me they loved me have been after one thing. They didn't give a damn about me. But you're not like that. If you say you love me, then, for whatever reason—and I can't fathom why—you really do love *me*. I've never had that before." Joe ran his thumb over her cheek, fought for the courage to say words he'd never said to any woman. "The truth is ... I love you, too."

Her eyes filled with tears, her lips curving in a tremulous smile. "I kind of figured, but it's really nice to hear you say it."

He wiped the tears from her cheeks, his heart soaring. "I love you, Rain. I've loved you since that first time you bought Bear supper."

"Really? That was so long ago." She cupped his cheek, leaned in, kissed him. "What happens now? Can I have my job back, or is that still breaking your rules?"

He hadn't thought that far ahead. "I don't want people gossiping about you."

Rain laughed. "This is Scarlet, remember? People talk."

Oh. Yeah.

Hell.

"Do we have to talk about this right now?" He needed time to think it over. Besides, there were other things he'd rather do.

"We don't have to talk at all." Rain slipped her hands behind his neck, drew his head closer to hers, and kissed him.

He let her set the pace, awed by her, overwhelmed by his love for her. She was as close to heaven as he'd ever get, his church, the source of his salvation, his beginning and end. He opened his mouth to her, yielded to her touch, her will be done.

She took her time with him, kissing him slow and deep, the heat between them on a slow build. He cupped her breasts, teased her nipples to erectness, blood rushing to his groin, making him erect, too. Then she reached down between them, took his cock in one hand, and stroked him.

He fought to keep his eyes open, not wanting to miss a single thing—the sensual light in her eyes, the flush that came over her breasts as she grew aroused, the little smile on her lips. She lifted herself up, and for a moment he thought she meant to take him inside her. He was about to reach for the condom he'd brought into the bathroom when she rubbed her clit against the underside of his cock.

Whoa.

This was something new. Could she come like this?

Rain rocked against him, stroking him with her clit and labia, the friction enough to keep him hard but not enough to make him come. That was fine with him. It turned him on to see her like this—aroused, uninhibited, hungry for him. He toyed with her breasts, determined to make it as good for her as he could.

She pressed him harder against herself, holding him in place with the flat of her hand, her eyes drifting shut, her breath coming faster now, an expression like pain on her face. She gave a frustrated moan, her eyes flying open. "I want you inside me."

He reached for the condom, tore it open with his teeth, and rose onto his knees to roll it down the length of his aching cock. "Turn around. Get on your knees."

She did as he asked, water sluicing down her creamy skin as she turned away from him, exposing that beautiful ass of hers. She spread her knees as far apart as the tub would allow, gripped the sides of the tub, then looked back at him over her shoulder. "Hurry."

He guided himself into her, burying his cock inside her with a single, slow thrust that made both of them moan. Then he took hold of her hips and began to move, thrusting slowly at first, blown away by the feel of her—so tight, so perfect.

He shifted the angle of his hips, trying to hit the most sensitive place inside her, driving into her faster. She turned her face to the side, and he could see that her eyes were squeezed shut, her lips parted, her every exhale a breathy moan. He reached around to play with her clit.

"*Yes!*" She rocked back against him, pressed her hips into his hand. "Fuck me. Hard."

She didn't have to ask twice.

He let himself go, pounding into her, one hand still busy between her thighs. If only his anatomy would cooperate, he'd stay inside her forever, driving into her *just ... like ... this*. Though he had more control now than he'd had in his twenties, he knew he couldn't last much longer.

She had to be close, too, her moans growing desperate, her fingers white where they clenched the edge of the tub. He willed himself to relax, kept his rhythm steady, wanting to please her ... wanting to satisfy her... wanting her to know. He loved her. Goddamn, yes, he loved her. He loved her so fucking much.

She gave a quick inhale, and her breath broke on a cry, her inner muscles contracting around him as orgasm carried her away. He followed her over that bright edge, climax washing through him in a surge of incandescent bliss.

When he came back to himself, he took hold of the edges of the condom and withdrew from her, tossing it in the trash.

She turned in the tub to face him, looking flushed and sexy as hell. "I wish you could just stay inside me all night."

"Honey, I had the same thought." He got to his feet, stepped out of the tub, and reached for a towel, wrapping it around her as she, too, climbed out. Then he reached for a towel for himself.

They walked hand-in-hand back into his bedroom, where the candles on his nightstand had burned dangerously low. He blew them out, then crawled into bed beside Rain, drew her into his arms, light from the fireplace casting a warm glow across his bedroom.

"Please tell me this wasn't all a dream."

He kissed her, knowing exactly how she felt. "Get used to the new normal."

Chapter Thirteen

Twenty-two days till Christmas

Rain awoke the next morning to find herself in Joe's arms, the sun shining through his blinds. She smiled, stretched, her heart so full of joy she thought it might burst. It hadn't been a dream.

Joe kissed her. "Good morning, beautiful."

"Good morning."

They made love in the shower, Joe pressing her back against the tile wall and lifting her off her feet. She came hard and fast, and he was right behind her, nuzzling her neck, kissing her forehead.

"I can't get enough of you," he said.

While she dried her hair and dressed, he went downstairs to get breakfast started. She was supposed to meet the claims adjuster this morning. Then she would go to the pharmacy to pick up the morning-after pill and call her GYN for an appointment for an IUD or something. After that…

She and Joe hadn't talked about her job, so she had no idea whether he expected her to show up at Knockers today or ever again. If he didn't, she'd have to look for a job somewhere else—a prospect that didn't excite her at all. Where would she go? Food Mart? Arturo's, the Mexican restaurant? Juana's taco truck? The liquor store?

She went downstairs, the scents of coffee and bacon making her mouth water.

Joe was on his cell phone, his long hair hanging damp down his back, denim apron over his jeans and black Henley. "Thanks. I appreciate it. We'll see you soon."

He set the phone down, glanced over at her, smiled. "I reserved a rental for you. You need a way to get around town until they liberate your SUV."

"Oh." That was a surprise. She wasn't used to having people do things like that for her. "Thanks."

"I asked them to put chains on it. The drive up here can be a little tricky." He walked to the oven, pulled out the bacon, then went to work making scrambled eggs.

Rain poured herself a cup of coffee, trying to remember what the balance was on her credit card. "How much do I owe you?"

"You don't owe me anything."

"I can pay for it myself, truly."

"I know you can." He glanced over at her. "What good is my money if I can't spend some of it on the woman I love?"

He had a point, and yet the thought left her feeling guilty. "I can't do the same for you, and that feels wrong to me. I don't want this to be lopsided."

He shut off the burner, scraped the eggs onto plates, then set the pan in the sink and turned to her. "Come here."

She stepped into his embrace. "What do I bring to the relationship?"

He held her, kissed her hair. "I'm forty-seven, and in all those years, I've never loved a woman the way I love you. Isn't that enough? Besides, if you were wealthy and I were in your shoes, would you hesitate even for a moment to help me?"

Well, he had her there. "No."

He drew back, hands cupping her shoulders, and looked into her eyes. "Let me help you. Let me spoil you the way I want to. Let me be a part of your life."

"And if you go broke?"

He laughed, a true and genuine laugh, as if she'd just said something hilarious. "Honey, that's never going to happen."

How much money did Joe have? Never mind. She didn't want to know.

He kissed her nose. "Let's eat before breakfast gets cold."

She took their plates, carried them to the table together with her cup of coffee, and sat. If he wasn't going to bring it up, she would. "Do I come to work today or not?"

He took a sip of coffee, seeming to avoid her gaze. "Why don't you take another vacation day? You've got that meeting with your claims adjuster."

"That won't take all day." She didn't want to pressure him, but he needed to know. "I need the job, Joe. I can't be dependent on you."

Brown eyes looked into hers. "I promise I'll have a decision tonight."

So he still hadn't made up his mind. Did he have to be so damned ethical all the time? Even as she asked the question, she knew the answer. He fought every day to prove to himself that he wasn't like the other men from his family.

She tried to cover her disappointment. "I hope the claims adjuster can give me some real information. I'd love to know when I'll be able to get my stuff—whatever is left of it. Also, someone needs to go to the grocery store. I thought I'd make up a list and drop by Food Mart this afternoon. I have to stop by their pharmacy anyway, so I might as well pick up a few things."

Comprehension dawned on his face. "Pick up some condoms, too. I checked the box this morning. They expired. That's probably why the one broke. Sorry about that."

"Why, Joe, is that your way of telling me it's been a long time since you've been with a woman?"

"Honey, you have no idea."

Joe dropped Rain off at Scarlet's only car rental place and gave her his debit card and PIN. He saw the misgiving in her eyes. "I trust you, Rain. Get whatever we need. I'll be home for supper."

She tucked the card inside her handbag. "You're not closing?"

"Why would I hang around Knockers when you're waiting for me at home?"

That made her smile.

"Tell everyone I said not to be mean to you. Have a good day." She leaned over, kissed him.

He slid his hand into her hair, held her, made the kiss last, reluctant to let her go even for a handful of hours. "You, too."

Joe arrived at the pub walking on air. Had he ever been this happy? He settled in at his desk, booted up his computer, and checked his email, images of Rain making it hard to concentrate. The sweetness of her smile. The light in her eyes when she laughed. The bliss on her face when she came.

God, he was a lucky son of a bitch. It made him feel like a better man just knowing that she loved him.

He reined in his thoughts, tried to focus. The utility bill. An update from a promoter about booking a popular Irish band. A half dozen invoices from their suppliers. A message from Victoria saying that she'd be late because today was ovulation day.

Well, Joe knew what she and Hawke were up to this morning. They'd been trying for a baby for a while now.

Libby stuck her head inside his office, orange industrial earmuffs hanging around her neck. "Is Rain coming in today?"

"I gave her the day off. She has to meet with her claims adjuster."

Libby's face lit up. "But she is eventually coming back?"

Joe couldn't keep the grin off his face. "She and I are working on that."

"Are you two together?"

"That's no one's business."

"You are! God, that took long enough!" Smiling ear to ear, Libby disappeared back down the hallway. "Finally!"

Did everyone have an opinion about this?

Joe put Libby out of his mind. He wasn't about to divulge the details of his relationship with Rain—not to Libby, not to anyone. He answered email and then logged into the payroll system. He'd begun verifying payments, which were distributed by direct deposit, when Cheyenne and Marcia walked in.

"What can I do for you two?"

Cheyenne, who was Austin Taylor's younger sister and as hot-headed as her brother was mellow, had a hopeful expression on her face. "Is Rain coming back?"

"That hasn't been decided yet."

Cheyenne's face fell.

Marcia crossed her arms over her chest. "Is her work going to fall to me?"

This was getting out of hand. "I'm in the middle of payroll right now. We'll talk about it later."

The two women walked away, grumbling to each other.

Joe buzzed the kitchen. "Hey, Rico, I need you in my office. Now."

Rico walked in a few minutes later, apron over his chef's coat, hairnet on his beard. "What's up, boss?"

"Catch the door." Joe waited until he and Rico had privacy. "I don't have the time or the patience to deal with questions about my private life from staff today."

"Dealing with staff would normally be Rain's job."

So, Rico wasn't letting him off the hook either.

"She's meeting with her claims adjuster, so today it's yours." Just talking about her soothed Joe's irritation. "She and I still need to decide what happens next."

Which reminded Joe...

"Thanks, by the way. What you said yesterday—I owe you."

Rico chuckled. "Judging from the shit-eating grin on your face, you and Rain are good again."

Joe tried to quit smiling, but couldn't. "We're better than good."

Rico reached out, slapped him on the shoulder. "Way to go, my man."

"I'm still trying to decide how to handle this. I don't want to subject her to gossip or give people the wrong impression of how I run this place."

"You can't control what other people think. Hell, why not make an honest man of yourself and marry her? That ought to shut people up."

"Yeah." Joe laughed—then realized what Rico had just said.

Marry her?

Joe cleared his throat. "Could you let the staff know that my relationship with Rain is not to be a topic of discussion here at work."

"Okay." Rico nodded. "If that's how you want it."

"That is exactly how I want it."

"Got it. I'll handle it."

"Thanks—and shut the door behind you." Joe sat there for a moment, staring at the back of the door.

Marry her?

He set the thought aside and got back to work.

R ain fought back panic. "My policy won't cover rebuilding my home?"

Agnes, the claims adjuster, spoke without a hint of sympathy in her voice. "Your policy covers the actual cash value of your home, not the replacement cost."

Heat rushed into Rain's face. This felt like a betrayal. She hadn't known there were different kinds of policies. "Shouldn't you tell people that when they buy a policy? It's not really insuring your home if you still don't have a home when you're done."

"Here's a list of contractors who can help you get started." Agnes handed Rain a sheet of paper with names, phone numbers, and websites. "The price will vary depending on whether you choose to demolish the house, soft strip it, or have it deconstructed, but they can explain all of that."

Rain couldn't let it go. "How am I supposed to come up with an extra twenty thousand? I'm switching insurance companies after this. I promise you that."

"I'll get your claim started as soon as I get back to the office." Agnes turned and walked away, leaving Rain standing in her driveway fighting tears.

It had been a long time since she'd felt this frustrated and powerless. This wasn't just a house. It wasn't just four walls and a roof. It had been her home. Now, it was a pile of twisted lumber, the garage held up by the roof of her poor, trapped SUV.

"Rain, honey, are you okay?" Mrs. Beech called from her porch across the street.

Rain wiped the tears from her cheeks. "Yes, Mrs. Beech, I'm fine."

"You poor thing. Why don't you come in and have a cup of tea? I've got shortbread cookies."

Cookies.

Wasn't that just what Rain needed now?

She crossed the street, deep, icy ruts making it hazardous going, and found herself drinking tea and eating cookies at a red Formica table with chrome accents and matching red-and-white vinyl chairs that looked like they'd come from a 1950s diner. Mrs. Beech's house was so desperately retro that it was almost hip—a big console TV that still worked, an end table with a built-in lamp, mint green appliances.

Rain told Mrs. Beech what the claims adjuster had said. "I don't know how I'm going to be able to afford this. I guess I'll work it out somehow. I've always managed before."

"That's a dirty trick to play on someone as hard-working as you," Mrs. Beech said. "It just doesn't seem right. Maybe Joe Moffat will hold a fundraiser at Knockers like he has in the past for others. He's such a nice boy. The night your roof collapsed, he climbed up on my roof to clean off the snow so the same thing wouldn't happen to me."

How like Joe that was. "I'm glad he was able to help you."

"My family has lived in this house since it was built after that second big fire. I'd have been upset to lose it. We helped build this town."

"Is that right?" Rain's eyes might ordinarily have glazed over, but reading Silas' journal had given her a new interest in local history.

Mrs. Beech nodded and picked up her teacup. "My great-grandfather, John Craddock, worked for the Moffat family."

Rain stared. "John Craddock was your great-grandfather?"

Mrs. Beech must have mistaken Rain's shock for something else because she smiled and nodded. "Yes, I'm a Craddock. That's my maiden name. John Craddock ran the Caribou Silverlode after the first Moffat moved back east with his son. He played such an important role in the history of this town."

Rain wondered whether Mrs. Beech knew that John Craddock had procured young women for his boss to rape and abuse and had helped to frame an innocent man for murder. Whatever else he might have done, Craddock was not a model citizen.

Mrs. Beech took Rain's interest as a chance to tell stories from her childhood, which might have been interesting if they'd been told by someone else. Rain stayed for another hour to be polite, then thanked Mrs. Beech for the tea and the cookies.

"Stop by anytime, dear." Mrs. Beech walked her to the door. "It's a shame you never finished high school. I always thought you were a smart girl."

Rain bit back the words she wanted to say. "Thanks again, Mrs. Beech."

She climbed into the Ford Explorer that Joe had rented for her and drove to Food Mart. She'd made a list before she'd left home and moved quickly through the store. It was mid-day, so she didn't run into a lot of people she knew. She stopped last at the pharmacy counter.

Herb, who'd been the town's pharmacist for more than 40 years, met her with a warm welcome. "I hope you're not coming down with something."

"So do I." The last thing she needed right now was to get pregnant. "I need to buy a packet of Plan B."

He nodded, walked to the shelves, and returned with a small box in his hands. "You're lucky. This is my last one. I guess lots of people found a way to pass the time during the storm."

Rain couldn't help but laugh. *Guilty as charged.* "Thanks."

She tossed a new box of condoms into her cart, too, then made her way to the checkout lane, wanting to get back to Joe's so that she could read and find out what had happened to Cadan Hawke.

December 3, 1880

*T*oday was a day I shall not soon forget.

Cadan Hawke was set to be hanged at noon, but I woke to the news that Sheriff Taylor had just left for Boulder, where he believed he would find proof of Hawke's innocence. This put me in a state of great agitation, as proof of Hawke's innocence might lead to evidence of my guilt. Taylor has been seeking for a way to exonerate Hawke since the day the jury found the man guilty.

I immediately sent two of my men to follow Sheriff Taylor down the canyon and through town and to report back each place he went and to whom he spoke. Then I sent a telegram to my hotel in Boulder, setting a man to guard Jenny and giving him orders that no one was to speak with her. Nor was she to leave her rooms.

Mr. Craddock thought it might be prudent to pack our bags and leave town at once, but I told him that was cowardice. I assured him we would find a way to stop Sheriff Taylor and make certain this hanging took place. I would not suffer that whoreson Hawke to live, not after the way he has spoken to me, not after the trouble he has caused.

A telegram arrived shortly after 10, stating that my men had been to visit a gunsmith on Pine Street and that the prey they'd been hunting had gotten away. I knew then Taylor's purpose in Boulder, for the Colt my men had hidden in the rafters of Hawke's henhouse had come from that very gunsmith.

Taylor had to know now that Hawke had not purchased the firearm, and he would be able to prove it. The thought caused me a moment of panic, but it was one thing to prove Hawke's innocence and something else to establish my guilt.

I sent my two most trusted men to eliminate the man who'd bought the pistol and hide his body somewhere it would never be found—at the bottom of Moose Lake or down a discarded mine shaft. I sent two more to a high point above the canyon with orders to delay the sheriff without being seen or caught.

At about 11, I dressed as I would for any important social event and made my way down the snowy and muddy streets with Mr. Craddock to the jailhouse. I asked for Sheriff Taylor. His deputy, a lout by the name of Quintrell, told me Sheriff Taylor had gone to Boulder on official business. I discerned by the way he looked at me that he did not trust me, but I refused to be sent away and insisted on waiting.

Who better to provide my alibi than the sheriff's own deputy?

It wasn't long after I arrived when Quintrell was called away to settle an armed dispute at the saloon. I seized this chance to speak with Hawke.

He stood in his cell in his best clothes, looking out the window toward the gallows, his face freshly shaved. He glared at me. "I know this is your doin'. Sheriff Taylor knows the truth, as do the men. They know I spoke against the violence and didn't own a pistol. You cannot cow them by murderin' me. Aye, I know that's what you're after. You'll not find them so easy to manage after this."

I told him that he was speaking nonsense but assured him it was likely normal for a man to protest his innocence and make far-fetched claims on the day he was to be hanged. "I still want to believe you are innocent, but I must trust in the jury's verdict. I'm told that the pain does not last long if the neck breaks. If not, hanging can be a long and torturous death."

He laughed at this. "Have you come to gloat?"

I did my best to mask my hatred with pity. "I came to tell you that I forgive you, and to promise that I will look after your wife and children. I'll see to it they receive candy and new shoes for Christmas."

His face contorted into a look of such rage as I have never seen. "You stay away from my family, Moffat! They need nothin' from the likes of you."

"Do you want them to starve in the streets? Do you want your wife to feed your children with money she earns on her back?"

He pressed up against the bars and would likely have killed me had he not been constrained. "My wife is a good woman and true. Speak of her again, go anywhere near her or my children, and I'll kill you, if I have to come back from the grave to do it!"

It was then the Methodist minister arrived. I left the two of them and went to wait once more with Mr. Craddock, who told me that one of my men had just returned with the news they'd tried to stop the sheriff with a rockslide but had failed. He expected Taylor to reach Scarlet Springs in the next twenty minutes and awaited my orders across the street.

I ought to have had them shoot Taylor, but it was impossible to kill him so near town without raising suspicions or risking being seen.

It was Mr. Craddock who seized upon the solution. He walked to the clock, opened its face, and moved the big hand forward fifteen minutes so that it was now almost noon. He shut it again and resumed his seat.

"Great men make the world as they wish it to be," he said.

He and I both changed the time on our pocket watches to be safe.

Wanting to seem in every way a law-abiding and helpful citizen, I went across the street and ordered my man to ride down the canyon and to tell Sheriff Taylor that I had heard about the dreadful rockslide and wanted to make sure he was safe. "Tell him that I sent you to ensure his safety. Accompany him into town, acting as his guard. Do nothing to harm him. Do you understand?"

A crowd had already gathered around the gallows by the time Quintrell returned. I saw Hawke's wife with her oldest son standing near the jailhouse.

"What has kept you, man?" I demanded. "Do you not see what time it is?"

Quintrell looked at the clock, saw that it was five past noon. "I should wait for Sheriff Taylor. He said he'd be here afore noon."

"Did the judge not set the hanging for noon?" Mr. Craddock asked me, making certain that Quintrell overheard. "The deputy will be held in contempt, I fear. He'll likely lose his badge as well."

Quintrell called to some of the sheriff's men and reluctantly went to retrieve Hawke from his cell, returning a few minutes later with the minister and the prisoner, whose hands were now bound behind his back.

Hawke glared at me but seemed unafraid. "You'll go to hell for this."

"I'm not a murderer. You are." I followed the others outside, Mr. Craddock behind me.

Hawke's wife ran toward her husband the moment he appeared.

"He is innocent! He could not have done this. Please, wait for the sheriff to return. It's not yet time." She tried to reach her husband, but the minister held her back.

It was the only time I saw remorse on Hawke's face. "All shall be well, Molly. Be strong, my girl. Moffat is determined to see me hanged, and so he shall."

Quintrell and the other deputies led him up onto the scaffold, and it was Quintrell who positioned the noose around his neck. The minister mounted the steps and spoke quietly with Hawke for a few minutes, then stepped back.

"Do you have any last words?" Quintrell asked him.

Hawke looked down at his wife. "I love you, Molly. I always have. Promise me you'll never let my children work in a mine."

His wife choked back her sobs and smiled at Hawke. "I promise, my love."

But Hawke hadn't finished. "Stay away from Moffat. Don't trust him. Tell the children I died an innocent man, my conscience clean."

"They know, my love, and they won't be forgettin' it."

Hawke tried to reject the hood, saying he wanted to look upon his wife's face, but Quintrell forced it upon him, assuring him that it was a mercy and meant to preserve his dignity. Then Quintrell stepped back, and the executioner released the trapdoor.

Hawke's neck broke in the fall, and he died almost instantly to the sound of his wife's screams. I can tell you I felt such relief when his struggles ceased!

It was not two minutes later when Sheriff Taylor rode in, his horse lathered.

"What have you done? Cut him down!" he shouted at Quintrell, leaping from his saddle and helping to lower Hawke's body to the ground. He attempted to revive Hawke until he saw that the man's neck was broken.

Molly threw herself on her husband's body, wailing and caterwauling as women do. The minister knelt beside her, but she rejected even his consolation.

Taylor glanced at his pocket watch and showed it to Quintrell. "What in God's name have you done? The hangin' wasn't until noon. I've brought a witness who might have been able to free him."

"But it is past noon."

I stepped forward. "If you had evidence, why did you not think to send a telegram, man? Your incompetence has cost this man his life!"

The stricken look on Taylor's face at my words brings a smile to mine tonight.

I offered to pay for Hawke's grave marker, but his wife spat on my boots. I assured her that I shared her grief, told her that she had misjudged me, and tossed a few silver coins onto his body. Mr. Craddock and I made our way back to my office, where we celebrated with a bottle of fine whiskey.

Chapter Fourteen

Joe arrived home to find Rain in the library crying, Silas' journal and the photograph of Cadan Hawke, hooded, noose around his neck, on the coffee table in front of her. He didn't have to ask why she was upset.

He sat beside her, drew her into his arms. "Hey, come here."

Some part of him was afraid she would pull away, reject him, but she didn't.

She rested her head against his chest, a tissue crumpled in one hand, her cheeks wet with tears. "Silas killed that poor man. He murdered him. He took Cadan from his wife and his kids. I hate him. I really do. I *hate* him."

"So do I." Joe had felt sick to his stomach when he'd read what Silas had done.

Unfortunately, Joe got his DNA from Silas and from three men who'd been very much like him—ruthless, selfish, immoral to their core.

"I can't read anymore. Please tell me there was justice, that Sheriff Taylor found some evidence to exonerate Cadan, that Silas paid for this somehow."

Joe kissed her hair. "I wish I could."

He told Rain how Silas had been right. Cadan's murder broke the spirit of the miners for a time, enabling Silas to lower their wages while meeting their demand for an eight-hour workday. He told her how the hostility between Sheriff Taylor and Silas grew fierce after this and how Silas decided it would be better to leave things in Craddock's hands and head back east to be with his son. "He threw Jenny out of her suite at his hotel and left her, pregnant and addicted to laudanum, on the street. She made her way back to Scarlet, moved into Belle's place, and died from a botched abortion one month later.

"Silas got away with all of it. He invested his profits—about five million a year by today's standards—wisely. When the price of silver crashed, he had already shifted most of his fortune to steel, railways, and hotels. He died not long after that, making his son one of the wealthiest men in the U.S."

"That son of a bitch. That's so unfair."

"There's nothing fair about life."

"What happened to Molly, Cadan's widow?"

"I don't know. The journals never mention her again."

"Poor Jenny. If Silas had left her alone, she might have lived a normal life, gotten married, had kids. I wish her family had done more to help her. Why couldn't they go to the sheriff and push him to charge Silas with rape?"

"Are you kidding? Wealthy men still get away with sexual assault and harassment today. Back then, an unmarried rape victim from a poor, immigrant family didn't stand a chance. Society always blamed the victim."

"Well, fuck them!"

Joe knew this was personal for Rain not only because she was distantly related to Jenny, but because she'd lived through something similar. She'd been manipulated by an older man—and then rejected by her family when she'd returned with a baby. Joe had met her parents once and had found them to be self-righteous prigs. "Yeah. Fuck them all."

"Where are they buried?" she asked.

"Cadan is buried in the Scarlet pioneer cemetery, though the headstone is worn. It's almost impossible to make out his name. Jenny was buried in an unmarked grave. The Scarlet Historical Society has a map showing where she was laid to rest. We can visit when the snow melts if you'd like."

"I'd like to buy a headstone for her, maybe get a new one made for Cadan someday." She tilted her head back, looked up at him. "Does Eric know? Does his family even remember Cadan?"

Joe nodded. "I went to see them not long after I moved here. I didn't want to make the journals public, but I wasn't going to cover for

Silas. I photocopied the pages that mentioned Cadan, blacked out everyone's names apart from Silas', and gave them a folder. Eric sat there listening—he was just a skinny kid, maybe fourteen. His mother, Robin, who is a direct descendant of Hawke's oldest son, was gracious. She thanked me for coming and sharing the pages with her. She even invited me to stay for dinner. I hadn't imagined in a million years that the descendants of the man Silas murdered would show me such kindness."

"Craddock!" Rain drew back, sat up, stared at him wide-eyed. "You kept the journal private to protect Mrs. Beech, didn't you?"

Rain had figured that out.

"Mostly Mrs. Beech, but also Rico and you. It was one of Rico's ancestors who put the noose around Cadan's neck. Given what you'd been through, I didn't think it would help you to read about something similar happening to one of your female ancestors."

"You're probably right."

"As for Mrs. Beech, she is so proud to be Craddock's great-granddaughter. I couldn't take that from her. Every time I run into her, she reminds me that her family used to manage the mine for my family. She acts like we're old friends or something. I don't know what she'd do if she found out the man she reveres was an accomplice to rape and murder. I figure justice has waited this long. It can wait until she passes. After that, I'll happily donate all of Silas' journals and photos to the library."

"You'll need to build a library first."

"True."

They both laughed.

"Oh, Joe, I couldn't love you more." Rain pressed her palm to the left side of his chest. "You have such a good heart. You're not Silas. You're nothing like him. You've been trying to prove that to yourself for so long. Please believe me. You have nothing to prove to anyone."

She brushed her lips over his, then kissed him.

Hungry for her, needing the absolution she offered, he kissed her back, then caught her face between his hands and drew back. "Let's go upstairs."

They sank together to his bed, locked in a kiss, limbs tangled, hands seeking the quickest way past clothing to skin. He yanked her shirt above her breasts, tugged down the cups of her bra, and suckled her until she writhed beneath him. While she wrestled herself out of her jeans, he grabbed a condom from the new box on his nightstand and rolled it over his erection. Then he was inside her, her body sheathing him, her nails biting into his back, her hips thrusting upward to meet him.

He fought to hold on, to rein himself in, wanting to please her. He was on the brink when she arched beneath him, cried out his name—and came. He kept up the rhythm, carrying her through her climax, the sexual ecstasy on her face shattering what remained of his control. Then he let pleasure carry him away.

They made a late dinner of grilled cheese and tomato soup, ate at the breakfast counter, then settled on the sofa near the warmth of the fire with a plate of Rain's fudge to watch the lights on the Christmas tree sparkle.

Rain told him she'd bought the last packet of Plan B in Scarlet. "I'm so glad I got there before it sold out."

"Yeah, me, too."

Then Rain told him about her frustrating meeting with the claims adjuster. "The cash value of the house is lower than the cost of rebuilding something similar, so I'm going to have to make up the difference. It feels like they're cheating. It's going to cost tens of thousands of dollars that I don't have."

That thought didn't overwhelm her quite as much with Joe's arms around her.

"Let me send the paperwork to my attorney. Maybe he can get them to bend."

"Okay, but I doubt that will accomplish anything."

He nuzzled her cheek. "I'm not going to let you fall, Rain. You are not alone."

"I can't let you pay for it."

"Sure you can—but we'll argue about that some other time." He kissed her temple. "I got a few calls today from people wanting to know when I'd be holding a fundraiser for you."

"Really?"

"You're one of the most beloved people in Scarlet. You know that, don't you?"

Rain's throat went tight. "No. I mean ... I know I have friends here, but ..."

"I'm not the only one who loves you."

"And to think I'd thought about leaving."

"Please don't." He kissed her again.

"Do I have a job?"

Before he could answer, Rain's cell phone buzzed. She drew away from him, picked it up off the coffee table.

It was Lark.

"Hey, sweetie, how are you?" Rain barely got the words out before Lark went off.

"I heard you quit Knockers and that you're thinking of moving away. Why would you do that without telling me? You're my mom. I don't want you to leave me and live somewhere far away."

"Oh, honey, I'm not leaving. That's just gossip."

"Then you're still working for Joe?"

"Do you mind if I put you on speaker phone? I'm still staying with Joe, and he's sitting right here."

"I need to talk with him, too."

"Hey, Lark. How's it going?" Joe asked.

Lark didn't bother with small talk. "Why did you let my mom quit?"

Joe met Rain's gaze, his lips curving in a grin. "Your mom hasn't quit. I never accepted her resignation, and now she's changed her mind."

"Why did she quit in the first place?"

Joe waited for Rain to answer, leaving it up to her.

Rain offered a simplification of the truth. "I turned in my resignation because I didn't want people getting the wrong idea about Joe and me now that we're together."

A loud squeal came out of the phone's speaker. "You and Joe are sleeping together? It's about time!"

Rain's cheeks flamed. She shot Joe an apologetic look. "Well, we... uh..."

Joe grinned, stepped in. "I'm not sure you're old enough to ask that sort of question, young lady."

Lark laughed. "I'm older than my mom was when she had me. But if you were wondering how I feel about this, all I have to say is *what took you so long*! My mom has been in love with you for as long as I can remember. You're the closest thing I had to a dad anyway. This *so* rocks!"

Rain squeezed her eyes shut, did her best to change the subject before Lark could say anything else embarrassing. "How would you like to come for dinner at Joe's place some night? We need to talk about Christmas, too. It looks like I'll be spending Christmas here."

Rain brought Lark up to date on the house, and they agreed Lark would bring her boyfriend for dinner on Friday, Dec. 14, after her last final.

"She thought of me as a father figure?" Joe asked when Rain ended the call.

She slipped into his arms. "I might have encouraged that—just a little."

He raised an eyebrow. "And I didn't know about this?"

"Nope. Still, you always managed to say the right thing to her."

"I did?" He sounded utterly taken aback.

"Always."

Twenty-one days till Christmas

Rain went back to work the next morning to the sound of cheering from the staff.

"You're back!" Cheyenne ran up to her, hugged her.

"It's about damned time!" Marcia called from behind the bar.

Rico winked when she walked into the kitchen. "Sorry about your house. That sucks. How was your ... uh... snowcation?"

She hugged him. "It was amazing—thanks in part to you."

She did her best to act like nothing had changed, but it wasn't easy. Just meeting Joe's gaze from across the room made her face flush. There was something arousing about it, too—being close to him, but not being able to touch him. She found herself thinking of all the things she would do to him when they got home. She could tell he was doing the same thing—undressing her with his eyes and fantasizing about what would happen tonight.

Thanks to the storm, Rain was behind on lots of projects, and that included the Christmas Tots Tree—a tree with paper ornaments on which were written the ages and genders of children from impoverished families in the Scarlet area. People who wanted to participate took down an ornament, bought clothes and Christmas gifts for a child of that age and gender, then brought the wrapped packages to the fire department for delivery by the firefighters on Christmas Eve.

But she wasn't the only one who was behind. Eric hadn't yet dropped off the paper ornaments. She asked Vicki if she would mind texting her husband and asking him to bring them by, then Rain went to work decorating the small artificial tree, which usually sat in a corner near the front door.

"He says he'll bring them by at lunch," Vicki told her.

When Eric walked through the door in his turnout pants and jacket, it wasn't the Christmas Tots project that popped into her mind. It was Cadan.

She hugged him, suddenly fighting tears. "I'm so sorry about Cadan."

"About ... who?"

"Cadan Hawke, your great-great-great-grandfather."

"Oh, yeah." He stepped back. "That was a long time ago, but thanks."

"Do you know what happened to his wife, Molly?"

Eric nodded. "My mom says she ended up marrying some Methodist minister and had a few kids with him."

Rain wondered if that had been the minister who'd been with her when Cadan had been hanged. "Do their kids have any descendants in town?"

Eric pointed toward the bar. "Yeah, the Rouses. Marcia and I are third cousins—or something like that."

Rain laughed. "You and Marcia? Really? I didn't know that."

Eric handed Rain the box of paper ornaments, each a little circle cut from red construction paper and threaded with a green ribbon so that it could be hung on the tree. "There you go. We've got sixty-eight kids this year—a dozen more than last year. I hope enough people participate to cover all these kids. I hate to disappoint any family."

"I'm sure it will work out." Rain knew what Eric didn't.

Joe always took the leftover ornaments home with him and bought gifts for those kids himself. In all the years they'd done the Christmas Tots project, not a single child had been left out. Thanks to Joe.

"Hey, Eric, your lunch is on me," Rain said. "Thanks for rescuing me."

Eleven Days till Christmas

Joe drove with Rain to the bus stop to pick up Lark and her boyfriend Zander—a surfer dude who instantly got on Joe's nerves—then took them to see the concrete slab that had once been the foundation of Rain and Lark's house.

Rain had allowed Joe to bring in a deconstruction crew, insisting that she pay him back when the insurance money came through. She'd been afraid that waiting until sometime in January—the insurance company didn't seem to be in a hurry—would mean greater property loss from snowmelt. Her SUV was now in the shop getting body work done, and her car insurance was covering that. She wouldn't have enough money to rebuild the house, but Joe had a couple of ideas about how to manage that. He hadn't shared them with her yet. One day at a time.

He turned the corner onto Rain's street, drove slowly over deep ruts in the ice.

"Oh, my God!" There was genuine shock in Lark's voice. "It's just ... *gone.*"

"The deconstruction crew finished a few days ago," Rain said. "Everything they were able to salvage is in boxes in Joe's garage. Your baby photos made it—thank God! My box of keepsakes from your school years survived, too. That's what worried me the most. All of our Christmas stuff made it. We lost most of our dishes and most of the furniture too. Grandma's crystal vase was broken, but Joe says he can get it fixed."

Joe had already shipped it off to Tokyo, where an artist he knew "glued" crystal and porcelain objects back together using gold or platinum. The vase wouldn't be what it had been before, but it would be in one piece and usable again. More than that, it would be a work of art with a history. Joe thought Rain would appreciate that.

"You're the only thing I care about." Lark's voice quavered. "You might have been killed, Mom."

Joe parked in front, and mother and daughter climbed out of the vehicle, walking hand in hand up the driveway, Lark now in tears.

Zander started to follow, but Joe held him back. "Give them some space, okay?"

"Yeah, okay, man." Zander watched him. "Lark said you've known her and her mom since she was a baby."

"Yep."

"Are you going to tell me that you'll kill me if I hurt her?" There was a note of humor in Zander's voice.

Joe didn't laugh. "I don't have to tell you if you already know. Besides, you won't have to deal with me. Lark can take care of herself."

Zander shifted uncomfortably in his seat. "Dude, I was just joking."

Joe met the kid's gaze. "I'm not."

When the women were ready, Joe drove them up to his house.

"You live here?" Lark's words reminded Joe of Rain's reaction.

He said the same thing to Lark that he'd said to her mother. "I live at Knockers. This is just where I sleep."

"Dude, you must be loaded," Zander said.

Joe pulled into the garage.

"That's it?" Lark looked at the stack of boxes. "That's all that's left?"

"It's more than I'd hoped for," Rain said.

The women stayed in the garage for a time, looking through the boxes, while Joe got started on dinner, drafting a reluctant Zander to cut and seed acorn squash while Joe sautéed Italian sausage with celery and onion. By the time Rain and Lark stepped inside, the squash were baking and stuffed with the Italian sausage mixture.

Lark looked around her, eyes wide, a smile on her face. "This is beautiful! I wouldn't mind staying here."

"You're welcome anytime." Joe hoped this would be the first of many visits from Lark. If he had his way, this would be her mother's new home.

His phone buzzed. It was his jeweler. He needed to take this in private. "I'm going to grab a bottle of wine. After that, I can give you a tour."

"I'd love that."

Joe disappeared down into the wine cellar. "Moffat here. Is it ready?"

Seven days till Christmas

Rain lay in a gown on the exam table, her feet in cold stirrups, a blue paper sheet draped over her knees. Why did rooms where people got naked always have to be cold? "Is this going to be painful?"

She hated pain.

Leah Voss, her gynecologist, pressed on her belly to feel her uterus and ovaries—not the most comfortable thing in itself. "Some women have bad cramps after insertion, but you've had a baby, so it probably won't be worse than a PAP smear."

That didn't sound too bad.

"When are you expecting your next period?" Leah asked.

Rain had to think for a moment. "Day after tomorrow."

"Have you had unprotected sex in the past month?"

Rain assumed this was a routine question. "We had a condom break, but I took Plan B within the seventy-two-hour window."

Leah inserted a speculum—they were always cold, too—and then a moment later removed it. "I don't think we'll be doing the IUD today. I'm almost certain you're pregnant, sweetie."

"What?" Rain raised herself onto her elbows, adrenaline shooting through her, her pulse throbbing in her ears. "I ... I can't be. I took the pill."

"Hormonal contraception is only about seventy-five percent effective after intercourse." Leah patted her thigh. "Get dressed, and then we'll talk."

Rain sat, staring after Leah as the door shut. She didn't want to get dressed. She wanted her IUD. She wanted to go home and have her life be normal with no bad news.

No. No. No.

The doctor had to be wrong. This couldn't be happening—not again. She was thirty-seven. She couldn't have a baby now. She didn't ever want to go through that again. She wasn't ready to start from scratch with a newborn.

God, what was she going to do?

Joe didn't want kids. He'd never wanted kids. He would be so angry with her, and this precious thing they had together would be ruined just because a condom broke.

Rain got down from the exam table, tears blurring her vision. Her fingers fumbled with her bra clasp and the buttons of her blouse, panic making her almost sick.

A knock came at the door. "May I come in?"

Rain zipped her jeans and sat, pressing her hands into her lap to keep them from shaking. "Yes."

Leah sat across from her. "I take it that this isn't welcome news."

Rain shook her head. "I can't go through that again."

"Having a baby in a hospital with a good epidural and a supportive partner and caregiver is a completely different experience than giving birth alone in a minivan as a terrified teenager."

They could *not* be having this conversation.

"Wh-what makes you say I'm pregnant?"

"Your cervix is soft as if you're about to ovulate, but you should be past that point if you're expecting your period to start in just a couple of days. Also, there are certain changes in cervical mucus early in pregnancy, and I see those quite clearly. Are your breasts sore?"

Rain nodded. "But they're always sore before I start my period."

"Have you been tired or felt nauseated?"

"No nausea. I've been tired, but it's really hectic at the pub with Christmas season and ski season. Plus, my house collapsed, and I've been dealing with that."

"I heard about that. There's certainly a lot on your plate."

"The man I'm with—he doesn't want kids. He's always been really clear about that. He's going to be so angry."

"I have to ask—is there any chance that he might hurt you? If so, there are shelters and people who can help."

Joe? Harm her? Never.

But that didn't mean he wouldn't break up with her.

Rain shook her head. "No, not at all. But what am I going to tell him?"

"Let's do a blood test today to confirm. If the test comes back positive, my advice would be to give yourself some time to think about it and decide what decision is right for you. Then talk it over with the father when you're ready."

Rain didn't know whether to laugh or cry—or throw up.

Chapter Fifteen

Joe got a text from Rain just before lunch saying that she didn't feel well and needed to go home and rest. He texted back.

Is there anything I can do?

After a few minutes, he got her reply.

Just love me.

He replied immediately.

I do.

He messaged her later in the afternoon but didn't hear back. Worried and not wanting to leave her alone, he ordered one of Vicki's deep-dish pizzas to go and left Rico and Marcia to manage the place.

He arrived home to find the house dark and Rain asleep on his bed, still in her clothes, the fireplace casting an orange light over her features. He walked over to her, drew up the covers—and saw the tear-stains on her cheeks.

Shit.

Something was wrong.

He left her to sleep and went downstairs to eat a slice of pizza while it was hot. He'd just put his plate into the dishwasher when she appeared at the top of the stairs. "I brought home a pepperoni deep-dish for supper."

"Thanks, but I'm not hungry." She walked down the stairs and over to the sofa. "Can we talk?"

Hell.

That couldn't be good.

He went to sit beside her on the sofa. "What's wrong?"

She sat with her hands in her lap, looking at the floor, misery on her face. "I... I'm pregnant."

Her words hit Joe like a fist, made his head spin. "You're ... what?"

"My GYN wouldn't insert the IUD because ... I'm already pregnant. I guess there are changes, things she can see inside."

"You're *pregnant*." There didn't seem to be enough air in the room.

"She did a blood test to confirm. It came back positive."

Joe's mind struggled to keep up, shock making him stupid. "I thought you took the morning-after pill."

"I did." Tears spilled down Rain's cheeks. "She says it's only about seventy-five percent effective. I ... I guess I'm in that twenty-five percent. I know you don't want kids. I didn't want to have another baby either. Never. I don't want to go through all of that again. But I've thought about it all afternoon, and I can't just get rid of it. I know I couldn't put it up for adoption either. The moment I see it, I'll love it. That's how it was with Lark. The moment I held her, I knew I couldn't give her away."

Joe caught most of what Rain was saying, his mind racing with denials. This could *not* be happening. He didn't want kids. He didn't want to continue the Moffat line. He was supposed to be the last. Besides, he wasn't cut out to be a father. He didn't know the first thing about love or family. He wouldn't know what to do with a child.

Then Rain lifted her gaze to his, and he saw it—the fear in her green eyes, the doubt, the despair.

The sight of her anguish cut through the maelstrom of his own emotions, clearing his head, slowing his pulse, making everything crystal clear in a single heartbeat. He would *not* be the next man to let Rain down.

He set his own emotions aside, reached out, cupped her face between his palms, wiping her tears away with his thumbs. "What you're telling me is that we're going to be parents."

She nodded. "I-I'm sorry. I didn't mean for this to happen. I'm not trying to trick you into anything or manipulate you."

"You don't have to apologize. I was there, remember? The condom broke. I let the condoms expire. If you're pregnant, we know who's to blame." He drew her into his arms, held her tight. "God, honey, you're shaking like a leaf."

"I'm so afraid. I don't know how I can face this again. I'm thirty-seven now, not sixteen. It was so hard when Lark was born. It was terrible—like a nightmare. The pain was so bad. I thought I was going to die."

Something twisted in his gut at the thought of her suffering like that.

He held her closer, stroked her hair. "It won't be like last time. I'll be right there. If you want all the drugs in the world, I'll make sure you get them. If you want to skip straight to a C-section, we'll do it. Whatever you need, I'll make sure you get it."

His money had to be good for something, right?

You're going to be a father, man.

But first Joe had to be a man worthy of his child's mother.

Rain took refuge in Joe's embrace. "So you're truly not angry with me?"

He drew back, a warm smile on his face, his gaze gentle. "How could I possibly be angry at you? It's not like you managed this on your own. I'm not like him. I'm not going to abandon you. I'm not going to leave you to face any part of this alone."

He meant it. He truly meant it.

Relief washed through Rain, leaving her almost weak and bringing fresh tears to her eyes. "I didn't know how I was going to tell you. I didn't want to see the love in your eyes disappear."

He reached out, placed a hand on her lower belly. "Never be afraid to tell me anything, okay? A man who stops loving you when you tell him that he got you pregnant is a man who never loved you in the first place."

She sniffed, managed a smile. "People are going to gossip, you know. They'll probably say I was trying to trap you into marrying me or something."

"Yeah? Well, fuck them." He frowned, seemed lost in thought for a moment. "I need to run upstairs for something. I'll be right back. Are you okay?"

"Yes, I'm fine—now." While he walked upstairs, she blew her nose, then went to the kitchen sink and splashed her face with cold water, her mind fixed on a single thought: Joe wasn't going to abandon her.

She turned on the Christmas tree lights and the fireplace, then went to sit on the sofa again just as Joe came back downstairs.

Joe walked over to her, knelt in front of her as if he were about to propose, which was absurd because he wouldn't do that. He didn't want to get married. She knew that. Everybody knew that.

"I was saving this for Christmas Eve, but I want you to have it now," he said.

She looked down. "Oh, God! It's *beautiful.*"

A ring sat in a satin-lined box, a large pink oval diamond surrounded by a halo of small white diamonds. The band, too, was inset with little diamonds.

"Rain, I have loved you for so long. Will you marry me?"

Stunned, she looked from the ring to the man, who knelt there, waiting for her answer. "You're really asking me to *marry* you?"

"I was going to wait till Christmas, but I decided to do it now. I don't want you to think for one moment that I asked you only because you're pregnant. I want you to believe that I wanted this before I found out about... er... the ... um... baby."

That *right there* melted her heart. "Yes, Joe, I'll marry you."

He kissed her, then took the ring from the box, slipped it onto her finger. "The gold is recycled from my grandmother's wedding ring. The diamonds are Canadian."

Rain stared at her finger, at the glittering stones. She didn't know much about diamonds or carats or Canadians for that matter. She'd never even seen a ring like this, much less imagined owning one. "How did you know my ring size?"

"I took one of your rings from the bathroom counter, dropped by a jewelry store on the way to work, and asked them to size it for me."

"Sneaky." Rain knew exactly which ring he'd taken, because she'd thought she'd lost it, only to find it that evening right where it was supposed to have been. "Is this really happening? Am I dreaming?"

"I'd originally thought we could get married this summer, but we should do it right away, before anyone knows you're pregnant. I don't want people saying that you got pregnant just to force me into marrying you."

Could he be any sweeter?

"Do you want to go to a judge tomorrow?"

He shook his head. "You deserve better than that. How about on December twenty-third? We can do it at Knockers and invite the whole damned town."

"That's only three days from now."

"Then I guess we'd best get busy planning."

They both agreed Lark should hear the news first—all the news.

Rain called her, then handed her cell phone to Joe, who put it on speaker.

"Hey, Lark. I'd like to ask your permission to marry your mom."

"Are you serious?"

"Of course, I'm serious. I've got a ring and everything."

Lark's happy scream made Rain and Joe both cover their ears. "Oh, my God, yes! Please, marry my mom! You'll make her so happy."

"I will do my best. I promise you that."

Rain leaned forward, spoke into the phone. "I'd like you to be my maid of honor if you're willing."

"Are you crazy? Of course, I'm going to be your maid of honor."

"I'm going to need your help finding a gown and all that. We'd like to get married at Knockers on Sunday, and there's a lot to do between now and then. But there's more news, and this has to be a secret. Promise us that you won't tell anyone."

"I won't tell anyone. I promise."

"I'm pregnant."

"Oh, my God!" Lark laughed. "Did you not listen to the lectures you gave me when I was a teenager? 'Don't get pregnant.' You said that every day for half my life."

Rain met Joe's gaze, nodded. "It's true."

"It's important to me that you know I'm not marrying your mother because she's pregnant. I already had the ring. We're just speeding things up now."

"You're protecting my mother's reputation. How sweet!"

"Also, I don't want the wedding preparations to wear your mom out. She's feeling pretty tired these days. I was hoping you could stay here for—"

"I'm already packing my backpack. Can you come get me?"

"Sure thing." Joe grinned. "You're not planning to bring Surfer Boy, are you?"

"Zander? Joe, he is *so* last week."

Joe and Rain held a meeting at Knockers the next morning and told the staff the news that he and Rain were getting married. He'd figured they'd be happy about it, but he hadn't expected the pandemonium of cheering and applause that broke loose. When things quieted down again, he went on. "After Sunday, she will have equal ownership of this establishment. A request from her comes with the same authority as a request from me. Is that clear to everyone?"

Heads nodded.

"Hell, Joe, we already take her more seriously than we do you," Rico said, laughing at his own joke.

"Look at the rock on her finger!" Cheyenne pointed.

"That has to be a two-carat stone, right?" Marcia asked.

"I don't know." Rain looked over at Joe. "I didn't think to ask."

That was one thing Joe loved about her. She hadn't asked him how much the ring had cost or how many carats worth of diamonds it held. It hadn't mattered to her.

Joe answered for her. "The center stone is two and a half carats."

The women stood, crowded around for a better look.

Vicki hugged her. "It's beautiful. I'm so excited for you two."

"Thanks."

When the meeting ended, Joe called Rico into his office. "I'd like you to be my best man."

Rico stared at him. "Me, boss?"

Joe nodded. "You're the closest thing I've got to a brother."

Rico laughed, pulled Joe into a bear hug. "Hell, yes, I'll be your best man. What do I have to do?"

"Help me pull this off." Joe had never been involved with a wedding, much less planned one. "I want this to be special for Rain, and I don't have much time. We need to order decorations, flowers, food, booze, and a cake. We have to arrange music, get the marriage license, find someone to officiate, get a photographer, put out invitations…"

"I got you covered on that last one." Rico pulled out his cell phone, tapped in a number. "Hey, Rose, yeah. It's Rico. Joe and Rain are getting hitched on Sunday at five here at Knockers. The public is invited. I thought you'd want to know."

Rico ended the call. "Done. Doesn't Rain want to be involved with this?"

Joe thought for a moment about what he was going to say. "I'm going to share a secret with you, and if you tell anyone else—"

"You got her pregnant." Rico cackled. "I love it. Okay, so she's probably tired and has other concerns. You ought to talk to Belcourt. His old grandpa got stuck here in Scarlet thanks to the snow and hasn't made the drive back to the reservation yet. He did Chaska and Naomi's ceremony."

Chaska's grandfather was a Lakota Sun Dance chief.

"Thanks. I'll ask." Joe saw Rain and Lark waiting in the hallway. "Let me have a moment with the bride and maid of honor, and then help me plan a menu and order food and alcohol."

"All right, then." Rico stepped out, still grinning.

Rain and Lark came in. Rain shut the door behind them and started to speak, but Lark cut her off.

"Don't let her buy something here in Scarlet. Tell her it's okay to go to Denver and get something she really loves."

"Lark, honey, I just don't think we have time for that. Besides, I don't want to spend all of Joe's money. He's paying for all of this."

Lark rolled her eyes. "I don't think you *can* spend all his money. I mean, look at his house. He's got to be a millionaire, right?"

"Lark! Do you know how tactless it is—"

"It's okay." Joe cut in. "Can I talk?"

The two women looked at him.

"I think Lark is right. You should go to Denver and find something you love. You won't be able to order anything custom-made, but there will be a lot more to choose from there than in Scarlet."

"Thank you." Lark looked over at her mother. "See?"

"As for spending all my money, I told you—it's not going to happen. I've got—"

Rain held up her hand. "I don't want to know how much money you've got—not until after we're married."

God, he loved her.

He closed the space between them, took her into his arms. "What I was going to say was that I've got *a car* on its way for you. The driver will pick you up and take you and Lark to the florists here in Scarlet so you can pick out flowers. After that, he'll drive you wherever you want to go. Shop for gowns, shoes, whatever. Have lunch. Do that mani-pedi thing. If you don't find what you want today, you can go out again tomorrow."

"Wow!" Lark beamed. "This is going to be so fun."

"Who's going to do my job while I'm shopping?"

"The staff aren't going to have any problem covering for you."

Rain smiled up at him. "You're spoiling me."

"Get used to it." He kissed her, let her go, then reached into his back jeans pocket for his wallet. "Here's my debit card again. We'll get you your own card soon. In the meantime, put everything on here. And, Lark, don't let your mom buy anything she doesn't truly love, okay? Money isn't an issue. I'm counting on you."

Lark stood on her toes, pressed a kiss to Joe's cheek. "Thanks, Dad."

As Joe watched mother and daughter leave his office together, Lark's words wrapped themselves around his heart like a big, warm hug.

Rain sat in the limo with Lark, scrolling through photos of wedding gowns on her smartphone. "This one is too quinceañera."

"Oh, yeah. Too many ruffles."

She scrolled further, not seeing anything she liked so far. "Look at this. I can't believe you could actually wear that in a church. It looks like lingerie."

"It's sexy though," Lark said.

"I'd wear this if I were dressing up as a cake for Halloween." Rain held the phone so Lark could see again.

"A layer cake." Lark laughed. "Hey, here are some cute maternity gowns."

"Stop teasing." At least Rain wouldn't have to wear one of those. "I'm not sure I'll find anything I like."

They'd been to four bridal shops already, and nothing had been available in a size eight that had appealed to Rain.

"You can always get a pretty evening gown if none of the bridal gowns suit you. You are getting married in a pub, right?"

"I suppose that's true, but…" How could she explain this? "I never thought I'd get married, so I'd kind of like to look like a bride."

Lark lowered her own cell phone, gave Rain's hand a squeeze. "We will find you the most beautiful wedding gown in Denver."

The driver pulled up in front of their next stop, The Bride's Studio, and came around to open the door. It was a new experience for both of them, and Rain couldn't help but feel like an imposter.

"I'll park in back, ma'am," the driver said. "Text me when you're ready."

"Thank you."

Rain walked up the stairs with Lark and stepped inside. The place was elegant and spacious, with high ceilings, crystal chandeliers, polished wooden floors, and long racks of gowns arranged by color.

"Over here, Mom." Lark started toward the bridal gowns, when an older, immaculately dressed woman stepped out from behind a curtain.

"Good afternoon. Do you have an appointment?" The woman's gaze moved over them, and she pressed her lips together.

Because of her nose piercing and the dreadlocks she used to wear, Rain was accustomed to people making judgments about her based on her appearance. Still, she felt self-conscious standing in her blue jeans and snow boots in a place like this. "I'm getting married on Sunday, and I need to find a gown."

"We carry exclusively designer and bespoke gowns, and our prices start at two thousand dollars. I'm not sure we'll have what you're looking for."

What the hell did that mean?

Lark gave the woman a sweet smile. "Money isn't an issue. The quality of the bridal gowns has been our problem, but if you don't think you can help…"

Rain stared at her daughter, amazed at her boldness.

"My name is Sally. I've got a little while before our next client arrives. Do you have a specific style or designer in mind?"

"Oscar de la Renta, Alexander McQueen, Vera Wang…" Lark was completely making this up, probably listing the designers she'd heard of watching the red-carpet coverage of the Oscars. She looked over at Rain and shrugged. "I guess I left the list in the limo."

Rain was onboard now. "I could text our driver, but it would probably be faster if we just look."

"This way." Sally smiled and motioned for them to follow.

Lark walked beside the saleswoman. "We don't want anything that's too high school prom or quinceañera or that looks like lingerie or resembles a layer cake."

Sally laughed at this and led them toward the bridal gowns. "I think we can avoid those styles. You look like you're a size seven or eight, Miss…"

"Rain Minear. You're right on. I'm a size eight."

They had spent ten minutes looking at gown after gown, when Rain saw it. She walked over to a locked display case. "This is beautiful."

It had a sweetheart neckline, three-quarter-length illusion sleeves, and a gathered satin and tulle skirt. The bodice and the sleeves were beaded with thousands of small crystals and pearls arranged into delicate flowers and vines, the needlework done in silver metallic thread. It was the most beautiful gown she'd ever seen.

She turned toward the woman. "What size is this?"

"I think it's a size eight," Sally said. "It's a one-of-a-kind bespoke gown being sold on consignment at a considerable discount by the bride. It has never been worn. The groom backed out, I'm sorry to say. It's quite lovely. Those are real freshwater pearls and Swarovski crystals, and the thread in the bodice is platinum. I'm afraid it's far outside most people's price range."

Surely, Sally didn't mean *real* platinum. She was just referring to the silver color of the thread.

"It's not outside *our* price range," Lark said before Rain could ask. "Would you like to try it on?"

Rain hesitated, then remembered that Joe had wanted her to find a gown she loved. "Yes, please."

Sally's entire demeanor changed. "Why don't you and your sister go sit down in our fitting area, and we'll bring the gown to you."

Rain bit back a smile. "Okay. Come on, *sister*."

People had been mistaking them for sisters since Lark reached puberty.

The two of them laughed and whispered together while they waited.

"When did you get so cheeky?" Rain asked her daughter.

Lark smiled. "I wasn't being cheeky. Everything I said was true."

"Right."

A woman they hadn't met came over and offered them tea. Then Sally appeared, carrying the gown with the help of two young women. Together, they hung it on a high rack so that the chapel train wouldn't touch the floor. Then the two assistants drew curtains around the area, making it private.

"If you would undress, please." Sally motioned Rain toward a raised platform at the center of the space.

Rain pulled off her boots and her two pairs of wool socks, then stripped out of her jeans and T-shirt. She walked to the platform, waiting in her bra and panties while Sally and the two other women took the dress from its hanger and brought it over to her.

"We'll help you put it on," Sally said.

Rain was enveloped in light, silky fabric as they lowered the gown over her head. The bodice was heavy, the sleeves so delicate she was afraid she'd tear them. Sally buttoned the dress in back, the bodice drawing tight—but not too tight.

Rain adjusted her breasts, looked down at yards of creamy tulle that hid her feet, then turned to Lark. "What do you think?"

Lark had a hand over her mouth, and there were tears in her eyes. "It's perfect. You are … so beautiful."

Rain turned toward the mirrors and stared. "Oh!"

She looked like a fairytale bride.

"They say every gown is meant for one special bride." Sally, too, seemed genuinely moved. "This dress is meant for you. You have the perfect figure for it, and it's got just enough sparkle to be perfect for a Christmas wedding."

As the saleswomen fussed with the gown, making sure it fit without need for further adjustments, Rain met Lark's gaze. "This is the one."

It was late afternoon when Joe got a call from the bank. There'd been some unusual charges, and they wanted to confirm with him that he had, indeed, authorized them. "Go ahead."

"We have charges from the Bridal Studio totaling two hundred twenty-five thousand dollars, and charges totaling nine thousand from Saks."

Joe's heart skipped a beat. He kept his voice casual. "Did you say two hundred twenty-five thousand on that first one?"

"Yes, sir."

Jesus!

A quarter of a million dollars. This must be one hell of a wedding gown.

Well, it served him right. He'd told Lark that cost didn't matter, and she had quite clearly taken him at his word.

He fought back a burst of laughter. "That sounds about right."

"You did authorize those charges, then?"

"Yes, I did." He'd told her to get something she loved, and it sounded like she'd done just that. "I'm getting married on Sunday."

"Congratulations, sir."

Two hours later, Rain and Lark walked into his office at the pub. Joe got to his feet, hugged Lark, then wrapped his arms around Rain. "I got a call from the bank."

Her eyes went wide. "Did we spend too much? Lark didn't let me see the price tags, and I was afraid—"

Joe kissed her to still her. "Hey, everything is fine. They just wanted to know whether I authorized the charges."

Lark hadn't let her look at the price tags. That certainly explained things.

"I filled out the online form for the marriage license. We need to drive into Boulder to pick it up tomorrow morning. Chaska's grandpa—remember him?—he has offered to officiate. I hope that's okay. He wants to meet with us tonight to talk about the ceremony."

Rain face lit up. "Oh, that's great. I love Old Man Belcourt."

"Rico and I set the menu and got the food ordered. What do you think of a prime rib buffet with a champagne toast?"

"Prime rib for a thousand people? That would mean roasting…" she did the math… "a *hundred* prime ribs. We don't have the oven space."

"We're planning on feeding about five hundred. We hired a caterer to help. They're bringing up a trailer with extra ovens."

"That will be incredibly expensive."

He rested his hands on her shoulders. "I know you've always had to worry about money, but you don't have to worry now."

She looked doubtful. "It's going to take me some time to get used to that."

"Fair enough." But he had more to tell her. "Libby has renamed 'Plow Me' to 'I Do' Christmas Wedding Stout in honor of the occasion. She's bottling it now."

Rain laughed. "So we have our own wedding beer, and I don't get to drink it. Doesn't that just figure?"

"You can have a taste, right? I'll save a few cases for you."

Rain told him how she and Lark had gotten everything they needed to wear for the ceremony and described for him the kind of flowers they'd chosen. "I went with red and white roses for our bouquets and your boutonniere and roses with holly and evergreen for hanging decorations."

Joe had gotten the receipt for that, too. "I'm sure it will be perfect. Marcia has volunteered to decorate. She wants to talk with you when you get the chance."

"I'll talk with her now, but then I need to go home and take a nap."

"She fell asleep in the limo," Lark said. "Isn't that cute?"

"Let me know when you're ready to go, and I'll take you home."

When Rain disappeared to talk to Marcia, Joe leaned over and spoke for Lark's ears alone. "Thanks for keeping your promise about the dress."

"I knew you could afford it."

Joe raised an eyebrow. "Did you?"

"You're a millionaire, right?"

Joe shook his head. "No, I'm not. Replace the 'm' with a 'b.'"

Lark's jaw dropped and her eyes went wide. "*Billionaire?*"

Joe chuckled at the shock on her face. "Keep that to yourself, please. I'm not in the habit of talking about my finances with anyone, but you're family now. And don't tell your mother because she doesn't want to know."

"O-okay. Why not?"

"She doesn't want anyone to think she's marrying me for money."

Lark laughed. "Anyone who knows my mom knows she would never do that."

"That's true, but people love to talk. Also, never let your mom know how expensive that dress was. She would have a heart attack."

"It will be our secret." Lark smiled. "But trust me—when you see her, you'll think it was worth every penny."

"I can't wait."

Chapter Sixteen

Two days till Christmas

Rain woke Sunday morning in the Matchless Suite at the Forest Creek Inn, the best suite Bob and Kendra had. Rain had cleaned it many times, but she'd never thought she'd be staying here. Joe had rented the suite for her so that they could observe at least one wedding tradition and not see each other the night before the wedding. As superstitious as it seemed, Rain hadn't wanted to risk bringing bad luck their way—not now, when all of her dreams seemed to be coming true.

Today, she was marrying the man she loved.

She had just climbed out of bed when a knock came at her door.

Sandrine, the French pastry chef who baked the croissants for which the inn was known, stood there with a breakfast tray, a bright smile on her face. "How is the bride this morning?"

"That looks delicious." The scent of food hit Rain—followed immediately by a surge of nausea.

Oh, great.

Sandrine set the tray down on the table. "We are all so happy for you."

Rain sat, fixed a smile on her face, did her best to look like she wasn't on the verge of throwing up. "Thank you, Sandrine. That means the world to me."

"I hear Joe has a special day planned for you."

Rain nodded, breathed deeper. "Yes. He has been amazing."

Shawna Evans, who owned a salon in town, would be coming with one of her assistants to give both her and Lark mani-pedis and to style their hair. Victoria, Lexi, and Kendra would be there to help her and Lark dress. Then a limo would pick them up at 4:45 to drive them to Knockers.

Rain didn't have to do a thing—except not throw up.

"I'll be there tonight. I think the whole town is coming. You must be so excited."

Rain nodded, almost afraid to open her mouth. She swallowed—hard. "I can't believe it's happening."

"It *is* rather sudden, isn't it?" Rose appeared in the doorway, Kendra behind her.

Kendra gave a snort. "Right. After twenty years of being in love, they *suddenly* decided to get married. I'd say it's about time."

Rose looked embarrassed. "Well, I… um…"

Kendra shifted her gaze to Rain. "I just came up to give you today's paper. I thought you'd want a copy."

"Thanks." Rain took the paper, saw that the wedding was the day's top story.

"If you need anything, let us know," Kendra said.

Rain wondered if she would give her pregnancy away if she asked for herbal tea and crackers. She decided not to risk it. She would text Lark and ask her to stop by Food Mart. "I appreciate that. I'm good for now."

She waited till the women had left her alone, then dashed for the bathroom.

Joe stood in the dining area at his pub, looking around at the sea of boxes. Flowers. Greenery. Ribbon. White Christmas lights. He'd closed the place until 4:30 to give them time to cook for roughly five hundred and to decorate the place. Staff had already moved the tables to make room for the buffet and to create an aisle for the bride. Now it was time to decorate.

"How many lights did you buy exactly?"

"I think twenty thousand," Marcia said. "We bought pretty much everything that was left at the hardware stores in Boulder. I hope it's enough."

"That will work." He unfolded the ladder, then caught sight of Lark heading out the door. "Hey, are you going to see your mom?"

God, he'd missed Rain last night.

Lark nodded, then motioned for him to come over. She waited until he was standing right beside her, then dropped her voice to a whisper. "She wants me to pick up crackers and herbal tea. She's nauseated and throwing up."

Shit.

Joe had really hoped she'd be spared morning sickness. He knew she hadn't wanted to go through the physical ordeal of pregnancy again. This was *his* doing.

He handed Lark a twenty. "I know you'll take good care of her. Tell her hi."

Lark shook her head. "No contact, remember?"

Well, this sucked.

When Joe walked back to Marcia, he found Cheyenne helping her.

"We've got this, Joe," Marcia said. "Go help Rico."

Joe found Rico in the kitchen talking with the catering staff, the scent of roasting prime rib filling the air. "Sorry to interrupt, but I need you to put me to work. Marcia just threw me out of the dining room."

Rico pointed toward a pile of roasting pans in the sink. "Start scrubbing."

Joe rolled up his sleeves and got to it, grateful for the distraction.

Rico came up beside him. "You nervous, boss?"

"What's there to be nervous about?"

Rico laughed. "You're such a shitty liar."

Okay, so Rico wasn't going to let Joe get away with that. "I just want it to be perfect for her."

"Rain loves you, man. She'd be happy with less. No one but you could have put together an event like this in three days. She is going to be amazed."

Joe looked over at his friend. "I couldn't have done it without your help."

Rico clapped him on the back. "Don't get mushy on me. Just keep scrubbing."

Joe had made good progress when Bear wandered into the kitchen. "Hey, Bear, we're closed till four-thirty today."

Bear glanced around the kitchen. "They said there was going to be a wedding and we could all come here."

"Rain and I are getting married today, and you're invited to join us."

Bear's beard shifted as he smiled ear to ear. "Is she coming back?"

"Yes, she is." Then an idea came to Joe. "Hey, Bear, would you like to do something special for us during the wedding?"

Bear nodded.

Joe turned to Rico. "Do we have anything we can heat up for Bear?"

Rico started toward the walk-in refrigerator "You like macaroni and cheese?"

"Yes, sir."

"Fill up your stomach," Joe told him. "Then we'll talk."

While Shawna fixed Rain's hair, Lark read the newspaper article aloud.

"'The couple has requested that people make donations to Scarlet Springs Fire and Rescue, which recently rescued the bride from her collapsed home, instead of gifts.' Really? You don't want gifts?"

"I think it's more an issue of them not needing anything," Kendra said. "Not sure if you've noticed, sweetheart, but your soon-to-be daddy is loaded."

"Oh. Right."

"What do you think?" Shawna handed Rain a mirror.

"I love it." Rain felt like a princess, her hair swept back in a loose French braid, her makeup understated and perfect. "Thank you."

Vicki, Lexi, and Kendra were helping Lark get into her dress.

"You look like sex on a stick, girl," Kendra said.

Rain turned and stared at her daughter, whose body was sheathed in a beaded spaghetti strap gown in Christmas red. She looked stunning—and far too sexy. "Are you sure you want to wear that?"

Rain had seen the gown, of course. She just hadn't seen it on her daughter. Lark hadn't wanted to model it, and now Rain knew why.

Lark gave Rain her "whatever" look. "Mom, I'm twenty-one."

Shawna doused Rain with hairspray, then stepped back from the table. "Time for your hair and makeup now, Lark."

Rain got to her feet, still wearing her bathrobe. She'd begun to feel better just after noon. She'd given her breakfast to Lark but had eaten her lunch herself. Then Vicki and Lexi had arrived, and the day had turned into a party.

"This reminds me of the day Austin and I got married," Lexi called from the bathroom where she was putting on her makeup. "Do you remember, Vic?"

"I was the maid of honor, so, yes, I remember. Eric and I fell in love that day."

Rain walked into the bedroom, shut the door, and put on the sexy lace panties, pushup bra, garters and silk stockings she'd bought to wear beneath her gown.

"You two certainly put this room to good use," she heard Kendra say. "You thought you were being sneaky, but we knew. Bob said we ought to rename it the Hawktoria Suite."

Vicki laughed. "That's fine by me."

Rain stepped out of the bedroom. "What do you think?"

Kendra wolf-whistled. "I hope you either worked out the contraception thing or have hit menopause, because that's the kind of lingerie that gets a woman pregnant."

"I didn't know lingerie could do that," Vicki joked. "I'll have to buy some."

Lexi stuck her head out of the bathroom. "Sexy."

Lark pouted. "God, I wish I had your boobs."

"The limo will be here in twenty minutes. Let's get you into your gown." Kendra walked into the bedroom, carried out the gown, and laid it out on the sofa. "This thing is heavy. What's it made out of?"

"Platinum," Lark quipped.

"Really?" Vicki and Lexi asked in unison.

"How much did it cost?" Kendra ran her fingers admiringly over the beading.

"I don't know," Rain answered. "I don't think I want to know."

"And I'm not telling," Lark said.

Lexi and Vicki helped Kendra gather up the yards of tulle that made the skirt and lifted it over Rain's head. Kendra buttoned the bodice, and the three of them fussed and fidgeted, adjusting the sleeves and skirts.

Rain started toward the mirror. "How do I look?"

The women stared at her, tears in Vicki's and Lark's eyes.

She reached the mirror and found a beautiful bride looking back at her. Butterflies fluttered in her stomach. "My God, I'm getting married! Do you think Joe will like it?"

"Oh, honey." Kendra's voice broke. "You are going to knock his socks off. But your dress is going to drag in the mud. I'll have Bob put a rug down on our sidewalk, but I don't know what you're going to do at Knockers."

"I have an idea." Vicki got on the phone to Eric. "Hey, honey, we have a couple of beautiful women here who are going to need to be carried inside Knockers so they don't slip on the ice or drag their gowns in the mud. Can you and the Team guys or firefighters figure something out?"

Shawna finished Lark's hair, then retouched Rain's makeup and hair.

"The limo's here," Lark called from the window.

The women went down in the elevator and found Bob waiting.

"You look like a million bucks, kid." He gave Rain a hug and a kiss on the cheek.

They walked out onto the carpeted sidewalk and climbed into the limo, the other women helping Rain with her gown, for the short ride across town. The sun was low on the horizon, casting a pink glow on the white snow. Christmas lights twinkled from houses, trees, and lamp posts. People waved as they passed, cars and pickups honking.

It was beautiful, perfect, like being lost in a dream. Rain was on her way to marry Joe in her hometown with all the people she loved around her.

They reached Knockers five minutes later, and Vicki instructed the driver to pull up in front of the main entrance.

The door opened and Eric stuck his head in. "You all look fabulous. Let's start with the maid of honor."

Rain watched as Eric scooped Lark into his arms and passed her to Austin Taylor.

"Hey, kiddo. Don't you look pretty—and very grown up." Austin handed her to Jesse Moretti, who put her down inside the front entrance.

"There you go, darlin'."

"That was the best thing ever!" Lark said from the doorway.

"Now for the bride." Eric lifted Rain easily into his arms, Vicki helping him to gather up her skirts. "Congratulations, Rain. We're all so happy for you."

"Stop, or you're going to make me cry."

Hawke laughed, looking so much like Cadan for a moment that it made her heart hurt. "Don't let her skirts drag."

"Congrats, Rain." Austin took her, handed her to Jesse. "Joe is going to flip when he sees you."

"Hell, yeah, he is." Jesse put her down inside the front door. "Congratulations."

That *had* been fun.

Then a voice came from behind Rain "Wasn't that sweet? Maybe they'll start helping old ladies cross the street."

Megs Hill, the founder of the Team, stood there beside her husband, Mitch Ahearn, dressed up in a denim skirt and sweater. "Congratulations, Rain. Don't you look beautiful?"

Rain glanced around at the place she'd worked for twenty years to find it transformed. Garlands of pine, holly, and roses were draped along the walls and wrapped around the columns, thousands of white lights hanging from the ceiling like icicles.

Joe had done this for her—with lots of help from their friends.

Marcia stepped up to her and Lark with their bouquets—and burst into tears. "You look so pretty."

"Thanks."

A hush fell over the room, and then the Mudbugs began to play, first the keyboard and then the violin.

Pachelbel's *Canon in D*.

"Hey, beautiful." Rico walked up to Lark, wearing a black sports jacket over his best pair of jeans, and slipped his arm through hers. "They're playing our song."

They walked through the dining area toward the dance floor and the stage beyond.

Rain waited a moment or two, then followed them, her pulse racing. It was crowded, friends and neighbors parting to let them through, everyone smiling. Mrs. Beech dabbing her eyes with a tissue. Frank from the gas station. Hank with a beer. Libby standing together with Brandon Silver. Rose with miniature white lights in her silver hair. Bob and Kendra. Chaska Belcourt and his wife Naomi and sister Winona. Sasha Dillon along with the rest of the Team. Cheyenne and Marcia, both in tears.

Then Rain saw him—and her nervousness melted away.

Joe stood beside Grandpa Belcourt on the stage in that tux she'd seen in his closet, looking more handsome than any man should. Then his gaze met hers, the emotion in his eyes taking her breath away.

Joe's first thought was that Lark had been telling the truth. That dress was worth every damned penny. Rain floated toward him like an angel, her face radiant, the bodice of the gown sparkling. His second thought was that there were tears running down his cheeks and there wasn't a damned thing he could do about it.

Why had he waited for so long? Why hadn't he done this years ago?

Lark smiled up at him as she made her way toward the stage with Rico, looking beautiful in a dress of shimmering red, her face as radiant as her mother's.

His daughter.

She and Rico waited at the bottom of the stairs for the bride, lifting Rain's train so that it wouldn't get caught, then following her up to the stage.

And then Rain was there—beautiful, sweet Rain, the woman he loved, the woman he had always loved. There were tears in her eyes, too.

He took her hand. "You are *so* beautiful."

"You clean up nice, too."

The music ended.

Grandpa Belcourt chuckled. "It's good to see so many people together. In this world, true community is a hard thing to find. Too many people live for themselves without thinking of others or the future.

"This town is a community, in part because of this man and this woman. I have heard stories from many today and yesterday about how Joe and Rain have strengthened ties, built relations, and helped others. Now they ask us to join them together as husband and wife, to bless their union, to witness their becoming one."

The old man talked at length about how real love meant a willingness to sacrifice for the other person, to place their needs before one's own, and, if it came to it, to lay down one's life for the other. Then it came time for their vows. They hadn't had time to write anything themselves and so had left it up to Grandpa Belcourt.

"Do you, Joseph Michael Moffat take Rain Marie Minear to be your wife, to sacrifice for her, to put her needs ahead of your own, and to lay your life down for hers should there come such a day?"

"I do."

"Do you, Rain Marie Minear take Joseph Michael Moffat to be your husband, to sacrifice for him, to put his needs ahead of your own, and to lay your life down for his should there come such a day?"

"I do."

"Who has the rings?" Grandpa Belcourt asked.

Bear stepped out from behind Rico, dressed in buckskin, his long hair brushed and drawn back into a ponytail. He came to stand beside them and opened his hand to reveal the rings. He placed his other hand over them in a gesture of blessing.

Joe expected a Bible verse from him, but for a moment Bear said nothing.

"Father God, these are true, kind people. They feed me when I am hungry. They welcome me. They clothe me. Bless them on this day and always."

Shouts of "Amen!" filled the pub.

Bear handed the rings to Grandpa Belcourt as they'd planned, then went to stand behind Rico once more—but not before Rain pressed a kiss to his cheek.

"Thanks, Bear."

Grandpa Belcourt talked about the importance of the circle, or hoop, in Lakota culture. "May this circle that unites you remain forever unbroken."

He handed Rain's wedding band to Joe. "Joe, as you put the ring on her finger, repeat after me. 'I give you this ring as a symbol of my abiding love for you, my life-long fidelity, and my devotion."

Joe repeated the words, slid the ring onto her finger. Then she, too, repeated those words and slipped a platinum band onto his finger.

"You are now husband and wife."

Joe didn't wait to be told to kiss Rain, but drew her into his arms and covered her lips with his as the pub filled with cheers.

They opened the buffet, the servers cutting prime rib, filling plates, distributing champagne for the toast.

Hawke came up to Joe, along with the members of his crew who'd come with him—Brandon Silver and Jenny Miller among them. "Amazing ceremony, man. Thanks for inviting us. I'm so happy for the two of you."

"You're not leaving already, are you?" Rain asked, looking disappointed.

"I'd love to stay, but I've got to go play Santa Claus."

Christmas Tots.

"Right," Joe said. "That's tonight, isn't it?"

"Once again, the people of Scarlet came through. Not a single child was left out."

Rain glanced at Joe, a knowing smile on her lips. "I'm so happy to hear that. Thanks, Eric."

"I should thank you. We've gotten a lot of donations in honor of the two of you." He kissed Rain's cheek, then shook Joe's hand.

Joe went to the seats that Rico had saved for him, Rain, Lark, and himself, glasses of champagne already poured, slices of prime rib sitting next to mashed potatoes, salad, and slices of baguette.

He leaned over to check on his bride. "How are you feeling?"

"Starving," she said. "Happy."

"Good." Joe waited until most people had finished their meals, then tapped the side of his glass with his knife. "This is an informal situation, so we won't be doing any big speeches or anything—

Rico stood. "Oh, yes, we are. I didn't stay up till three this morning writing this for nothing. Sit down and shut up, Joe."

Laughter.

Joe sat next to Rain, the happiness on her face lighting his world.

Rico cleared his throat. "I've known Joe Moffat and Rain Minear since I came to work here, almost twenty years ago. Joe hired me despite my prison record, trusted me with knives, helped me get back on my feet. He never treated me like an ex-con, but like a trusted member of his staff. He helped restore my sense of dignity after it had been stripped away. I stayed out of trouble because of him."

Rain looked over at Joe, her gaze soft. "That's my man."

"I've heard people call Joe cold, aloof, eccentric. If you believe that, then you don't know this man. None of us—not even Rain and I—know everything Joe has done for the people of this town, but that's how he wants it. He doesn't want attention. He just wants to make things better. Joe, you're my hero, and you're a hero to this town."

Shouts of "hear, hear!"

Joe looked up at his closest friend, his throat strangely tight. "Thanks, Rico."

Rico went on. "What can I say about Rain? We all love her."

Cheers, shouts of "yes!" and "we do!" and applause.

"When I first met her, she had a baby and was serving drinks— illegally—to try to make ends meet. I had a thing for her. I admit it."

Rain smiled up at him. "That's sweet."

"I never acted on it."

"Smart man," Joe muttered.

Laughter.

"I realized within the first week here that any man who went after Rain would have to go through Joe. I outweigh Joe by about forty pounds, and I've come out of prison fights not even bleeding. But there was *no way* I was taking him on. The man was crazy in love with her even if he didn't yet know it."

Joe looked into Rain's eyes. "It's true."

"Rain is one of a kind, the sort of woman who raises up everyone around her. Her kindness and generosity have touched us all. Whether she's only served you food and drinks or whether you know her personally, she's made your dark moments brighter and your happy days happier still. She's the best friend a person could have, a wonderful mother, and the soul of this pub."

Rain dabbed at the corners of her eyes. "Stop! You're making me cry."

Joe squeezed her hand, leaned in, kissed her cheek. "It's all true."

"Please stand for a toast." Rico raised his glass, gave people a moment to get to their feet. "To the bride and groom!"

"To the bride and groom!"

"And Merry Christmas!"

Joe drank his champagne, while Rain took only a sip, then deftly switched her almost full flute for his empty one, the two of them sharing a secret glance.

Joe stood, thanked Rico and Lark, the staff, the catering company, the Timberline Mudbugs, and all of those who'd come to celebrate with them. "Now that we're done eating and talking, it's time for music. May I have this dance?"

He took his bride's hand and led her onto the dance floor, just as the Mudbugs started playing their own rendition of *Je Suis Tout Pour Toi*, the Cajun Wedding Song.

"Rain and Joe, this is for you."

Rain stood with her husband by the front entrance saying goodnight to their guests and thanking them until only the staff and a few diehards were left. Hank sat at the bar. Bear ate from the buffet like it might be his last meal. Team members sat at their usual table cheering one another on as they took turns on the climbing wall.

"How do you feel?" Joe asked her.

"I'm doing great."

"Good." His lips curved in a sexy smile that told her he had plans.

That was fine with her. She had plans, too—like getting him out of that tux and jumping his bones.

Rico walked up to them. "You want us to take down the decorations tonight?"

Joe shook his head. "No, leave the decorations up. It's Christmas. But, hey, can you clear everyone out of here? I'd like to be alone with my woman—*completely* alone."

Rico grinned. "Sure thing, boss."

"What are you up to?" Rain asked.

He took her hand, kissed it. "You'll see."

It took ten minutes or so to round everyone up and get them out the door. The Team guys moaned when Rico told them it was time to quit climbing.

"Time to go home," he told them. "You can come back and play with your favorite toy tomorrow. The wall isn't going anywhere."

Bear thanked them for the food.

"Where will you be for Christmas?" Rain asked him.

"Winona and Chaska want me to stay at their house."

Rain felt relieved. "Merry Christmas. Thank you for your blessing."

Bear shuffled away.

Hank was the last customer to leave. "You won't even let me drink one last shot to you and your woman, Joe? That's just mean."

"Thanks for the thought, Hank, but I'd like you to get the hell out of here so I can be alone with my bride."

Then there was only staff. Rain and Joe thanked them one at a time as they left— Marcia and Chey for decorating and serving drinks; Libby for the Christmas brew, which had been drunk to the last bottle, apart from the cases Joe had locked in his office; the kitchen staff for their hard work in feeding an estimated six hundred guests.

"You were the most beautiful bride ever," Marcia said.

Chey gave Rain a wink. "Have fun tonight."

Rico was the last to leave. "The place is all shut down and locked up. Congrats to the two of you. Don't do anything I wouldn't do."

Joe's eyes narrowed. "I've heard about some of the things you've done."

Rico nodded and laughed. "Yeah."

"Are you sure everyone's gone?" Joe asked "No one is hiding in the bathrooms?

"I'm sure."

Joe reached behind the bar, pulled out the bottle of Macallan 1940 that he'd brought from home, and handed it to Rico. "Thanks for being my best man. You did one hell of a job. I couldn't have pulled this off without you."

Rico's jaw dropped. He took the bottle from Joe as if it were a baby, cradling it in his arms. "M-M-Macallan 40? This is… Oh, my God. Jesus. Thanks, Joe. You are one crazy son of a bitch. You know that?"

"So I've been told."

Rico kissed Joe full on the mouth. "Take care of that beautiful bride of yours. She's a keeper."

Rain watched Rico go. "You just made his year."

"Come dance with me." Joe threaded his fingers through Rain's and drew her with him toward the dance floor. He walked to the sound system and put on John Legend's "All of Me," a song Rain loved, then took her into his arms.

They held each other close as they danced, Rain singing along, the lyrics coming alive for her in a way they hadn't before. She would never hear the song again without thinking of this night, without thinking of Joe.

He nuzzled her ear. "You have such a beautiful voice. I want to hear you sing every day of my life."

The song ended—and Joe walked toward the stage, his lips curving in a grin just as "My Eyes" by Blake Shelton started to play. He stopped at the control panel, flicked on the spotlight, then walked up the stairs, loosening his tie, unbuttoning the top button of his shirt. "What are you waiting for?"

"Oh, my God." Rain gaped at him, laughing. "Do you want to…?"

"I am *not* going to be the only person in Scarlet who hasn't fucked on my own stage. Come here, woman."

Still laughing, Rain lifted her skirts, walked up the stairs, and into Joe's arms.

He crushed her against him, brought his mouth down on hers, his kiss slow and deep and warm with the taste of whiskey.

Oh, she wanted him already. "You look so freaking sexy in that tux."

He backed her up against the back wall, his mouth moving to her throat, raising goose bumps on her skin. "I've wanted to fuck you in that fine dress all night."

"Yeah?" She reached down between them, fumbled with the hook and fly of his trousers, and freed his erection, impatient for him. "What are you waiting for?"

He lifted her skirts, grabbed her ass, and lifted her off her feet. She wrapped her legs around him. They moaned in unison as he buried himself inside her and started to move, fucking her hard and fast. She held onto him, light from the spotlight blinding her, and she realized that anyone could be standing there, watching Joe fuck her, watching him pound into her, and she wouldn't see them.

To her astonishment, the idea turned her on.

It didn't take long, orgasm quickly overtaking her, pleasure singing through her, his breath hot on her skin as he groaned out his climax. For a time, they stood there, bodies still joined, out of breath, hearts pounding.

"We have to do this again," she said.

"Fine by me."

"I didn't know a person could feel this happy," Rain said as Joe lowered her feet to the floor.

"Yeah?" Joe kissed her, soft and slow, then looked into her eyes. "Want to know a secret? Neither did I."

Chapter Seventeen

Christmas Eve

It was hard to have a romantic morning in bed with your new husband when you felt hideously nauseated. Forget sex. Forget breakfast in bed. Forget breakfast, period.

Joe brought Rain tea and crackers—then held her hair when it all came up again.

"It's like having stomach flu half of the day every day for three or four months," she told him, kneeling beside the toilet.

"I've been doing some reading. They say it's a good sign."

"It doesn't *feel* like a good sign." She moaned, threw up again.

She brushed her teeth, then let Joe tuck her in bed again. She managed to fall asleep despite the nausea. When she awoke two hours later, she felt good enough to take a shower and dress. She left the bedroom to see what Lark and Joe were doing and overheard them talking.

"I wish you really were my dad."

"I could be. I could adopt you."

Rain's stomach did a flip. *Oh, Joe.*

She'd never imagined anything like that.

"Adopt me?" Lark laughed. "I'm an adult."

"Adult adoptions happen all the time. You'd be a Moffat then—and my legal heir, along with your mother and the baby."

Rain smiled to herself. He'd said *baby* without stammering this time.

"You would do that?" Lark asked.

That's when Joe spotted Rain on the stairs. "Hey, how are you feeling?"

"Better. Thanks." She went to sit at the table beside them, saw a small stack of printouts sitting in the middle of the table. "What's all of this?"

"Joe was thinking about taking all of us to Hawaii for Christmas. As much as I love the idea, I told him that he shouldn't surprise you with this because you might not feel up to it."

Good girl.

Rain had known Joe would try to do something like this. She'd asked Lark to do her best to intervene if she got wind of any plans. Then she'd told Lark how Joe had never really had a true Christmas.

"You mean he had never decorated a tree before?" Lark had stared at Rain, clearly shocked and sad for him. "I always thought you and I had it rough because there was never much money. But Joe grew up wealthy, and he had less than we did. You always told me that money didn't matter. You were right, Mom."

Rain shared a smile with her daughter. "Lark and I have other plans."

Joe looked over at Lark. "Aha. The truth comes out."

Lark laughed. "This year, you're having a *real* Christmas."

"A real Christmas?" Joe looked from Lark to Rain, one dark brow raised.

Rain took his hand. "You know—strings of popcorn and cranberries for the birds, cookies—"

"You *ate* the cookies," Joe said accusingly, a hint of humor in his voice.

"*More* cookies, games, stockings, ghost stories, yummy food—"

"Turkey and mashed potatoes," Lark blurted. "Or more prime rib."

Rain went on. "Singing carols, watching *It's A Wonderful Life* and *How the Grinch Stole Christmas*, sitting together by the tree to watch the lights, opening gifts on Christmas morning."

She could see that Joe still didn't get it. But then how could he understand something he'd never experienced?

She tried to explain. "This is our first Christmas as a family." Oh, it felt incredible to say that. "You've missed out on so much. Let us give you a true family Christmas."

Joe sat back in his chair, a bemused expression on his face. "Okay. I'm game. What do we do first?"

They made a shopping list for everything from craft supplies to food. Then the women got dressed up—Joe knew they were up to something—and they drove into Scarlet. Joe tried to give Rain one of his credit cards, but she refused.

"Whatever we get you, it's going to be with our own money," she said.

They all went their separate ways, agreeing to meet at the Food Mart parking lot in two hours, when they would shop for the items on the list and then head home.

The streets of Scarlet were crowded with locals doing last-minute shopping like they were, the shop windows decorated with holiday themes, lights hanging in garlands across the street. People called to him when he passed, waving.

"Merry Christmas!"

"I heard you got hitched. Congratulations!"

"Hey, Joe, congrats! Where's your better half?"

Despite the friendly faces, Joe felt like an outsider. Christmas had always been impenetrable to him, a hollow and empty holiday. Since leaving home, he had ignored it, apart from giving his staff holiday bonuses. But now he had a family—the thought made him smile—and he would do his best not to be a Grinch, no matter how he felt.

He made his way down Scarlet's only retail street, hoping to find something special for Lark, as well as a few smaller things for Rain. The ring had been her big gift, but she'd already gotten it. He knew it probably wouldn't matter to her, but he wanted her to have something to open.

He went to the bookstore, the jewelry store, and then found himself inside Tanagila's, Naomi Belcourt's shop. He glanced around, saw Naomi, Chaska, and Winona Belcourt standing behind the counter. "Hey, how's it going?"

They smiled when they saw him, offered their congratulations.

"I think that's the most fun Old Man ever had at a wedding," Chaska said. "He's still talking about the food."

"I'm glad he enjoyed himself. We're grateful that he agreed to officiate with so little notice. Rain adores him."

"Can I help you find something?" Naomi asked.

"I'm not sure what I'm looking for. I'd like to get something for Rain. The trouble is that she's very easy to please."

Naomi nodded as if she understood. "Let's see if we can find something special."

"She doesn't need jewelry." Joe realized the moment he said it that jewelry made up most of Naomi's inventory. She was, after all, a jewelry maker.

Naomi came out from behind the counter, led him around her store. "We've got nativity sculptures. These are all made by Native American artists. Does she like photography or painting?"

Joe was about to answer when he saw it—a silver, heart-shaped ornament with two crystal snowflakes hanging from its top by little silver chains. He walked to the display, lifted it from its hook, read the engraving.

Our First Christmas Together.

He stared at it, something about it putting an ache in his chest. It was nothing really. Just a bit of polished silver. Less than thirty dollars. But he knew Rain would love it. "Can I get this gift-wrapped?"

Naomi nodded. "Of course."

He left the store, his spirits lifting. Maybe buying Christmas gifts wasn't about trying to find something expensive and cool. Maybe it was about giving the people you loved gifts that held meaning for you both.

The idea struck Joe as a revelation. Could it really be so simple?

Excited now, he walked the short distance to Knockers, ideas filling his mind. He went to his office and logged onto his computer.

An hour later, he made his way back to their meeting spot. He stowed his gifts in the back of the Land Rover, covered them with a tarp, then looked around for Rain and Lark. He found them, huddled together against the cold, listening to a small group of carolers from St. Barbara's Church.

"God rest ye merry, gentlemen / let nothing you dismay."

Rain and Lark smiled when they saw him, Rain reaching out her gloved hand for him, her cheeks pink from the cold. "There you are."

He took her hand, came to stand beside her, drawing both women close, doing his best to shelter them from the wind with his bigger frame. The music drifted over them, the sun dipping behind the mountains and turning the sky pink, cheery Christmas lights twinkling all around them.

"Isn't this beautiful?" Rain asked.

He looked down at her. "Beautiful."

And for the first time in his life, Joe thought he might just understand what people meant when they talked about the Christmas spirit.

"Bananas!" Lark cheered.

"I can see now why you like this game." Joe frowned, but there was a light in his eyes that told Rain he was joking. "You always win."

"Lark dominates Bananagrams." Rain was proud of her daughter, proud of how much she knew and how smart she was.

Joe got to his feet, went to check the stuffed shells. "These are almost done."

Rain stood, looked over at Lark. "Want to help me set the table?"

Joe had shown her his grandmother's fine china when they'd gotten home, wanting her to know she was free to use it if she chose. "I almost forgot it was here."

White with dark blue flowers and lacy edges, it was obviously old but still beautiful. Rain and Lark had liberated what they would need from dusty boxes and had washed it by hand. Some of the pieces were chipped, but that only added to the charm. There was everything a person could possibly want for a dinner party—lots of place settings, serving dishes galore, platters, candleholders, a gravy boat, and some things Rain couldn't identify.

They ate dinner—stuffed shells, salad, French bread— then popped corn and poured cranberries in a bowl to make a garland for the birds.

"It's not going to be much of a garland if you eat all the popcorn, Larkness," Joe had teased, calling Lark by the new nickname he'd started using.

They'd ended up with about six feet of garland in the end. They'd gone out together and hung it from the boughs of a nearby pine tree, then come back inside where it was warm.

They settled in front of the TV to share their favorite Christmas movies with Joe, Rain resting her head against Joe's chest. By the time they reached the end of *It's A Wonderful Life,* she was in tears.

"She always cries when we watch this," Lark told Joe.

Rain sat up. "It hits closer to home this year. A month ago, I was thinking of leaving Scarlet, of moving somewhere and trying to start over. I felt like my life was going nowhere. I was certain you would never notice me, and I thought I would have to spend Christmas alone. I'm so glad I didn't leave. This is my home."

She could see on Joe's face that he understood. So much had changed in such a short time for both of them.

Joe reached over, wiped the tears from her cheeks. "That feels like a hundred years ago now, doesn't it? Everything turned out so much better than either of us could have possibly imagined."

She wiped her eyes, smiled. "Yes. *Much* better."

"Should we hang our stockings now?" Lark asked.

"Stockings?" Joe frowned. "We have stockings?"

Rain and Lark had picked matching stockings of gray embroidered velvet, along with stocking holders, from a little Christmas market behind Food Mart. Lark dashed upstairs to get them.

"Are you having fun?" Rain asked Joe. "Truly?"

He drew her into his arms, kissed her. "My family never spent time together like this. By the time I was ten, I opened Christmas presents alone that staff had bought for me because my parents couldn't stand to be in the same room. How could I not be having fun? Every moment I'm with you and Lark feels new and exciting."

Lark returned, the stockings and stocking holders still in the bag. She walked over to the gas fireplace. "Is it safe to hang them on the mantel?"

Joe stood, walked over to the wall, turned off the fireplace. "Now it is."

Lark handed the bag to Rain, who drew out Lark's stocking first. It was embroidered with silver stars. "Here you go."

Next, she reached in for the stocking holder—a small silver picture frame that held a photo of Lark from the wedding, looking brilliant in her red dress.

"Cool," Joe said. "How did you get the photos?"

Rain had asked the photographer to print a few and to leave them in her mailbox, which was still standing, even if her house was not. But she didn't tell Joe this. "I have connections."

Joe's eyebrows rose. "Is that so?"

Then she pulled out Joe's stocking, which was embroidered with the shape of a reindeer with antlers.

"We figured the antlers meant this had to be yours," Lark said.

Joe leaned down, whispered loudly, "Female reindeer have antlers, too."

"Really?" Lark looked up at him, surprised.

Rain handed the stocking to him, together with his stocking holder, which contained a photo of him in his tux. "I love this photo of you."

Rain pulled out her stocking next. It was embroidered with silver and gold snowflakes, her stocking holder complete with a photo of her in her wedding gown. She put hers up between Joe's and Lark's. "There."

Rain watched Joe's face as Lark took the bag from her and pulled out a fourth stocking, this one with little silver snowmen. Its stocking holder held no photo.

He exhaled—a little gust of air—and reached out to touch the empty picture frame, tenderness on his face. There was awe in his voice when he spoke. "Next year, there will be a new little face here, someone we know and love."

Lark beamed. "I can't wait."

Joe made love to Rain with so much finesse and tenderness that night that it made her heart ache. He showed her how much she meant to him with every kiss, every touch, every caress. Never had she felt more cherished. Then he'd kissed her and held her as she drifted off to sleep in his arms.

Christmas morning got a somewhat later start than usual, as it took Rain a couple of hours to get away from the bathroom. Joe made breakfast for himself and Lark in the meantime, warning Lark repeatedly to stay away from the tree and the stockings.

"No cheating!"

Rain was finally able to join them in the late morning, pale but happy.

There weren't a lot of presents around the tree, but Joe didn't care. There'd been lots of packages to open when he was a kid, lots of gifts, but everything had been purchased by his mother's staff. None of it was personal. None of it was heartfelt. By contrast, everything under *this* tree meant something to the person who had placed it there. That's what mattered.

Lark went first. Rain had gotten her some pretty clothes and some sniffy stuff—lotion, body wash, foot cream. "Thanks, Mom. I love this scent."

"Merry Christmas, baby."

Then Lark opened the small box from Joe. "Oh, my God. My own diamond studs. Are they real?"

Joe couldn't help but laugh. He reached over tousled Lark's hair. "Of course, they're real."

Lark crawled over to him and threw her arms around his neck. "Thanks, Dad."

Joe hugged her back. It meant so much to him when she used those words. "Merry Christmas, kiddo."

"You're going to spoil her, you know," Rain said.

Joe shrugged. "Father's privilege."

Rain opened her gifts next—a pretty silver barrette with turquoise stones. "That's beautiful. Thanks, honey. I love it."

"I figured you could use something pretty now that you're done with dreads for good. You are done with them for good now, right?" Lark asked, hopeful.

Rain pulled back her hair and clipped the barrette into place. "I make no promises."

She reached under the tree, drew out the box from Joe, and unwrapped it, her face lighting up like a thousand sunrises when she saw it. "Oh, it's beautiful. I love the crystal snowflakes."

He'd known she would like it.

She held up the ornament. "It's our first ornament."

Lark reached out, turned it so she could see it. "That's so cute!"

Rain got to her feet, walked to the tree, hung it front and center, stepping back to adjust it until it faced forward perfectly. "There."

There was more love in that single action than Joe had ever seen his mother put into anything at Christmastime.

Rain sat beside Joe on the floor, kissed him. "Thanks. It's perfect."

"You've got something else under the tree." Joe pointed to the envelope.

Rain picked it up. "This scares me."

"Why?"

"With you, the smaller the package, the more expensive the gift."

Joe wasn't sure why his spending money on her bothered her, but they had time to sort through that later. "Open it."

She tore through the envelope, took out the piece of paper and read through it, her eyes filling with tears. "Oh, Joe. Only you…"

"What is it?" Lark leaned closer, trying to see.

Rain handed the piece of paper to her daughter.

"A year's worth of singing lessons." Lark reached out and took her mother's hand. "This is perfect. You had to give all of that up when I came along, and now you can have it back."

"I don't know. I'm not very good."

"Stop." Joe had heard that so many times, and he'd always let it pass. Not any longer. "You've got one of the sweetest voices I've ever heard. You have perfect pitch, an intuitive sense of harmony and rhythm. You sing like an angel. Don't let the past stop you from doing what you love."

Rain sniffed. "You really think I can do it?"

He wiped a tear from her face. "You'll never know if you don't try. If I learned anything this past month, it's to grab onto your dreams with both hands, or they might just get away from you."

"Your turn." Lark reached under the tree for the last remaining package and pushed it across the floor to Joe, a look of anticipation on her face.

Joe tore off the paper, opened the box, and drew out a silver triptych-style picture frame. He opened it, expecting photos from the wedding. Instead, there were three portraits that had clearly been taken yesterday—an 8x10 of Rain and Lark together, and one of each of them alone. "My new family."

The only true family he'd ever had.

They were beautiful, professional portraits. Joe would bet Rain had paid a bundle for them, too, given that it had been a rush job.

"Do you like them?"

"I love them."

"They're for your office," Lark said. "It needs some sprucing up."

"Now you'll have us with you all the time."

"I'm a lucky man." It was the best Christmas gift he'd ever received.

Rain took down Joe's stocking and dropped it in his lap. "You went last with gifts, so you get to dig into your stocking first."

Joe reached in, drew out a few candy canes. Next, he found the gift card for the cinema that Lark had gotten him. "This will be fun. You'll have to tell me what movie you want to see. Thanks, Larkness."

Last of all, he drew out the tiny pair of white newborn baby booties Rain had bought. He unwrapped them, tossed aside the tissue paper, and set them side by side on his palm. "There is no way that babies' feet are *this* small."

Rain couldn't help but laugh. "Oh, yes, they are."

Rain found a gift card to the coffee shop in her stocking. "Caffeine! This is proof you love me. Thanks, Lark."

There were candy canes, too, and a small box.

"Is this from you?" she asked Joe, knowing full well that it was.

He gave her a sexy grin. "Just open it."

She peeled back the lovely embossed wrapping paper, took off the top, and stared down at two pink diamond earrings, each surrounded by a halo of tiny pavé diamonds. "Oh, they're beautiful! Joe, you really shouldn't You're spoiling me."

"Oh, nice, Dad!" Lark said.

"Husband's privilege." He winked at Lark. "This was part of your original Christmas present. You needed something to go with the ring."

"I have *you* to go with the ring." Rain took the earrings one at a time from the box and put them on. "How do they look?"

"Beautiful," Lark said. "Mom, you're so pretty anyway."

Joe agreed with that.

"My turn." Lark hopped up, hurried to the fireplace, and took down her own stocking, which she dumped out onto the sofa. "Candy canes. Yum. A gift card to the university book store. Thanks, Mom. And a little box."

"Joe," Rain said. "Seriously."

Joe shrugged, grinned.

Lark sat down between them, opened it—and shrieked. "Car keys? Oh, Joe!"

In the next instant, she was on her feet again. "Where is it? What is it? Can I see it? Can I drive it today? Is it really mine?"

"They delivered it late last night. It's out in the driveway, and, yes, it's yours—unless you fail to make the insurance payments."

Lark took off at a run toward the garage. "My own car!"

Joe helped Rain to her feet. "Come on."

Rain held him back. "You really are going to spoil her—and me, too."

"What's wrong with a little of that? It's just money."

"Yes, but she's never had it. Neither have I. I don't want to change, and I don't want her to change. I don't want my daughter becoming some privileged brat you read about in the tabloids with drug problems and car wrecks and pet monkeys."

"Pet *monkeys*?" Joe laughed. "I will definitely draw the line there."

A scream of delight came from outside.

"Okay, I hear what you're saying, but you raised that kid right. I don't think either of you is in danger of becoming the next brainless heiress. I don't like to throw money around. You know that. But the two of you have had a hard life. I want to make things easier for you, give you a few luxuries. Money has only ever been a burden in my life. It destroyed four generations of my family. It has soured every relationship I've ever had. Now, for the first time, it feels like a *good* thing because I can share it with you. I hope you'll let me. If you start to change, I promise to let you know."

Rain drew a deep breath. "Okay. All right. It's just so new to us."

"I get that. I really do. We can make rules if you want, set limits for Lark." Joe kissed her. "Which reminds me… I haven't told you."

"Told me what?"

"My net worth."

Rain shook her head. "Oh, you don't have to—"

"Yes, I do. Everything I own is now yours, too, so it's important that you know. My attorney is drawing up the paperwork, so I'll have documents from the banks for you to sign sometime next week."

"*Banks*. In the plural?"

He nodded, gave a little laugh. "Believe it or not, I don't keep all of my one-point-eight billion in the Scarlet Springs Savings and Loan."

"What?" Rain couldn't have heard him right. The breath left her lungs, dizziness overtaking her, the floor seeming to rush up at her. "One point eight *bill… bill…*"

"Breathe, Rain. Deep breaths." Joe caught her, steadied her, led her to the couch.

Lark ran into the room. "It's beautiful!"

Joe settled Rain on the sofa, concern on his face. "Lie down. Breathe. It's okay."

Rain's mind still reeled. Joe was a freaking billionaire? That was *a thousand million dollars*. She couldn't even imagine that much money.

Then it hit her as it hadn't before that she and Lark would never face hardship again. She would never have to choose between food and gas. Or work two jobs to make ends meet. Or wonder if she would ever be able to retire.

"What's wrong with Mom? Is she okay?"

"I just told her my net worth, and she almost fainted."

Rain had never fainted before, not once in her life.

"Oh." Lark sounded unimpressed. "Geez, Mom, Dad's a billionaire. Get over it. Sometimes good things happen, you know?"

Yes, sometimes good things happened.

Rain drew a breath to steady herself and sat up, the dizziness ebbing. "I'm okay. I'm fine, really. That was just… I mean I knew you had money, but… Really?"

Joe rubbed one of her hands between his. "Really."

"Can we please go for a drive?" Lark's excitement made Rain smile. "We don't have to go far. I just want to see how it feels."

"Sure." Rain sat up, got slowly to her feet, and walked with Joe to the mudroom, stopping to grab her parka and step into her boots.

Billionaire? That was crazy!

She followed the excited sound of Lark's voice outside, and there the driveway stood a shiny white Mazda CX5, gleaming brand new in the midday sunshine.

"Isn't it amazing?" Lark asked.

"It certainly is," Rain said.

All of this was amazing.

Rain climbed into the backseat, leaving Joe to sit up front to explain the vehicle's features to Lark, who was all but bouncing in the driver's seat. Joe had had the dealership add additional safety features, which made Rain happy, but holy shit! *A billionaire?*

She laughed to herself, shook her head.

Lark stuck the key in the ignition, started the engine.

Joe turned to look back at Rain, reaching for her hand. "You okay?"

Rain nodded. "I am now."

Those delicious lips of his curved into a big grin. "Well, hang on, honey, because it's going to be one hell of a new year."

Epilogue

August 14

Joe walked into Scarlet Springs Town Hall, hand in hand with Rain, letting her set the pace. She was due in twelve days and easily got out of breath. "Stop if you need to. We're in no hurry."

She halted just outside the entrance, breathing as deeply as she could with eight pounds of baby taking up all the space in her abdomen.

Joe hadn't given much thought to the things women endured during pregnancy, but he'd been witnessing it up close and in stereo for the past eight-and-a-half months, as Vicki was almost due to have her first, too. Between the nausea, backache, sore breasts, swollen ankles, and mood swings, it sure didn't seem like fun to him.

He'd done what he could to make things easier for Rain, bringing in extra help to cover for both of them when they'd gone through morning sickness. He'd put a sofa in his office so both women could lie down and take naps at work. He'd brought in a massage therapist to the pub once a week to give Rain massages. But he couldn't take away the visceral reality of pregnancy from her—or go through labor for her. All the pain, all the risk to health and life, was hers.

That was the part that scared her, and he could do nothing to change it. All he could do was assure her that she wouldn't be alone.

He waited for Rain to catch her breath, then opened the door for her.

"Thanks." She waddled past him. "There are a lot of people here tonight."

"I'm betting the articles in the Gazette have something to do with that."

Mrs. Beech had died in her sleep in January. Joe and Rain had attended her service, along with most of the rest of the town. A month after she'd been laid to rest, Joe created an anonymous nonprofit foundation to build and stock a library in Scarlet Springs. Then, as a private citizen, he had announced his intention to donate Silas' journals to the library for research purposes. The paper had covered this news, too, and published key passages that revealed Silas for the man he was.

It was the most-read series of stories in the paper's recent history.

Tonight was the next step in what felt to Joe like settling a very old score. Tonight, the Scarlet Springs Town Council would vote on Joe's request to rename Moffat Street, stripping Silas of an honor he had never deserved.

Hawke and Vicki were already inside the crowded council chambers. Hawke waved them over. "I saved you a few seats."

"Thanks." Rain sat, caught her breath.

"Is Lark coming?" Vicki asked. "She's a Moffat, too, now."

Joe had adopted Lark, starting the process shortly after the New Year. She was now officially his daughter and a legal heir to his estate. "Chey was going to cover for her tonight but got caught up in traffic."

A moment later, Lark breezed in and sat next to her mom. "Did I miss anything?"

"The meeting hasn't started yet," Rain said.

Lark had moved back to Scarlet after graduation to be close to Rain during this pregnancy and now lived in Rain's rebuilt house. She had developed an interest in brewing beer and had asked Joe to teach her the business from the ground up.

She glanced around. "It looks like the whole town is here."

The chamber only held two hundred people, so that wasn't literally possible, but it seemed to Joe that most of the people he knew well were here. Mitch had come, of course, because Megs was on the council. Austin and Lexi were there with most of the rest of the Team. Kendra was sitting with Rose. Ellie and Jesse Moretti were there with their twins. Brandon Silver had come in his turnout pants. Sheriff's Deputy Julia Marcs was also in uniform. Bear stood in the back. Even Hank had showed up.

The six council members and the mayor came out of the back room and took their seats, among them Megs, Bob Jewell, and Marcia.

The mayor, Michael Taylor, Austin's father, opened the meeting. "Our first piece of business tonight is to decide whether to rename Moffat Street. This is a request made by Joe Moffat, the only living descendant of Silas Moffat, in whose honor the street was named back in 1920. I think we're all aware of the recent revelations regarding Silas Moffat. The man was a rapist and a murderer. Of that, there is no doubt. I would like to open up the mic to input from the public."

A couple of homeowners on Moffat Street said they were concerned the switch would cost them time and money as they would have to change their address with everyone from their banks and credit cards to the DMV.

Joe could appreciate that. He just couldn't see a way around it.

Then Hank stepped up to the mic. "This happened a long time ago. Does anybody really care what Silas did? What do I say if someone asks me for directions—'Turn left on the street formerly known as Moffat Street'?"

Laughter.

"Well, Hank, that's part of what we have to decide," Mayor Taylor said. "Does anyone else have anything to add?"

Rose got up, walked to the mic, and said, "I just want all of us to appreciate this present moment. We are agents of karma tonight. If you do vote to change the name, we could rename it Ellery Street, in honor of my great-great-grandmother, who was a woman ahead of her time."

"Name it after a whore?" Bob blurted from the dais.

"She was a sex worker," Rose snapped.

More laughter.

Joe gave Rain's hand a squeeze, then stood and walked up to the mic. "Silas Moffat got away with murder. He got away with raping and abusing young women in his employ. Changing a street name can't undo any of that, but it does set the record straight. It gives his victims the only justice we can give them by ensuring that future generations won't grow up thinking of Silas as anything other than a criminal."

Applause.

Joe went back to his seat, threaded his fingers through Rain's.

"I love you," she whispered.

Mayor Taylor turned to his fellow council members. "Ready to vote?"

Six heads nodded.

Joe found it hard to breathe.

"All in favor of stripping Silas Moffat's name from the street say, 'Aye.'"

Six voices said "aye" in unison.

"It's unanimous. The name Moffat Street is to be changed."

Joe let out the breath he hadn't realized he'd been holding, a weight he'd carried for more than twenty years finally lifting from his shoulders.

It was done. It was over.

Rain leaned closer. "I'm so proud of you."

Looking like he was fighting a grin, Taylor glanced over at Marcia, who nodded. "There is a motion before the council to change the street's name from 'Moffat Street' to 'Moffat Street' in honor of Joe Moffat, a man of outstanding character who has done so much for our town."

The room exploded into laughter and applause.

Joe stared open-mouthed. "What? No! I—"

"You deserve this, Dad," Lark assured him.

"This wasn't my intention. What the hell…?"

"All in favor of changing the name of Moffat Street to Moffat Street in honor of Joe Moffat say, 'Aye.'"

This time, the audience said "aye" right along with the council members.

"Shit." Joe shook his head, stunned.

Rain laughed. "It's okay, Joe. You'll live."

He was about to stand and say something—he had no idea what—when Rain gasped—and looked down. "My water. It just broke."

"Oh, my God!" Lark jumped to her feet. "My mom is having the baby!"

"Not here she's not." Joe helped Rain to her feet, looked up to find the whole room watching them. "Thanks for taking this seriously, and thanks very much for the honor. It means a lot to me. Marcia, you and I will be having a long conversation. But right now, I need to go."

Shouts of "good luck!" and "take care!" followed them out the door.

Rain surfed through TV channels while Joe and Lark played Bananagrams—again. There was nothing on that she felt like watching. She glanced at the monitor, saw another contraction begin, rising until it reached the top of the graph.

She couldn't feel a thing.

Thank God for epidurals.

They had arrived at the hospital a couple of hours ago, after driving home so that she could get her overnight bag and change out of her wet pants. By the time they'd gotten to the hospital, she was having regular contractions—nothing too strong. Leah had checked her and the baby and found that she was already dilated to three centimeters. Leah had kept her promise and called in the anesthetist, who had given Rain her epidural. Having a needle stuck in her back hadn't been fun, but it had been worth it. Rain had suffered through just a few hard contractions before going blissfully numb.

"Bananas!" Joe exclaimed.

"Want to play another round?" Lark asked.

"We ought to let your mom get some rest." Joe turned to Rain. "It's almost midnight. You're going to need your strength later."

"You're probably right." Rain turned off the TV, turned onto her left side, facing Joe and Lark. She watched while they put away their game and then sacked out, Lark on a folding chair near the foot of the bed, Joe on the chair beside her.

He bent over her, kissed her forehead, turned out the lights. "Sleep."

"I'll try."

"Are you afraid?"

"A little. Mostly, I'm just excited for this to be over with and to have the baby in my arms. How about you?"

Joe looked confused, as if he had no idea how he felt. "I'm good."

She threaded her fingers through his, closed her eyes, and quickly fell asleep. She woke once when a nurse came in to check her vitals, then once more when Lark's cell phone rang, but fell asleep quickly.

It was pain that finally woke her.

She moaned, the sensation muted but still intense. "The epidural is wearing off.

She shifted onto her back, and the pain grew stronger.

Joe took her hand. "Lark, go get the nurse. It's going to be okay, Rain. I'm sure they can do something."

The pain grew worse until Rain found herself trying to remember the breathing exercises from her childbirth class. "This doesn't help!"

Unlike a contraction, this pain didn't come and go. It just got worse.

The nurse came in, Lark behind her. "Are you having pain?"

"Yes," Joe answered for her. "We need you to fix the epidural."

"Let's check her first." The nurse put on a glove on one hand, sat, and lifted the sheet with the other. "Bend your knees, and let them fall open."

A moment later, the nurse sat back, pulled off her glove. "What you're feeling isn't contraction pain. It's pressure. This baby is plus-two station. It's almost here."

"Did you hear that, Mom? It's almost here."

Rain was too focused on coping at this point to pay attention to what was happening around her, her world constricted by pain.

Joe held her hand, kissed her forehead, reassured her. "It's going to be over soon, and you won't ever have to go through this again."

Then Leah was there in her blue medical garb. "We don't have time to break down the bed. She's crowning."

That brought Rain's eyes open. "I'm crowning?"

"Oh, my God, Mom! I can see its head. It has lots of dark hair."

"It's going to be a boy," Joe said. "Moffats always have boys."

"It's going to be a girl," Lark said. "Times change."

"You don't know the sex?" the nurse asked.

"They wanted it to be a surprise," Lark answered.

Leah sat at the foot of the bed, near Rain's feet. "Rain, give me your hand."

Rain reached down between her legs, let Leah guide her fingers until she felt the wet, hard top of the baby's head. She smiled, despite the pain, genuinely excited now. "Oh, my God. My baby."

"Dad, do you want to catch? Yours can be the first hands to touch your baby."

Joe shook his head. "I'll stay with this end of Rain."

Something about the way Joe said it, combined with the overwhelmed look on his face, made Rain laugh.

"There you go," Leah said. "Laugh that baby out."

Rain laughed, then shrieked in pain—and it was over.

"Oh, Mom!" she heard Lark say.

Instinctively, Rain reached down for her baby and drew it up between her legs and cradled it against her chest. The nurse unsnapped her gown so that she could put the baby to her breast and give it skin-to-skin contact. The baby didn't cry but looked around as if trying to figure out what had happened. "Hey, sweetie. Aren't you beautiful?"

The nurse rubbed it with a towel. "Happy birthday, little one."

Rain looked up at Joe, found him staring, wonder on his face, tears in his eyes. He reached down, stroked the baby's head. "It's ... so *little*."

"Is it a boy or a girl?" Lark asked.

Rain turned the baby so that Joe and Lark could see.

"It's a girl." Joe looked astonished. "She's a girl. We have a girl."

"She's beautiful!" Lark had tears on her cheeks, too. "I have a little sister. See, Dad? Times change."

While Rain slept, Joe held his newborn daughter, amazed by her. Eight pounds nine ounces. Ten fingers. Ten tiny toes. Itty-bitty eyelashes. Dark, downy hair.

She was perfect.

She sucked on her little fist, making tiny baby noises that melted his heart, her eyes bright and alert, her scent sweet.

"Are you hungry, baby girl?" It was almost four in the morning, and she hadn't nursed for a couple of hours.

Joe hadn't realized it was possible to love someone so quickly—or so fiercely. He'd seen her emerge from Rain's body, had watched her draw her first breath, and in the next heartbeat couldn't have imagined his world without her. She was a part of him as if she'd always been there. He could think of only two events that had affected him as much as the birth—the night she'd been conceived and the night he had married her mother.

He glanced over at Rain, glad to see she was still asleep, relieved that this was behind her. She would be sore for a long time and needed to heal. The past nine months had given him a whole new respect for his wife and all women.

He walked the length of the room, bouncing the baby gently in his arms, humming to her—some Mudbugs tune that probably wasn't suitable for a child. But then he didn't know a single lullaby.

"I love watching you with her." Rain sat up, wincing as she shifted her position.

Joe walked back to the bed. "I think she's getting hungry."

He placed the baby in her mother's arms, helped Rain open her gown so that she could breastfeed. The baby latched on quickly this time and began to suckle. Joe stroked her little head with one hand, his other hand on Rain's shoulder, emotions stirring behind his breastbone that were too sublime to name or even fathom.

"This time a year ago, I fought every day to pretend I wasn't attracted to you. I was set on never marrying, never having kids. Now, I have a wife, an adult daughter, and a new baby girl. Somewhere, God must be laughing."

Rain was laughing, too. "A year ago, I was trying to figure out how to face life alone because my daughter had moved out and my boss was too much of a good guy to jump my bones."

"Idiot."

"Lark grew up with nothing—hand-me-downs, thrift store toys. This little girl is going to grow up with everything, including a father."

"Lark had you."

"I was always afraid I wasn't enough."

"You have nothing to worry about this time around. You're not going to raise this baby alone."

Rain leaned her cheek against his hand. "I've been thinking about names again."

"Uh-oh."

Rain had talked about naming the baby after Jenny if it was a girl, but Joe had found it morbid to name his daughter after someone her own ancestor had destroyed, a woman who'd lived a short and tragic life. He wanted to leave the past in the past.

"What about Angel?"

"Angel." He looked at his daughter and had no objection to that. "I like it."

They played around with middle names for a while, shooting down Rose, because it reminded them of, well, Rose, and tossing out a half dozen others as well—Grace, Skye, Isabella, Storm, Snow, Ivy, Holly and so on.

"Angel Noelle." The name popped into Joe's head. "She *was* conceived around Christmas."

"Angel Noelle Moffat," Rain said, testing it.

They agreed to sit on it for a few days. There was no rush, after all.

"Where did you come up with Lark's name?" Joe had never asked.

"She made me think of a hungry baby bird—tiny, helpless, always wanting to eat. Today was so much easier than Lark's birth. Thank you for helping me through this. I couldn't have faced it without you."

He bent down, kissed Rain's temple. "I wish I could have done more."

Now that he'd witnessed a birth and been beside her through an entire pregnancy, it left Joe feeling sick to think of her at age sixteen giving birth alone in a goddamned vehicle. If that bastard ever set foot in the pub again…

"What are you feeling?" Rain asked. "You look upset."

Joe took a breath, let it go. "No. Not at all. I feel like I'm just starting my life. It's like the past forty-eight years have been lived in black and white, and now everything has become color. Loving you has changed everything. How do I feel? I feel *happy*."

Yes, times certainly had changed.

Also by Pamela Clare

Romantic Suspense

I-Team Series

Extreme Exposure (Book 1)

Heaven Can't Wait (Book 1.5)

Hard Evidence (Book 2)

Unlawful Contact (Book 3)

Naked Edge (Book 4)

Breaking Point (Book 5)

Skin Deep: An I-Team After Hours Novella (Book 5.5)

First Strike: The Prequel to Striking Distance (Book 5.9)

Striking Distance (Book 6)

Soul Deep: An I-Team After Hours Novella (Book 6.5)

Seduction Game (Book 7)

Dead by Midnight: An I-Team Christmas (Book 7.5)

Contemporary Romance

Colorado High Country Series

Barely Breathing (Book 1)

Slow Burn (Book 2)

Falling Hard (Book 3)

Tempting Fate (Book 4)

Close to Heaven (Book 5)

Historical Romance

Kenleigh-Blakewell Family Saga

Sweet Release (Book 1)

Carnal Gift (Book 2)

Ride the Fire (Book 3)

MacKinnon's Rangers series

Surrender (Book I)

Untamed (Book 2)

Defiant (Book 3)

Upon A Winter's Night: A MacKinnon's Rangers Christmas (Book 3.5)